O'BRIEN, BUCCANEER

H. BEDFORD-JONES

TABLE OF CONTENTS

I

O'BRIEN, BUCCANEER

*A Novelette of High Adventure
on the Spanish Main.*

THE PINNACE was a large, clumsy, heavy craft with blunt bows and a stumpy mast on which a square canvas was rigged with a makeshift gaff and boom constructed from unbarked tree limbs and rope.

Under a blazing morning sun, she ploughed relentlessly across the blue-green rollers of the Caribbean, almost dead before the wind, toward the rising blue growth of land that broke the sword line of the horizon. The sun tanned and shriveled bodies of two men were huddled beneath her midship thwarts, as though they had there sought some shelter, and died. Up forward, face down across the bow thwart beside the mast, was the body of a huge, red haired man, a dirty, blood stained bandage about his chest, and dried blood black on the thwart and gunwale beside him.

The only living thing in the boat was the man sitting at the helm, arm crooked over the tiller, his head on his breast.

Except for tattered breeches, he was naked, sun blackened; he was wide in the shoulder, his arms and torso a mass of smooth, rippling muscle. His face was blurred behind a week's growth of yellow-gray beard, and sun bleached yellow hair hung long about his ears, and both hair and beard were encrusted with brine. Water sloshed unheeded in the boat's bottom.

The man at the tiller lifted his head. Blue eyes came wide open as he saw the purpling rise of land ahead. He stared at it, then stooped over stiffly and opened a locker in the sternsheets of the pinnace. From this he produced a little wooden keg, balanced it in his hand, and held it to his lips. He drank thirstily, dragged out some ship's biscuit wrapped in canvas, and munched away. His wrists showed half healed scars, as from handcuffs.

It was obvious that the other three men had not died of thirst and starvation.

The sun mounted higher in the brazen sky, reached meridian, slowly drove on in his course westward. The blue-purple land widened and changed in color, brightening to a vivid green. From the long wave crests, as the pinnace rose beneath their hissing drive, the land became more distinct.

"An island," muttered the man at the tiller. "Lord knows what island!"

The sun was halfway to the horizon when, from the top of a wave, he first saw the smoke. He was closer, now; gradually the smoke grew more distinct, apparently rising from the shore ahead. The steady breeze, however, was failing fast, and it was evident that he would not gain the land before night.

He shrugged, ate more biscuit, emptied the water keg without losing a drop, and presently, with his canvas flapping idly and the boat rocking gently to the sunset, he fell asleep.

Cold white light wakened him; the moon was just risen, almost at its full—but under the moon was a ruddier glare. A windless current had brought him closer to the island; a breeze

was coming down from the north, and he drew in his sheet and caught the tiller. Not more than a couple of miles off shore, he calculated; but the glare puzzled him.

"Fires on the beach, but I can't make 'em out," he muttered, squinting at the veiled shore. "Must be a headland—that argues a cove or a bay, eh? Fires argue men. An island argues a ship, egad! Either Spaniards turtle fishing, or brethren of the coast bucaning meat—what matter? On with you, worthy Colonel O'Brien, and devil take you if you guess wrong!"

He laughed and swung the tiller as the pinnace heeled over a trifle to the wind. In this year of grace 1692, he was not the only man without a country haunting the Carib keys.

The pinnace drove in ever closer to the island, O'Brien heading for the ruddy glare. He could tell now that it was the reflection of firelight against high trees, and the steadily droning boom of surf came drifting back athwart the breeze. Then, suddenly, the point of a headland was gone and the fires themselves came into the sight. And more—much more!

Between the moon, now high, and the half dozen great blazing fires, was disclosed the curving shores of a wide and pleasant cove, backed by a wall of circling forest green. Through the sound of the surf outside lifted voices; a sudden wild burst of them in a rousing lilt of song, whose chorus came clearly to O'Brien as he brought the pinnace around:

> "Down among the dead men,
> Down among the dead men,
> Down, down, down, down—
> Down among the dead men, let him lie!"

O'Brien's lips parted in a laugh.

"A Jacobite catch, eh? Come, here are no dons, at least!"

Dark figures showed here and there against the fire glitter, but O'Brien had abruptly lost interest in all the scene ashore—a scene of carousal, as his ears testified. He had caught sight of something far more interesting, and closer at hand: a trim brigantine, her spars and lines picked out by the light, anchored bow and stern in the cove.

No glimmer of light showed aboard her; she hung there like a dead thing in the tide, half a mile from the curving sandy shore, where two boats lay on the beach above high water mark. O'Brien chuckled as the puffy airs of the cove filled his canvas and sent him slowly ahead.

"Faith, what better could I want, now? They'll all be ashore till sometime tomorrow when they wake up, and if I can gain her unseen…."

He bore down upon her steadily, with never a hail nor a light from her deck. The shrieks of women came from ashore—delighted, drunken shrieks of laughter—and were drowned in a wild French rouse swept up by a mad chorus of voices. The night was well begun, obviously, and O'Brien hoped there was liquor enough on the beach to keep it going heartily.

The pinnace slipped through the still water without a ripple, and presently the stern of the brigantine slid between her and the shore. O'Brien cast loose his sheet, let go the halyard and his splotch of canvas rustled down. The ship was still all silent and deserted, evidently; he forged slowly alongside, and the pinnace came in against her with a crash and a groan. In her waist, O'Brien came upon a great gap in the bulwarks, whence hung a tangle of cordage. He caught a line, made the pinnace fast and, after testing the tangle, mounted to the deck.

"A yard shot away, eh?" he observed. "And everything topsy-turvy—ha! They've taken a prize after a fight, and now they're digesting the loot. So much the better."

The moon showed him her disarranged and cluttered deck, empty of life, and he turned aft. Here, sheltered by the deck-house, he found a dim burning lantern. Beside it a man lay snoring, a man nearly naked to the warm night, his right leg a peg of wood and leather, an open keg of rum close beside him. O'Brien took the pannikin from the deck, dipped it at the keg, and tasted the rum. With a grimace, he dropped it.

Catching up the lantern, he turned up the wick a trifle, got a better light, and started aft.

He was not long in discovering that the ship was an untidy mess, but he found all he sought in the way of food, with good wine to wash it down. The after cabin was a litter of splendid garments, weapons, and miscellaneous loot strewn about. When he had eaten and drunk his fill, O'Brien washed and shaved luxuriously, the operation revealing a lean and long jawed face that wore a cheerful smile. The blue eyes twinkled at those in the mirror.

"Faith, Colonel, you look a bit white where the beard lay. Well, a bit o' sleep won't hurt a bit—but there are a few things to do first."

Naked and shaved, his long hair trussed back into a knot

behind his head, he filled a long clay pipe from its rack and lighted it at the lantern. Puffing at this with sheer pleasure, he laid it down presently and went on deck again, and paused beside the snoring man with the wooden leg. He sat down and bumped the man's head, repeatedly, against the deck, until a drowsy oath rewarded his pains.

"Is that you, Hardinge, blast your ruddy eyes?" muttered the man.

"Aye," said O'Brien. "D'ye know what island this is, lad?"

"Aves, you drunken fool. Go away and let me sleep, or I'll have Cap'n Vernier truss you up!" His head sank back on the deck, and he muttered again as he resumed his snoring, "Vernier or a new cap'n—all one to me—Vernier or—the devil…"

O'Brien straightened up. Aves—the little Island of Aves, haunt of Mansfelt and the great Morgan, where a debauch might be held or a ship careened and scraped without interference of any man! And he was aboard Vernier's ship—the Frenchman who had been off the Jamaica coast a short month ago! Buccaneers in all truth.

"Well, so much the worse for Cap'n Vernier," observed O'Brien pleasantly, "since I ha' most pressing need of his ship and crew—French and English, no doubt. Ho, hum! I think I'll turn in—and let destiny bide until the morrow. A pleasant good night to you, Cap'n Vernier!"

Chuckling softly, he went below, with a snatch of drunken song from ashore to set him on the road to sleep.

II

CAPTAIN RAOUL VERNIER was not a particularly nice person, either in his personality or in his tastes. He was black bearded, barrel chested, his nose had been broken and was askew, and he made no pretensions to gentility. Of St. Malo origin, he was an excellent seaman, extremely brutal, and cautious in a fight. Rather, about getting into a fight, for once in, he was the very devil.

Toward noon he left one of the huts at the side of the old careening ground, and stood stretching himself in the sunlight, his head rocking after a night of debauch. He was of the general type of his day, which made no concessions to decency of thought or act, and he grinned sourly as he surveyed the scene of the night's carousal—whose details might well please him, but would please no one else.

Half a dozen of his men were seated about a fire, broiling meat and groaning over their aching heads. Vernier looked about, found a half emptied wine keg, and helped himself from it; then he strode to the fire.

"Four of you lads tumble into a boat and take me out," he said curtly, and passed on toward the boats on the beach. The men looked at one another, grimaced, then four of them followed him with muttered curses.

Vernier halted by a sprawled figure and kicked it twice. It wakened and evolved into a tall and spindly man with enormously long arms and a beak nosed face—his lieutenant, Rocher, once a French officer and a gentleman, now drunken and given over to the devil with no hope.

"Come aboard with me, Rocher," Vernier ordered contemptuously. Rocher stumbled after him.

The four men got a boat afloat and tumbled in. Vernier and Rocher followed, and they were taken out to the brigantine; naturally they saw nothing of the pinnace, which floated on the other side of her. When they came to the dangling ladder, Vernier turned to his four men.

"You needn't wait—I'm stopping aboard," he said. "Take those wenches in the huts, if you want them. All hands ready to come aboard two hours before sunset, mind. And no women."

"Eh, Captain?" said Rocher, staring at him. "But you promised to land the women at Tortuga! You can't leave them here."

"To the devil with them," said Vernier, and mounted. "Come on."

Rocher shrugged and followed him. Most of Rocher's life was a shrug, these days—he who had been a brilliant officer of French artillery. Vernier glanced at the one legged watchman, still snoring, and strode aft.

"Come down to the big cabin," he said. "We'll have to arrange our plans, and I want to look over the jewels and gewgaws we took out of the Spaniard—before the men see the stuff."

"A drink first—water," said Rocher. "My head's splitting."

He went to the water butt forward. Vernier passed on down the companionway.

When he entered the main cabin he came to a dead halt, and stood there stupefied at sight of O'Brien, who was sitting at the big table. O'Brien laid down his pipe, rose, and bowed with a certain dignified grace that told its own story. His hair was drawn back and powdered; he was wearing a flowered waistcoat and a suit of sky-blue silk; diamond buckles glittered at his knees and upon his shoes, and the jeweled rings on his fingers were half concealed by the rich Mechlin lace of his cuffs. On the table before him lay two ornate pistols, lately loaded, and a gold hilted Spanish rapier, out of its scabbard.

"Good day, Captain Vernier; good day!" he said. "I must apologize for my rusty French, which has suffered from undue repose in the Virginia plantations."

"Who in the devil's name are you?" blurted out the astounded buccaneer. O'Brien bowed again, and flicked a handkerchief over his lapel.

"Oh, yes! Allow me; Colonel James O'Brien, late regimental commander in the forces of his Majesty, King James, more recently aide-major of the Irish Brigade, serving his Majesty, King Louis; more recently yet, staff officer in the service of his Majesty, the King of Sweden—"

"Death of a thousand devils!" exploded Vernier. "Where did you come from? What madness is this? How did you get here?"

O'Brien paused. In the doorway behind Vernier, now appeared Rocher, and the eyes of the two men sat. The face of the Frenchman became overspread by a mortal pallor. He caught at the door as though he were about to collapse. O'Brien, ignoring him, turned to Vernier again, a slight smile upon his lips.

"Where did I come from? Why, my dear Vernier, from hell! Hark'ee: I sneaked back to Ireland to see a dying mother; they recognized me, caught me, sent me as a slave to the plantations! First Virginia, then to Jamaica—and on the way back to Virginia, when the Spaniards turned up and plumped me into a new slavery. From which, praise be, I delivered myself. And what madness is this? For you, a most unfortunate madness. How did I get here? Faith, my dear fellow, the devil caught me up under his arm and carried me just here—plumped me down in this cabin to await you! If you doubt it, look at these loaded pistols and this excellent rapier, placed so ready to my hand. There's a whole biography for you—aye, and your own destiny to boot, if you but knew it!"

His lightly mocking tone, his air of being completely at home, and perhaps a certain glint in his blue eye, brought a scowl to the face of Vernier.

"What do you want here?" he said harshly.

The blue eyes struck squarely on his, and the jesting voice became like steel.

"Your life," said O'Brien. "Your ship; your men—or some of them. You're the scoundrel who sacked Santa Margerita early this year, murdered women, carried others to the Tortugas; you're no man but a beast, to be treated as such."

Without taking his gaze from O'Brien, Vernier spoke quietly in Spanish.

"Get the men aboard, Rocher," he said, and then took a step forward, hand to belt. "Whoever you are, you damned popinjay, and however you got here, strip off those clothes and get for'ard, unless you want to be triced up and given a score of lashes!" His voice was imperious, harsh, brutal. "Off with 'em, hear me?"

O'Brien shrugged slightly. Rocher, in the doorway, had not moved; was staring at O'Brien.

"You mistake, Vernier," said the latter calmly. "You are not giving orders here. I am. Take one of those swords from the rack behind you—" And, reaching forward, he picked up the rapier, springing it slightly in his hands as he spoke. "Quick, man! Would you have me spit you like the dog you are, without a fight?"

Vernier half turned, with a sneer, as though to obey. Then, quick as light, his hand moved. A knife was in the air, swift as an arrow, singing straight for O'Brien's throat. The rapier swept up and around; the knife, deflected, clanged against the stern post and fell to the deck.

WITH THE throw Vernier lunged forward, flung himself half across the table to seize one of the pistols there; then he choked and strangled, and his body relaxed. It slipped from the table and crashed down on the floor, and threshed there for an instant or two, hand clutching at throat, all crimsoned. O'Brien looked at the reddened point of his rapier, and with a grimace wiped his handkerchief along the blade, then dropped the bit of lace distastefully.

"O'Brien!" burst out the voice of Rocher, who took a step into the room as he spoke. "You!"

O'Brien looked up, and warm friendliness lighted up his face. With a quick step he was around the table, catching the other man in his arms, gripping his hand.

"By all that's holy, my old friend the Vicomte de St. Rocher!" he cried out heartily. "I thought it was you, but had to keep my eyes on that rascal. St. Rocher! Remember the Boyne water, and how we stood against the Dutchman while the coward who led us was fleeing? And how we met in Riga—you were in the Polish service then, I think? Faith, this is a strange meeting, old comrade!"

"But—but you—look at you—and at me," stammered Rocher, passing a hand across his gaunt, unshaven face. Shame flooded into his eyes, and bitterness. O'Brien pressed his hand quickly.

"Nonsense, my lad! You should ha' seen me when I slipped aboard here last night. That pinnace of mine is still alongside, with three dead men in her. We were sold to Virginia again, after a year on Jamaica, but a Spaniard took the bark we were in and carried us down to the south, and there was the devil and all to pay. They put in for water at some island, and the four of us got cleared wi' the pinnace, then the Indians jumped us—it's not nice to think of, let me tell you; I don't like arrows. They near finished us all, but we got clear and rigged a sail—and here I am. What luck to find you!"

"Diantre!" Rocher stood back, staring at him. "You don't mean that—you're not alone?"

"Not while you're here, St. Rocher."

"I'm not that," said the Frenchman. "I'm plain Rocher the buccaneer, lieutenant of this ship, scoundrel, child of misfortune, stepson of crime—"

"Oh, devil take your nonsense!" broke in O'Brien, clapping him on the back. "Vicomte de St. Rocher, ally and lieutenant and friend o' Jack O'Brien—and we've work to do, me lad!" The warm glow in his eyes broke into a sparkle of whimsical humor. "You and I have to get away with this craft, for I've big news in my head. Away with you now; get shaved and into gentleman's clothes, and join me here after I finish my pipe. Time enough to talk later."

Rocher disappeared, looking dazed and bewildered, as well he might.

O'Brien did not resume his pipe, however. He went to the side of Vernier, who was quite dead, and stood looking down at the brutal face.

"So you preferred murder to fair fight, eh?" he mused aloud. "It's like you, you damned woman killer. But there—" he sighed—"I mustn't let my feelings run away with me. After all, you're dead, and that's the main thing. Now you can serve my purpose a bit further."

He picked up the body in his arms, heavy as it was, and strode out to the companionway and so on deck. Walking to the break of the poop he dropped Vernier's body into the waist, and turned away.

Back in the cabin again he took a weapon belt he had found, buckled it about his waist, and was presently girded with sword and pistols like any buccaneer. Then he set out wine and food on the table, and turned at a step to see Rocher—a changed man.

Pale was the Frenchman, newly shaven, wearing bits of the finery from the other cabin—and a glow in his dark eyes such as had not been there for many a day. He held out a hand to O'Brien and stood smiling.

"It's not a dream, then," he said softly. "You, my Colonel—"

"Down with you, Vicomte, and get some food and drink under your belt," exclaimed O'Brien, pressing the other into a seat. "There's long years to cover with our tongues, but we've not time for it now. Other things press. I wanted a ship, and got her—but I didn't look for a friend. Praise be, fortune's kind! Here's to the future—and revenge!"

"To the future!" exclaimed St. Rocher solemnly, and his eyes kindled as he drank the toast.

They ate rapidly, looking at each other as men will after long parting, with conjecture and surmise, noting the passage of time in the marks it has left. Each man realized that there would be bitter spots in the tale, heart searing places; no place for confidences now, with brusk action in the offing. O'Brien shoved away the wine chalice and reached for the long clay pipe.

"Don't you smoke? You'll come to it. Well, what's the temper of your crew? Good men?"

St. Rocher grimaced.

"Beasts like their master. Vernier owned the ship; a planter friend of his at Basse-terre helped to found her. She's paid well.

Three months and not a dernier; two days ago we took a Spaniard—sunk him, but cleaned him out first. There are some gold ingots and some silver bars under our feet in the lazaret; the men have much coin."

"Prisoners?"

"Vernier took none."

O'Brien nodded.

"And the men themselves? They're not all French."

"Over half are. Out of the hundred and twenty, we have a score of Dutchmen and others, a few Portugee rascals, and twenty-odd English and Irish. The others are all French or Canadian."

"Hm! Brethren of the coast?"

"No. Recruits on shares. An organized affair, my dear Colonel."

O'Brien puffed at his long stemmed pipe for a space.

"Think you they'll take my orders without persuasion?"

"You know how such men are, my friend."

"And you know who the chief men of this crew are. Hm! Have you a signal to call a boat?"

"Yes—the flag."

"Set the signal, then. It's a nuisance we're so far from shore. You go ashore and pick thirty men—the ones you can best trust. Fetch them aboard, with both the boats. No others!"

"And what shall I tell them?"

"That Captain Vernier wants them instantly for special work."

With a shrug, St. Rocher rose and departed.

O'Brien got the charts from their rack and spread them on the table, finishing his pipe as he studied them. Leaving one outspread, he replaced the others and then sauntered up on deck. A boat was coming out from shore, and St. Rocher, in the waist, was talking with the one legged man. O'Brien beckoned this latter and the man stumped up to the poop, staring blankly. "Come below, my man."

III

SEATED IN the cabin, O'Brien refilled his pipe and looked at the seaman who stood before him.

"Your name?"

"Piggoty, sir—Jem Piggoty o' Norfolk. I be the master gunner, sir."

"You're a long way from home—" and O'Brien smiled thinly. "Well, Piggoty, you've probably taken note that Cap'n Vernier has passed to his reward—a just one, I hope. You talked in your sleep last night. I gather that you had no love for Vernier?"

"Not a scrap, sir. A main black brute, he was."

"And you an honest God fearing seamen, I've no doubt." Under the cold blue eyes and the thin irony, Piggoty shifted his wooden peg uneasily. "You continue master gunner, my lad. Under the larboard counter, there's a pinnace wi' three men in her, dead. Go and drop Vernier's body into her. When Vicomte de St. Rocher comes aboard with the men he brings, point out the body to them and tell them that Colonel O'Brien is now in command of this ship. That's all."

"Aye, sir." Piggoty touched his forelock and stumped away.

O'Brien remained where he was for some time, until he caught the thudding of boats alongside and the murmurous sound of voices and bare feet pounding the deck. Then he rose and went up the ladder, and came out in the bright sunlight.

St. Rocher was just mounting the poop ladder. Along the larboard rail were thronged some thirty blowsy ruffians, staring down at the pinnace, and talking excitedly. Of a sudden they saw O'Brien standing at the poop rail, with St. Rocher beside him, and their faces turned to him, blinking in surprise and wonder.

"Good morning, my lads," said he blithely. "Those who understand English, lift your hands."

A score of hands lifted, then fell again, rather foolishly.

"Fair enough," said O'Brien. "As ye've learned, this is now my ship. You're my men. The gold and silver that's aboard will be divided among you—I'll have no share. I know where there's enough more to make us all rich men, and we're going to get it. Where's the bosun?"

"He's ashore, sir," said a voice.

"Leave him there, then, with the others. Piggoty, select a capable bosun."

"Couldn't have a better, sir, than this Hobbs, sir." Piggoty pointed out a massive, scowling fellow with a red beard.

"Hobbs, you're bosun," said O'Brien quickly. "Rating as such, with five shares out of the loot. Man the capstan, get up the anchor and that stern kedge, bring in the boats, then tail on the lines and we'll move out of here. Once out, you men select a committee of three to come aft and settle details with me."

The men gasped, stared up at him, then at one another. Hobbs spoke out.

"Aye, Master? And what of our mates ashore?"

"Leave them there with the wenches until we come back in a fortnight or so," said O'Brien coolly. "You men can be trusted; they can't. There's ticklish fighting ahead of us, lads, and gold for the taking. We're enough for the job."

"Oh, aye?" said Hobbs, with a rising mutter of voices behind him. "And who may you be?"

O'Brien smiled down at them lazily, and flicked a crumb from his silken waistcoat.

"Whoever wants to argue it, can find out, my lads. Why not wait and see? I'm not the man to cruise emptily for three months, take a ship and sink her clumsily, and then put into Aves for a carouse! Not I. This time a seven-night, you'll be carousing aboard a galleon, one of the plate fleet itself, with gold like dirt around you and every man rich as a lord! Those that don't like the prospect can go ashore with Cap'n Vernier.

St. Rocher, take charge for'ard! Hobbs, get your men to the capstan and fetch in the boats."

Mention of the dead Vernier, the evident allegiance of St. Rocher, the alluring prospect held out before them, stirred the upturned faces; but more than all else was the superb coolness and arrogant confidence of this man whose cold blue eyes commanded them, and who had proclaimed himself their master. Added to this was the element of mystery in him, and the fact that most of their company were still ashore. St. Rocher had picked his men well.

Two minutes later the boats were coming in, the capstan bars clicking, and the men laughed as they heard the wrathful shouts of those ashore, who now began to throng the beach in wild and helpless fury. All of them English, Irish or Dutch, they had small love for their Latin comrades.

O'Brien was still at the poop rail, watching, when a wizened, blear eyed man with ragged hair and beard broke away from the others and stood staring up at him.

"*Mhuire a-struagh!*" came the fellow's voice in Irish. "Is it yourself, Shamus O'Brien? And do you remember the breach at Limerick town, and Phelim who served your mess?"

O'Brien was down the ladder with a rush, and wringing the man's hand.

"So it's you, Phelim—what a rascal you were, eh? The best thief in all the regiment! Aye, I remember well enough. Where've you been since then, my lad?"

The other grimaced.

"A plantation slave, Shamus O'Brien, until I cut the Englishman's throat and ran for it. Praise be, it's a glory to the eyes to see you, sir!"

"Then tell your mates they need have no shame in sailing with me," said O'Brien quickly. "And once out of this, you'll be cabin steward, Phelim. Enough for now."

There was laughter in his eyes and in his soul as he walked the poop and saw the canvas flutter up, amid shrill and furious yells from the beach. St. Rocher for lieutenant, and one man whom he could trust from of old. Aye, fortune had favored him with full hand.

He ordered the pinnace cut adrift and left to float ashore, to tell her story, as the brigantine slipped from the cove and then heeled to the freshening breeze. The pleasant Isle of Aves fell away from behind them.

Presently three men came down to the great cabin where O'Brien and St. Rocher awaited them—red bearded Hobbs, stumping Piggoty, and a keen eyed Dutchman they called Dunker. O'Brien had doffed his weapons, but the Spanish rapier lay on the table before him, a splendid blade.

"Sit down, men; take your ease," he said, waving his long stemmed pipe at seats. "We're all comrades; but fix it in your heads that we're not all equal. I'm giving the orders. Now, there's sharp work to be done, and not many hands to do it."

"Cursed few there be for fighting," growled Hobbs.

"Aye?" O'Brien looked at him, smiling. "There are two-score and ten good men waiting for us, Hobbs—English and Irish all. Listen, now! A week ago I was in Spanish hands, d'ye see? And got away. The dons took two ships out of Jamaica for the Virginias, with prisoners for the plantations, Irish and English all—blown off the course, we were. The Spaniards meant to take us to the mines, Catholics or not, for it's small mercy they show any man. They were making for Chagres and Panama, but we met a craft with news that a galleon of the plate fleet had lost her rudder and been sore battered, and lay at Margarita for repairs. So our good ship headed thither. And thither go we, my hearties."

"Aye?" queried Dunker keenly. "With thirty men, Master?"

"With me," said O'Brien. "If I, single handed, could take Vernier's ship and the best of his crew, what can I do with that ship and those thirty men? Tell me that."

They grinned, and he knew he had them.

"Now, St. Rocher and I will work out details," O'Brien went

on. "Meantime, trick yourselves out in what Spanish clothes may be aboard—plenty of them, to judge from what I've seen. This craft is named the *Malouin*, I see. Get out your paint pots and change it to read *Sta. Teresa*. We'll have to leave the yards as they are, but rig up some false work on the poop in Spanish style and get it painted. We're sailing into Margarita, my lads, as a Spanish coaster from Hispaniola."

St. Rocher whistled at this.

"They've got a battery on the point there," he pointed out, "and the guns of the fort. And by your own account we'll find two ships, with enough guns to blow us out of the water."

"Aye, but we'll find fifty fighting men to aid us, likewise," said O'Brien gaily. "And no lack of Indians off the coast to give us information, d'ye see?"

"Who's talking the dons' lingo, Master?" demanded Hobbs.

"I am—Don Diego Ramirez, no less." O'Brien smiled at him. "And since you're so full of questions, let me give you a bellyful of information, lads. There'll be no more women aboard this ship, and no women will be harmed by any of you in our takings. Dunker, you'll ha' charge of the rum, to be handed out at my orders only. There'll be no questions when I give orders, on pain of death. Throw your cursed black flag overboard—I'll give you a better, later on. We have three days' sail to Margarita, and I want all shipshape aboard here before then. Are ye suited, my bullies?"

They were.

Alone with his friend, St. Rocher regarded O'Brien with a gleam in his dark eyes, and showed his teeth in a smile.

"Mon ami," he said, "what is in your mind?"

"Eh?" The blue eyes regarded him probingly. "You've heard."

"Exactly. I've heard—what the others have heard. But there's more to be told, unless I'm mistaken. Is it so?"

O'Brien looked down at the rapier and fingered it for a moment, and the lines of his face became drawn and old. He looked up at the other man suddenly, and nodded.

"You're right, St. Rocher," he said. "This is but the beginning. I'm aiming higher. This is the middle of April, eh? At the beginning of June I want to be at Guadeloupe."

"Yes? I know the island well."

"The Marquis de Fleury arrives sometime in May, as the new governor," went on O'Brien. "He's some relative of Pontchartrain, I believe; I heard talk about it in Jamaica."

"I happen to know him—or did," said St. Rocher quietly. "A capable man, very. He was in charge of the operations before Nevers."

O'Brien's lips were compressed thinly, so that all the color had run out of them.

"Yes," he said, after a moment. "I had just formed a regiment of the Irish Brigade, then. He was a friend of mine. I had a wife. She was carried off one night. Later, she died."

St. Rocher looked quickly at him, eyes widening. There was a little silence.

"I shall be honored, my friend," said the Frenchman, with grave comprehension, "to lend you my fullest assistance—at Guadeloupe and elsewhere—even to hell itself!"

O'Brien dropped the rapier on the table, drew a quick breath, and smiled.

"You understand? I aim at Guadeloupe. Meanwhile, there are stepping stones."

"You would do well to keep this ship, then," said St. Rocher thoughtfully. "Vernier has a roving commission from the governor—you'll find the document somewhere about."

"I've found it—" O'Brien smiled again, but his eyes were like blue ice—"and by its terms the command falls to you if Vernier is killed or hurt."

St. Rocher's lips curved a little.

"So!" he murmured. "It promises well, provided there is no stumbling—over the stepping stones."

"Faith—" O'Brien laughed out—"I've learned not to stumble,

my friend! Lay our course for Margarita, and leave the rest to me. Men and gold I must have, to come at my revenge later—so we sail to Guadeloupe by way of Margarita!"

I V

MARGARITA—RAVAGED BY Captain Vaugon's filibusters ten years afterward, and later quite destroyed by earthquake, and abandoned—was in those days a pretty place, built as it was at the mouth of the Santos River, with the hills behind.

Up the river and in the valleys were the fertile lands of rich *haciendados*. Enslaved Indian labor was plentiful at this period, before the pestilence had wiped out Indian and Spaniard alike, letting the rich fields relapse into jungle. The little port was small but afforded perfect protection, for a wide sandspit, engulfed at the time of the earthquake, ran out and curved about to help form a harbor. The white buildings along the rising shore, the plaza and church on the plateau above, the sheds and boat works on the beach, and the square stone building beyond, where silver from all the district was smelted down for the royal treasury, afforded a scene of activity and delight; the town looked much larger than it really was, indeed.

At the end of the sandspit was a battery of six twenty-pound carronades, so placed as to command either the channel or the harbor itself. Above the beach on the first rise of ground lay the fort, a solid stone structure, whose heavy guns had the whole of the harbor at their mercy.

In the harbor lay a few fishing craft and numerous Indian *pirogues,* over which towered the massive rising bulk of the *Santiago* galleon. She had been warped in as close as might be for the repairs, which were now practically finished. Beyond her lay the San Martin, the Spanish craft which had brought O'Brien and his fellow captives into these waters, a faster and trimmer ship, built for fighting alone. She was newly arrived from Spain, while the galleon was bound thither.

On the beach below the fort was a long double row of thatched huts—*barracoons* for the slaves, white or black or Indian, who labored on the rising bastions of the fort and on the new buildings of the town. The better part of these slaves were now white, being the crews and lading of two Virginia bound bark carrying plantation slaves; and now slaves and masters alike, Jacobites or no, were cast together into a more desperate and hopeless slavery.

There was little care spent in watching them. They were safe enough by day, and toward sunset were marched to their huts, fed, and then ironed by the overseers, whose dwelling, a small fort in itself, was at the end of the line of huts.

Self-sustaining, prosperous, a little out of the world even for this New World, Margarita had no worries; and her governor, Don Augusto Gonzalez, was very much his own master. At the present moment, the town had all the aspect of a *fiesta,* for every house held guests and the fort was crammed, and the governor's palace itself filled to the doors with nobility. All the soldiers from the galleon, a full hundred of them, were living ashore, and so were her two-score passengers—officials and their families, gentlemen, friars, returning to Spain and glad to spend this time ashore while the repairs were being made. Only her working crew remained aboard the *Santiago,* while the *San Martin* was even emptier, most of her complement being down with scurvy and encamped ashore.

Thus were matters on the day of the governor's ball—a grand *fiesta* to be held that same evening in the *palacio* on the plateau, in farewell to the chief guests. For, in two days, the galleon would be outward bound once more on her long voyage to Spain; she had been hauled out into deep water, and all this day the slaves had worked refilling her water butts with clear-water.

It was an hour before sunset when the *Sta. Teresa* was sighted, standing about Cape Formo with evident intent to make Margarita. Her rig caused swift alarm; bugles shrilled, drums beat, men ran to battery and fort, and the magazines were opened—she might be one of a filibuster squadron. The *San Martin* was brought around with her starboard broadside to bear on the channel.

The visitor, however, proved to be alone, and the alarm was stilled. The flag of Spain was seen at her main, scarce a dozen men were visible on her deck, and Don Augusto sent out a pilot to fetch her in; with the light air, she could not drop anchor before dark, so *flambeaux* and torches were ordered out, and the stately don went down to meet her captain at the landing.

Aboard her, O'Brien received the half-breed pilot with polite Spanish phrases and turned over the wheel to him. The men on deck were all Dutchmen, who spoke Spanish fluently; and O'Brien soon heard of the governor's *fiesta* and all else. He presently drew St. Rocher aside and spoke with him softly, as the little harbor opened out.

"See to it yourself," he concluded. "Don't trust one of our men to act independently, except Hobbs. You'd better aim those guns yourself; double shot them, to get her spars with the first broadside. Run up a lantern the minute you're back aboard, and I'll be ready."

The pilot laid the brigantine exactly where O'Brien wanted her—between the battery on the sandspit and the *San Martin*. Beyond the latter, under the guns of the fort, lay the great galleon. From the Spaniards' point of view, the newcomer was safely boxed.

Not that there was any suspicion of her, now. Indeed, there could be none after Don Diego Ramirez y Ribera stepped ashore and announced himself, with profound bows, to the governor. In some fashion his severe elegance outshone all the glitter of Don Augusto and his officers. The light of the *flambeaux* touched up ruddily his gorgeous black velvet with the richest of lace at throat and cuffs, his one jewel, the magnificent gold hilted rapier; and above, his bleached and powdered hair, and the bronzed face with the blue eyes.

"*Verdamente!*" ran the mutter through the crowd that gaped around. "*Viejo Cristiano!* One of the ancient Gothic blood!"

Don Augusto was impressed, and welcomed Don Diego most warmly. Then the visitor checked him, and looked him in the eye with some intentness. A few questions to the pilot had served him well.

"Is it possible, señor don," he demanded, "that you are of the Gonzalez family of Estramadura, of the strain of Aguilar that goes back to the ancient glories of the cave of Covadonga?"

"That is indeed the boast of my family, señor—" Don Augusto beamed.

"Embrace me, my more than cousin!" cried Don Diego with stately pride. "For you must know that we are indeed cousins of a sort, my father's sainted wife having been the offshoot of your glorious race! Have I not heard my worthy parent declaim upon the honor of this alliance with the house of Gonzalez? Closer are we than cousins. Indeed, we are brothers in blood and pride!"

Don Augusto was more than delighted, but as a matter of duty bethought to ask about papers. Don Diego snapped his fingers.

"Papers! I have none, good cousin—and why? Because a rascally filibuster laid me aboard two days out of San Domingo—you have doubtless observed the marks of his shot aboard us. Aye, and captured us, rifling our ship of everything; but he was dealing with a Ramirez y Ribera, let me tell you, and the noble blood of Gonzalez and Ramirez could not brook the affront. That same night I got free and overpowered him and his men. True, I did not get my goods back, for his ship was separated from us in the storm; but at least I had the pleasure of hanging him! And I have half a dozen of his rascally crew aboard. May I have the honor of presenting them to you for hanging?"

Here was news; great news. Don Augusto even forgot his *fiesta* momentarily, demanding the name of the filibuster.

"Some scoundrelly Frenchman—Vernier, I believe. Is there such a one?"

Was there, indeed! *Por los clavos de Cristo!* Don Augusto embraced his guest and cousin with new warmth. That scourge, that unspeakable beast, that louse of a Vernier—overcome by a cousin, an uncle, a very brother Gonzalez! The news provoked a tumult in the crowd, a clamor of wild delight, and Don Diego turned nonchalantly from the ovation to point to the boat just coming in.

"Here are the rascals, good cousin," he exclaimed. "See, I present them to you freely. Hang them or use them as slaves, at your pleasure."

Acclamations, vivas, filled the evening air as the huge, red bearded Hobbs and half a dozen of his fellows were trundled ashore and rescued by the governor's guards from the onslaught of the crowd. When he had inspected them, Don Augusto summoned a lieutenant of his guard.

"Place them in the slave quarters for tonight, señor," he commanded, "and leave them bound as they are—the dogs will not be hurt by tight ropes. In the morning we shall settle their fate. Come, my heroic cousin, you are my guest. I shall be honored in presenting you to the commander of yonder galleon, the Conde d'Aguilar, and to his officers and my own. My house is yours, and in honoring you I do myself untold honor!"

So, with the delighted Don Augusto at his side and the torches and guards round about, Don Diego Ramirez y Ribera was marched up to the *palacio* to become the guest of honor at the *fiesta* and to receive the stately felicitations of a score of stately Spanish men upon his great feat. If black eyed Spanish ladies fluttered and pressed about him likewise, they found his high courtesy and ready tongue as notable as his deeds at arms.

HOBBS AND his five companions, meanwhile, were marched up to the slave *barracoons* and with many a kick and cuff, were hurled into a hut where miserable chained-wretches already occupied the foul ground. Their feet were bound, and they were left until the morning.

"All safe, bullies?" said Hobbs in the darkness, and the others assented. A voice spoke out.

"Be ye Englishmen or not?"

"Aye," said Hobbs, with a chuckle. "And you?"

"Slocombe, o' the bark *Powhatan*, from the Virginia capes."

"Then stow your jaw, Master Slocombe, till I get rid o' these cursed ropes. We ha' files hid in our shoon and knives in our breeches, my bully, and a good ship awaiting. Stow the jaw, Master, for there's work ahead."

Now arose curious sounds from the long double row of huts where lay fifty-odd white men and a score of Caribs—low, hoarse voices, and the steady scrape of files on iron, and now and again that of a broken link. None of these sounds reached the guards and overseers in their own quarters, however; music drifted to them from the *palacio* and the town, and they had a girl or two of their own, and wine as they willed it; so who were they to bother with the safely ironed slaves in this night of celebration?

In the fort and the town was dancing, and the two taverns were crowded. Lanterns strung about the plaza lighted great merrymaking before the church doors. From the *palacio* came the sounds of fiddle and bassoon; and there was a glitter of uniforms and gay silken gowns. And the envious sentries on the fort walls had more eyes for the *fiesta* than for aught amiss beyond. Even in the battery there was drinking and the twang of a guitar, for the dozen men left there had no minds to miss all the fun.

Miss it they did, however. Out of nowhere suddenly appeared a tall, cadaverous man all in black, with immensely long arms and a pistol at the end of each, who commanded them to stand up and make no sound. Before they could collect their wits, other men poured in upon them, triced them up, gagged them, and then set to work spiking the carronades of the battery.

With not a shot fired, St. Rocher led his men back to their boat and was set aboard the brigantine, where he hoisted a lantern to the main yard. The boat, with eight men in her, crept ashore to the landing and waited there, a lantern ready but hid under a cloak.

Aboard the galleon and the *San Martin,* likewise, was music and wine, but no true gaiety for lack of female company. There was none to see the shadowy figures that flitted down from the slave *barracoons* to the beach, and there flitted aboard *pirogues* and boats, as directed by a huge man with a red beard. In all this part of the business was only one bit of ill luck—when a half drunken overseer stumbled out of his quarters and started off to find a certain wench of his acquaintance, and ran slap into a number of those flitting figures whom he had been wont to lash by day. That, however, was his ill luck, not theirs, as was proven when his body was found next morning.

Amid the merriment and feasting, meantime, was Don Diego Ramirez y Ribera, seated on the left of the governor, on whose right sat the Conde d'Aguilar. Worthy Don Augusto, full of Spanish pride and Xeres wine, blinked rapidly when Don Diego leaned over and whispered in his ear.

"Say you so, indeed, my cousin?" he returned under his breath. "A real treasure?"

"Hush!" said Don Diego sternly. "Not here. Can we speak a little apart?"

"Of a surety,"—and Don Augusto excused himself from the festive board, pleading a trifle of official business with his heroic cousin which could not well be put off.

Once outside, in the cool night air of the terrace outside the *palacio,* he turned to his guest.

"But you did not mention this treasure before, Don Diego!"

"It was for your ear alone, good señor don!" returned the hero. "Besides, it is a matter to discuss in private—whether it should be turned in to your agent of the royal treasurer, or otherwise disposed."

"Hm!" said the governor thoughtfully. "That depends upon its size, my cousin."

"Chests of it!" said Don Diego with enthusiasm. "There is a whole chest filled with pieces of eight, another of jewels—"

The governor caught his arm.

"What? A real treasure?"

"Aye. What say you, my honored cousin—would you care to inspect it? I ordered a boat to await me at the landing. We might go over it together and arrange its division, if such be your pleasure; we would never be missed—"

"Come, then," exclaimed the governor, trembling with eagerness and greed. "You are right, good cousin—this is a matter for private division. *Dios!* Only one of the Gonzalez strain could show such generosity, such true nobility, such scorn of base metal! Come!"

Don Diego, having seen the lantern at the yard of his ship, did not delay one moment.

Together the two men left the *palacio* and the town; arm in arm they turned their steps toward the landing below. The water was glimmering before them, when Don Diego uttered a soft whistle. The lantern in the waiting boat was uncovered.

At this moment the governor halted abruptly, and his jaw fell.

"What is that?" he exclaimed sharply, pointing toward the harbor. *"Nombre de Dios!* Am I mad, or do you see it also, my cousin?"

"See what, señor don?"

"That!" The governor pointed toward the dark mass of the galleon, rising huge before them. "She is moving. Listen! There are men's voices—there is fighting aboard her—"

Something struck him under the ear, and he toppled forward into the waiting boat.

"Give way, lads!" exclaimed O'Brien, as he leaped in. "No time to lose now—"

Aboard the galleon flamed out a shot, then another. A wild chorus of voices leaped out from her decks, and the clash of steel came clanging over the water.

A sentry on the fort fired his piece, as did another. Above the music and gaiety rose the sounds of alarm; a bugle broke in with shrill, strident blare, and a drum began to roll. Lights sprang on the deck of the *San Martin,* voices shouted forth. The great galleon, indeed, was moving, half a dozen boats strung ahead of her, towing, while wild figures streamed aloft and let go canvas.

The boat swept in under the counter of the *Sta. Teresa,* and O'Brien swarmed up the waiting ladder. He saw slow-matches along the deck, red points in the darkness.

"St. Rocher!" rang out his voice. "Let go, man, let go!"

"Waiting for you, *mon ami,*" came the voice of the Frenchman. "Fire, lads!"

The larboard broadside erupted flame and smoke with a shattering roar. As the deck reeled men leaped to the capstan; there was a clink of pawls, a sharp patter of feet, hoarse, panting voices growling oaths. The ship swung about slowly, steadily, until St. Rocher cried out an order.

A moment later the starboard broadside crashed out terribly. Before the echoes died, before the staggering ship came to an even keel, men were leaping aloft, shaking out the topsails to catch the light upper wind; while, from the riven and shattered *San Martin* came, not the roar of broadsides, but the shrieks and terrorized cries of men.

She, at least, would not pursue. And before the missing governor could be found to give orders, the two fleeing ships would be past reach of the guns in the fort above.

As, indeed, they were.

V

IN THE CHILL light of dawn, with the sun not yet up, the two ships came to anchor under the point of Cape Formo.

The prisoners taken aboard the galleon were kicked down into two boats—with oars only—and O'Brien ushered the unhappy Don Augusto to the gangway, amid the grins of his men.

"*Vaya con Dios,* my good cousin!" he exclaimed merrily. "Go with God, and may you not be too sun blistered ere you come into Margarita harbor and explain matters to the excellent Conde d'Aguilar. Pray convey my sympathy to him—"

The wretched governor fled down into his boat, and O'Brien turned to find St. Rocher rigging a gangway from the waist of the brigantine to a midships port of the galleon, and men flocking into the waist of his ship. There was no sea here, and the two craft were moored close.

From the poop rail, O'Brien looked down at the wild, tattered men who so far outnumbered his own crew—many of them with irons still fast to their wrists, though the chains had been filed or snapped. He lifted a hand to still their wild yells of rejoicing.

"Freedom, my lads, and no more slavery!" rang out his voice, provoking yet another shrill yelp. Then a wild Irish kern swung up both arms and waved them.

"Shamus! Shamus O'Brien!" he yelled, and there was a wild, shrill chorus. "Shamus *abu! Lamh laidir an uachtar!* The Strong Hand above!"

More than one man here knew him, and O'Brien's blue eyes kindled as he heard the old O'Brien war cry ring out.

"Well, my lads, you've pronounced your fate there," he exclaimed, a whimsical twist to his lips. "The Strong Hand above—aye; and those of you who sail with me will find it true enough, and heaven help ye! Now, then, to business. How many of ye want to sail under me?"

Another chorus of shouts, and waving arms; but there were some who shouted not, nor waved.

"Hear me, now—" his voice quelled them. "We'll fall to work looting everything out of the galleon yonder, which will take us most of the day or more. All hands on the job. Then, those who so desire, will sail with me. Those who do not can take the galleon and welcome, and I'll sail with her as far as Dominica or Port Royal, to see her safe. The Indios will want to take a boat now and steal ashore, and let them do it if they will. As to the galleon's loot—" he paused—"ten shares out of a hundred go to me, another ten to Vicomte de St. Rocher, five to the bosun and master gunner, and the balance is divided among ye. What's aboard us already belongs to my original crew."

There was a riotous approval, amid which Hobbs stepped forward.

"What about our mates, back there on Aves Isle, Master?"

"Why—" O'Brien laughed—"we'll go back and pick them up, and we'll set them ashore at Dominica. How's that, eh? I want none o' them in my crew. So get to work, now—hatches off! Larboard watch, remain here to stow cargo; take charge of them, St. Rocher. I'll go aboard with the others and strip out cargo—or what we want of it."

A half dozen men came to him as he stepped into the waist— the English officers of the two barks taken by the *San Martin*. Captain Slocombe faced him, bluntly enough.

"If ye meant your words, Master, it was well said. There be some of us who've no liking for service with you, though God knows we owe you deep thanks for takin' us out of bondage."

O'Brien clapped him heartily on the shoulder.

"Enough, Master! No man sails with me against his will. What I said shall stand. The galleon is yours when we've done with her, and I'll lend you what men you need until we're within sail of Port Royal. You'll find enough aboard her after we're through, to repay what you've lost. So fall to work, all hands!"

Fall to work they did, with a will.

All that day they labored shifting cargo, while the bulwarks groaned together and the seas glittered emptily under the hot sun. The freed Indian slaves took a boat and went ashore, but toward sunset appeared a score of *pirogues,* coming stealing out from the coast lagoons, all of them laden down with fruits and green things and fresh meat—gifts for these enemies of Spain.

And all that day O'Brien moved among men who knew him or had known of him from others, and some of them had slaved beside him on Jamaica plantations. When evening came, he and St. Rocher sat alone in the great cabin, with Phelim serving them, and listened to the hatches being battened down and made fast, as they ate and drank.

"It's a great treasure we have aboard here, my Colonel," said St. Rocher thoughtfully.

"Enough to gladden many a heart," said O'Brien.

"But not yours, eh?" The dark eyes of the Frenchman glittered at him. "What'll you do with this gold and silver, stamped with the royal stamp of the Spanish king, eh?"

O'Brien looked at him for a moment, and nodded.

"I see. Hard to dispose of, eh?"

St. Rocher shrugged.

"Not at Basse-terre, for example. Elsewhere, the English ships have made the seas none too safe for filibusters, and I'd hate to end on Gallows Point, at Port Royal."

O'Brien saw the point. If they returned and landed the treasure in Guadeloupe, whose commission they carried, all well and good; but the planters who had outfitted the *Malouin* would then share in the loot. Elsewhere, they might have difficulty in disposing of it, unless they stood up for New York or Boston, these places being clearing houses for the filibusters.

"You suggest—?" queried O'Brien, frowning slightly.

"Common sense. Petit Guave, on the East Coast, is the rendezvous and outfitting point at Guadeloupe. There are bankers and agents there, whom I know personally, who'll take over the gold—and no questions asked. We can land the stuff taken by Vernier on the regular account, and turn over our own stuff for your account. I'll act as captain, vice Vernier. Then we can sail around to Basse-terre, get our credits and cash from the bankers, less their commission, and do as we want with it. The planters will share in Vernier's loot, but will know nothing of our own. And when we've finished our business there—"

"We'll not want to return soon," and O'Brien smiled grimly. "Good enough; you have a head, my friend."

S O , A N hour later, they hauled off the land, the two ships, and headed for the Isle of Aves. How much treasure they had taken out of the galleon, O'Brien did not know in round figures. It was no enormous and spectacular haul, for the greater part of her lading had been useless to him; but it was enough to start his name flying through the middle seas, once the news of his exploit got out.

There was no further question, either among the old men or the new, as to his authority. This was settled for all time; he installed a discipline aboard the ship which was rigid, and was as great a gentleman on his own quarterdeck as the Conde d'Aguilar. Since this was no affectation but the man himself, the crew respected him the more for it. And the change in the lieutenant was tremendous. Become the Vicomte de St. Rocher once more, no longer a drunken, hopeless wastrel, but a gentle-man with a sword at his side and new keenness in his eye, this Frenchman was in all truth a new man. He fenced each morning with O'Brien in the ship's waist, spending an hour or more at it. Despite his long arms, he was invariably worsted, but the pair kept up their sport with a dogged insistence which came in time to fetch knowing looks and significant winks from the watching men. Some reason for it, they gathered—not quite guessing that O'Brien was getting his rusted muscles and eye in shape for particular work ahead.

At Aves they found, without any chagrin, that their birds were flown; another ship had obviously stopped here and picked up Vernier's men. They halted also at the careening ground on the northern beach, and while the galleon rested at anchor, all hands fell to scraping the foul bottom of the *Malouin*, whose name was likewise restored—temporarily.

Off again at last, and there came a day of pleasant weather when the blue hills of Jamaica lifted over the horizon. Dangerous ground, this, for filibusters, with the king's ships thickly about; so, shaking hands with Slocombe and his dozen men, O'Brien took his own men back again and parted company with the galleon, heading up for Petit Guave. An hour later the topsails of a king's ship lifted over the horizon with a white squall, but the *Malouin* dropped her again long ere sunset.

Colonel James O'Brien was rapidly becoming a navigator, thanks to his lieutenant. St. Rocher, pupil of Vauban and skilled artillerist, had found navigation a simple matter, and passed on his instruction readily to O'Brien. Unusual as this might be, in a day when such matters were left to professional pilots as beneath the dignity of gentlemen commanders, it was a distinct advantage; and when, one evening, O'Brien announced that they would raise the hills of Guadeloupe next day, his lieutenant nodded assent.

"Right. And now that it's all close at hand, my Colonel—does it look different?"

O'Brien's blue eyes were like ice.

"Very different, St. Rocher; very different. We can plan nothing, however, until we land and get the news."

"Eh? You don't mean that you'll give up your ideas about the yardarm?"

O'Brien smiled grimly.

"My dear fellow, I never give up ideas. I merely enlarge them. Will you muster all hands directly after dinner?"

They gathered in the waist, staring up at the poop rail, where O'Brien stood slim and elegant in his black velvet.

"Men," he said directly and simply, "we land tomorrow at Petit Guave. The gold taken by Vernier will be turned over to the account of the *Malouin* in the usual fashion. We'll go on to Basse-terre, and you who sailed with Vernier will get your money there from the agents. The gold from the galleon, however, is another matter. Say nothing of it. This will be handled separately, and your share will come to you at Basse-terre also. From the moment we sight Petit Guave, I no longer exist. M. de St. Rocher becomes your captain. Say no word of me ashore. Only Vernier's men will land at Petit Guave, mind that. We've work to do at Basse-terre, and the men who go ashore with M. de St. Rocher tomorrow night had best keep a close tongue or we'll all be hanged. Hobbs, you'll have charge of the shore boat. I'll depend on you."

"Aye, sir," returned the boatswain.

At sunset next evening they dropped anchor in the bight of Petit Guave, finding the roads empty of other ships.

St. Rocher went ashore, and O'Brien, at the forward rail, looked out over the blue and red hills of sunset toward Basse-terre—where the Marquis de Fleury, all unwitting, awaited him.

VI

A LITTLE AFTER dark St. Rocher came aboard, ahead of the boats coming for the gold, and he was filled with news; bursting with it.

"All arranged, my Colonel!" he exclaimed exultantly, coming into the cabin where O'Brien awaited him. "It goes ashore at once, will be weighed and valued tonight, and I'm to be present to check up. We can leave in the morning for Basse-terre—if we do leave for there."

"Eh?" O'Brien gave him a quick glance, pausing in his pipe filling operation. "Why not?"

St. Rocher shrugged.

"Fleury arrived four days ago. He won't take over his duties for a week or more, until the governor sails for France. Meantime, he's visiting with a M. de la Potherie, also a distant connection of Pontchartrain and a relative, who has a large plantation. All our Creole planters are extremely hospitable, my Colonel, keep open house, play for high stakes, and enjoy life to the utmost. There'll probably be a large assemblage at Potherie's plantation, both officers and gentlemen planters."

O'Brien tamped down his pipe, drew over the candle, lighted it, and sank back in his chair.

"Yes?" he said thoughtfully. "It looks different when close up, as you observed. Where is this plantation?"

"About three days' ride to the north, and a few miles back from the sea."

"Hm! Are there post houses in this island?"

St. Rocher broke into a laugh.

"My friend, every plantation is a post house! Travelers are welcomed with the true Homeric hospitality—welcome the coming, speed the parting, guest. You are thinking of riding north?"

"I am riding north," said O'Brien slowly.

"It was my thought that you might, so I got an advance if you need it." From his pocket St. Rocher brought out numerous *rouleaux* of gold pieces. "I know the island well. I can guide you and we may ride together—"

"Not so," broke in O'Brien. "Three days—hm! Suppose you arrange for horses and a guide, to leave at sunrise. I'll go alone. You take the ship around to Basse-terre and make collections. If you cannot get the sum in cash, as seems unlikely, get bankers' paper on Bordeaux or Paris, which we can always negotiate with any French house. Is this plantation near Basse-terre?"

"No; on the other side of the island. I could bring the ship around in a day's time and send a boat ashore—"

"Excellent!" said O'Brien, with a quick nod. "You may or may not meet with delays at Basse-terre; so as soon as you're ready to leave there, send one of the men who knows the island to report to me at the plantation, by road. He can apprise me of the rendezvous and the time."

"And you? What will you do then—alone?"

O'Brien smiled.

"Faith, my dear chap, how should I know that until the time comes? I think I'll take Phelim with me, to act as my servant. He speaks French and is a resourceful rascal. So it's settled."

And settled it was.

With sunrise, the *Malouin* weighed anchor for Basse-terre, and O'Brien, from the beach, waved her farewell. Then he turned to Phelim, who was getting their baggage lashed aboard a led horse, and nodded to the Creole guide.

"Allons, mes amis!"

O'Brien was not long in discovering that what the Creoles called a three day ride, he could have covered in one, if need be—but there was no need. He found himself welcomed at every plantation like a royal guest. The men whom he met on the road pressed him to visit them and would not be refused; all that was theirs was his, in a complete but indolent hospitality. His statement that he was an Irishman in French service, but now on private affairs, ended all queries; he was received as the gentleman he was, and this spirit of magnificent comradeship uplifted him. Soft tongued women, men who dreamed of Versailles and Paris, slaves to anticipate every wish—it was a land of luxury, of rich plantations; a land of tropic ease, in which even the horses drowsed along at a snail's pace and would not be hurried.

Upon the third afternoon they came to the plantation of M. de la Potherie. What was more to the point, they came upon M. de la Potherie himself—an energetic gentleman of fifty, who was hastening his overseers in the repairs of a bridge just outside his estate. Until the bridge was repaired, no coaches could pass—and several coaches were in a devilish hurry, it seemed. The worthy planter welcomed Colonel O'Brien warmly.

"A friend of M. le Marquis? My dear fellow, the house is at

your command! You shall have my own room; we are, it is true, a trifle filled at the moment, but there's no lack of space. Yes, your lackey shan't suffer—I'll ride along back with you myself. So you knew M. le Marquis in the field, eh? Ah, a great man, this Fleury! Sagacity—that's what we need in this colonial administration, my dear sir! Look at those fields of sugar cane—what has built them up? Not the wisdom of our governors, I assure you. With M. de Fleury at the head of things, you'll see Guadeloupe forge to the front. But your pardon. You are not upon the staff?"

"A private traveler, no more," said O'Brien. "Has any one been here seeking me? I was looking for a messenger from Basse-terre."

"None, to my knowledge. Come, m'sieu, let us go on to the house."

So they did, and a grand house it was—high ceilinged, of massive hewn mahogany, with spacious galleries, and surrounded by gardens and graveled walks. Presently O'Brien found himself installed in the satin walled bed chamber of La Potherie, and his luggage as well. Two slaves and a tub appeared, and he was bathed luxuriously.

Only then did he find himself alone with Phelim, who had opened up the packs. O'Brien chuckled and reached for the fine Spanish linen that had belonged to the Conde d'Aguilar.

"Phelim, me lad—off with ye," he exclaimed. "I've no need of a lackey. Look about, use your wits. Discover where the stables are, where the Marquis de Fleury is lodged—this most particularly. He's spending the day with a neighbor and not back yet. And, Phelim, no drinking, ye scurvy rascal, or it's my whip to your back, mind! Too much depends on sobriety, now. Above all, keep your eyes open for a messenger from the ship."

Phelim departed, grinning widely.

Darkness was gathering and a slave came, lighting the lamps of brass and crystal. O'Brien dressed with care in the most gorgeous that the galleon had afforded—and surveyed himself in the long mirror with approval. True, he lacked a wig; but in the colonies many gentlemen wore their own hair; and his was most becoming, powdered and drawn back in a silken knot. His deep lace was of the finest. The azure silk suit, picked out with gold, the diamond buckles, the jeweled rings, the splendid order of St. Jago—and, above all, the man himself—proclaimed at once that here was one who had walked with princes. When a slave came to inform him that the company was assembled for dinner, O'Brien followed, sure of his effect.

N O R   W A S he deceived. The officers, fresh from France, the wealthy planters and their ladies, fairly gasped at his magnificence, and he adopted the rather lisping, indolent air so much the fashion in France to increase the impression. His entry was something of a triumph, and then, at the far end of the glittering room, he found himself bowing before the Marquis de Fleury.

It came to him, with a shock, how the years had flown.

Here was no trim, elegant cavalier in the uniform of the Gardes Nobles—but a rather pompous man, heavyset, double chinned, imperious of manner, a great curled periwig adorning his head, the stars of St. Louis and St. Michel on his breast; and the powdered face turned white as death when O'Brien straightened from his bow.

"Death of my life!" exclaimed the marquis. "Not my old companion in arms, surely—not my friend O'Brien of the Irish Brigade?"

"The same, your Excellency—" and O'Brien smiled in his gay manner. "Older, it is true, and somewhat less honored, perhaps—but still O'Brien. Do you remember our dicing for English gold on the drum head, that night before Nevers, eh? Do you remember that tavern we found—"

Friendliness! The terror left the eyes of Fleury and with a great laugh he leaned forward, caught O'Brien in his arms, embraced him warmly.

Under the warmth of that embrace, O'Brien shivered.

And now there was talk of this and that—old campaigns, old comrades, dukes and princes and courtiers, and when they dined, the marquis insisted that O'Brien be close to him. It was as though, finding his swift and dreadful fear all groundless, he were pushed to the other extreme, to the utmost friendliness. And in this O'Brien gave him laugh for laugh, toast for toast, compliment for compliment.

Dinner over, there were music and dancing, when the wine and pipes had been finished, and one or two tales recounted that were not for ladies' ears; and straightway the card tables were set out, and the gold began to clink merrily enough. O'Brien played against the marquis, and for a time won heavily, for he scattered wagers with lavish hand.

"You have the devil's own luck, my Colonel!" complained Fleury, with a grimace.

"Unlucky at love, lucky at gaming, monsieur!" But O'Brien's laugh was so merry and light ringing, that the swift glance Fleury shot at him could detect nothing behind the words.

As it chanced, however, O'Brien fell into a losing streak, and presently had gambled away all the gold in his pockets. He rose from the table with a laugh, and a black slave touched his arm.

"M'soo, there is a man outside with your servant, asking for you."

The man was Dunker, the keen eyed Dutchman, who had just arrived from Basse-terre.

O'Brien walked with him and Phelim under the trees, in the starlight, and heard the message. St. Rocher had made his collections in due course, but had been forced to weigh anchor and sail in all haste, that very day. A ship had come in bearing certain of Vernier's men aboard, that morning, and there was trouble that might come to any length; so St. Rocher simply weighed and departed, after sending Dunker on his errand.

"Vernier's men will go to the governor most certainly," said Dunker, "and French waters will be too hot for us."

"They will, that's sure," and O'Brien chuckled. "Go on. The rendezvous?"

"The coast, east of here—there's a road goes to Turtle Bay from here," said Dunker. "We're to be there at noon sharp; a boat will come ashore for us. The weather promises good."

"Peste!" O'Brien was startled. "Not much time to act, eh? Good. Listen close, now, for our heads depend on it. How long will it take us to make the rendezvous?"

"I know the trail," said Phelim. "I was up here after turtle last year, Colonel. Afoot, it will take us a good four hours or more. It's the devil's own road, only used by turtle hunters in the season, for no one lives in the hills yonder."

"Good. Then both of you come to my room a trifle before sunrise—the house won't be astir until hours later. And come ready for the road."

O'Brien left them and went back into the gay rooms.

A little later, he contrived to find himself alone with M. de la Potherie. He beckoned that gentleman into a quiet corner and looked him in the eye.

"Monsieur," he said, "I owe you thanks for your hospitality, and as I shall be leaving in the morning, I wish to give you my thanks tonight."

The planter would have pressed him to a longer stay, but the chill blue eyes silenced him.

"That was not all I have to say," went on O'Brien, refusing the proffered snuff box. "There is more. Some years ago, monsieur, a certain gentleman abducted my wife; she died later, of illness and shame. It was as though he had deliberately killed her, but much worse."

Potherie, inexpressibly shocked, expressed quick sympathy. Again his voice died before the blue eyes and the rock hard face of his guest.

"That man, monsieur—" and O'Brien met his eye gravely, "is a guest in your house. When, tomorrow, you discover that one of your guests is missing, you will know why."

"*Diantre!* I'll gladly second you myself, monsieur!" exclaimed the planter heatedly. O'Brien shook his head and said calmly—

"No question here of a duel, my friend, but of an execution."

"Good! Let us speak now to M. le Marquis—as our governor, you understand—"

"Monsieur—" O'Brien bowed slightly—"what I have told you is a confidence between gentlemen, and to excuse what may seem an affront to your hospitality."

"I shall so consider it, monsieur," returned the other. "My only regret is that you refuse my active help."

O'Brien smiled thinly at this, in whimsical amusement.

"Faith, I think you'll have no regret tomorrow! Shall we rejoin the company, monsieur?"

VII

THE DOOR of the stately bed chamber offered no resistance to Phelim's deftly knavish fingers. The three—Dunker was with them—entered. O'Brien went to the high, curtained bed and abruptly flung open the drapes. Then he reached forward and plucked the nightcap from the head of the sleeping man.

Fleury, a bit heavy with wine, had only gone to bed a couple of hours previously. When a knife point pricked his throat, even, he was slow to waken; but the face of the man above him, clear cut in the dawn light, drove reality into his brain.

"M. le Marquis," said O'Brien in a cold voice, "there was something you forgot last night. You forgot to ask after my wife's health. No, I have no intention of putting my knife into your throat; but I shall do it if you call out."

He reached out, caught the coverlets in one hand and flung them back.

"Come, get out of bed!" he ordered harshly.

The great man was robbed of greatness, and knew it. His

bald shaved head looked like that of a vulture; his cheeks hung pendulous, red veined, and his teeth chattered with terror. He put both feet to the floor, and so lost his last chance of regaining dignity and courage.

No matter how brave a man may be, only let him be accustomed to boots—and in his bare feet he is a lost man. Besides, terror was mounting in Fleury's heart; a dreadful fear gathering from out the past. When he saw the two silent men looking on, he lost all hope.

"O'Brien!" he quavered, as he sat on the bedside. "I will make amends—"

"That is true…" O'Brien smiled grimly. He was clad in his black velvet now, a cloak about his shoulders, a hat beneath his arm. "Phelim! His Excellency's breeches! Nothing else."

"What—what do you mean to do?" stammered the marquis.

"That does not concern you," said O'Brien, as Phelim came with a pair of breeches. "Don these, put on your shoes, and come with me. One cry, remember, and this knife drives into your ribs."

The Marquis de Fleury was well assured that the threat was true.

"Lead the way out, Phelim," ordered O'Brien. "Dunker, take his Excellency's arm, and if he treads too heavily, sink your knife in his *derrière*. March!"

The marquis, in night gown, breeches and shoes, obeyed the commands of this grim specter from his past—this specter who had not forgotten, who was not ignorant, after all.

The four men left the great plantation house and walked down the road. None saw them, for as yet not even the blacks were up and around. The power of an evil conscience left Fleury hesitant and unnerved, until it was too late.

Too late, indeed, when he came to a sudden halt, a half mile down the road, and turned.

"Where are we going?" he demanded heatedly. "What means this masquerade, this folly?"

"You fool!" said O'Brien, looking at him steadily. "Do you think that I will bandy words with you? The knife, Dunker."

A quarter-inch of steel drove into Fleury's hip. He choked back a howl, and thereafter made no effort to summon up his indignation.

They strode on into the sunrise, along a good road which presently crossed another, turned into a trail, and led them among the hills—here a mere footpath. Time passed, but the miles fell slowly behind them, for it was all up hill and down dale, stony and in places dangerous, wending ever toward the sea by circuitous ways. The morning was half spent before they had their first glimpse of the sea, far below and ahead.

And now a dreadful sort of courage had settled upon the Marquis de Fleury. He marched on in silence, bearing himself resolutely enough, a shattered pride creeping back into his flabby cheeks. When they halted at a brook crossing for a drink in lieu of breakfast, he knelt and drank in turn, and rose to look O'Brien in the eye silent, waiting. His feet, naked in his gaily buckled low shoes, were bleeding.

"Bring him," said O'Brien to the others. "No need to torture him—take it easily. I'll go ahead. If he escapes, you hang."

"He will not escape," said Dunker.

O'Brien strode on ahead of them, spurred by sharp uneasiness. Well enough he knew that by now the search would be on, though none would come this way at first, until other roads had been run down. And this path was interminable. Well, at least they would know why their governor had vanished, and with whom, when M. de la Potherie told his story. A grim smile played about O'Brien's lips as he set feet to the stones.

Then, after another endless hour, he came suddenly out upon a cliff above the sea, where the path zigzagged down perilously to a little rounded, sandy cove, bordered by a wide white beach. It was wearing on toward noon, now.

He stood there, incredulous; the blood leaped into his face, and ebbed again as realization smote him—and cold, sharp dismay.

There, bearing down from the north and running close in to the steep shores, almost within biscuit toss of the cliffs, was the *Malouin*. She was not, indeed, above a half mile distant; and he knew that they had caught sight of him on the cliff, almost instantly. He could see men clustered about a boat, getting it ready, and her white flag, with the golden lilies of France, dipped and was run up again, as a signal from St. Rocher.

It was not at her that he stared, however. The sandy cove below lay in shelter of a promontory of rock, jutting out eastward from the north and south cliffs. Below this sharp headland, to the south, the land fell sharply away in a great sickle sweep of coast. Within this curve, tacking up as though to ram headlong into the cliffs, but in reality waiting to make a sharp tack that would take them out past the promontory, were two ships. They were, perhaps, a mile distant from him, and he could make out every clearcut detail of them there in the white sunlight.

One, evidently the faster of the two and well in the lead, was a smart twenty gun sloop-of-war. The other was a fifty-two gun ship. And both of them flew the red cross of England. He, up there on the cliff, could see both them and the brigantine; but they could not see her, nor she them. And she was running down slap into their hands.

"What the devil!" came an ejaculation behind him. He turned to see Phelim in the lead, just catching sight of the ships below, while Dunker brought up the Marquis de Fleury.

"Captain," said the Dutchman stolidly, "the prisoner has offered us a thousand louis to let him escape."

"Very well," said O'Brien indifferently. "You shall have two thousand for refusing. Make all haste. Dunker, can we signal them?"

"They would but think we were hastening them on," said the Dutchman, and with a suppressed groan, O'Brien knew that it was so. Then he rallied from his dismay.

"Come, then—drive him down!" he called vibrantly, and

hurled himself at the sharp descent like a madman. Every minute counted now.

Swiftly the English ships were hidden from him by the headland, as he descended. The boat was coming in, red bearded Hobbs at the tiller. O'Brien remembered how the two ships had been bearing, calculated their speed, knew that the *Malouin* could not possibly slip away from them. There was but one chance—one slim, desperate, utterly mad chance—if he could get aboard her in time. It depended on speed, on action, on luck, on a dozen things—and nothing else could save her. Nor could that, very possibly.

"Faith, why calculate it out?" A laugh broke from him as he came at last to the shingle, and ran down to the sand, where the boat was but fifty feet away. "Play the game and be damned to them—win or lose! Quick, lads—put your backs into it! Two English ships just around the headland—lean on your oars!"

Phelim and Dunker came ploughing along, forcing the sweating, cursing marquis between them. The boat ran in, the prisoner was flung into her bow, and amid a chorus of questions and sharp exclamations, O'Brien leaped to the tiller as she was shoved sharply out.

"Double bank an oar, Hobbs," he commanded. "You, Phelim and Dunker—that's right! Pull, lads—we're caught by two English ships—pull with the devil at your backs! Thank the lord we've got St. Rocher aboard there and not some slow witted fool—pull!"

Not half comprehending, yet sharp spurred by his furious excitement, the men bent on their oars and sent the boat flying through the water. The *Malouin* was close in, for all the cliffs ran down straight into the water, which was steep-to along this coast; and as the swirls of foam fell behind them, O'Brien waved a hand to quiet the yells of greeting going up from the crowded bulwarks ahead.

"St. Rocher!" his voice lifted and was thrown back by the cliffs. "Hurry, man—you're trapped! Drop sail, drop sail— Piggoty, double shot the guns! Jump to it! Down helm!"

The urgency, the stark desperation of his voice, lashed into them. The *Malouin* had been drifting along under backed top-sails alone, for there was a smart breeze bearing down behind her. Now her men leaped into life, as O'Brien's voice made the danger clear. Her yards, swung around, men swarmed aloft and canvas fell billowing out. The boat foamed in beneath her side and caught a line, and O'Brien went up like a madman, leaving the others to get the prisoner aboard as best they might. St. Rocher met him but there was no time for talk.

"Take the guns, St. Rocher—I'll take the helm! Keep the ports triced up till I give the word—double shot every gun! You take the larboard side—Piggoty, starboard battery! Hurry, lads—up wi' the powder and ball, there!"

"O'Brien!" St. Rocher paused, his dark eyes anxious. "One broadside from them would sink us. We can't hope to run from them—what's your intent?"

O'Brien laughed curtly.

"Faith, since we can neither run nor fight, I mean to do both! To your guns, man!"

And he leaped aft to take the helm, as the sails bellied out and the *Malouin* leaned over to the thrust of them.

"Silence on the decks!" blared O'Brien's voice from the poop. "Cease talking—be ready to jump when I give the order!"

She rushed for the headland as though to crash upon the rocks towering there.

VIII

DUNKER CAME dragging his miserable prisoner to the poop.

"What'll I do with him, Captain?"

"Lock him in a cabin and get to your station," snapped O'Brien, leaning on the wheel; no eyes now for the Governor of Guadeloupe—every attention was fastened on those high rocks ahead, on the headland for which he was making, his thoughts with those two invisible ships just beyond.

The sea opened out, abruptly he swung the helm, the man beside lending his weight. With the wind dead behind her, every sail drawing full, the brigantine swung up to an even keel and gathered new speed, a foamy bone in her teeth as she hurtled forward. A yelp sounded from the men, then silence— for dead ahead appeared the sloop and the ship-of-war, a scent two cable lengths apart.

"All but the gun crews—down behind the bulwarks!" rang out O'Brien's order, and the men obeyed, albeit sullenly.

For an instant the enemy seemed dazed by this sudden apparition of a ship thus leaping from behind the headland, rushing at them down the wind, the flag of France at her peak—a mere brigantine, which either one of them could sink with one broadside! Then men shouted, whistles shrilled, drums beat, men went rushing to battle stations.

"Ports down!" shouted O'Brien, and the ports fell with a crash and the guns were run out and made fast. "Aim for their rigging—the sloop is yours, St. Rocher; but await the word!"

Sharp as was the discipline aboard those ships, they had scant time to open magazines, bring up powder, get the guns loaded and run out. Straight in between them headed the *Malouin*, holding the weather gage of them, while marines were hastily flung into rank along their decks and muskets loaded in a wild flurry of haste, faces staring at the apparition.

"Piggoty, hold your fire until I give the word!" rang the voice of O'Brien. "St. Rocher—let her have it!"

They were dead abreast the sloop now, for she was well in the lead. St. Rocher was laying a gun himself; at the word he leaped back, applied the match. The ragged broadside roared out with a shattering crash and the *Malouin* reeled. Men shrieked out, a volley of musketry came with pitiful, feeble reports. A glance showed O'Brien that the sloop was out of it—her fore was down with a splintering crash, and they were past.

And now they were bearing down upon the fifty-two, her gun ports falling as they swept close alongside, her sides towering far above the brigantine.

"All hands—ready to come about!"

O'Brien's voice was hoarse with excitement now. Bullets were flying around them—marines plumping lead into the deck so close alongside. The man beside O'Brien gasped and crumpled, and another sprang to take his place. But not a gun let fire so swift was their coming; they were alongside and past ere the guns were run out.

And, sharp under her stern, O'Brien swung on the helm, the yards swung, and as she came around into the wind, his voice gave the order. Piggoty's guns roared out, with all the towering canvas above for their mark, and rents appeared in the white cloud.

"About!" shouted O'Brien, while the musketry sent bullets whistling over his head. "Ready, St. Rocher!"

St. Rocher was ready, his men furious with swab and charge, and as the *Malouin* swung about and came into the wind again, his guns crashed out. But now the fifty-two had luffed, also, and for a moment the brigantine was under her full broadside, and gun after gun roared. The balls went overhead, for the most part, but one crashed into the midship bulwarks and strewed the deck with dead or groaning. O'Brien stared up to find his canvas intact, though hole spotted, every sail bellying out full, and the *Malouin* darting like a wild thing down the green seas.

Crash!

Another broadside from the great ship, and O'Brien's heart sank at the shudder and thud; but exultation surged up again as he found all steady above. The stern work behind him was a mass of splinters, and he wiped blood from his eyes—a musket ball or splinter had grazed his brow.

Crash upon crash behind them—but they were away now,

almost beyond danger of the furious carronades. St. Rocher came leaping to the poop, his eyes blazing.

"*Diantre,* man! You've done it! Now we have but to outrun her—"

"Outrun her—that ship? Are you mad?" O'Brien glared at him. "We can't do it. If she's not crippled—"

He abandoned the wheel and swung about, staring. Well he knew that the brigantine, which had no great speed, could never outrun that ship with the huge spread of canvas. He had staked everything upon the chances of crippling both enemies aloft, and getting enough of a start to be clear of them ere night fell to cover the escape. But, if the ship were not crippled....

And she was not. Once again his heart sank as he saw her come about in stately fashion, men swarming black in her rigging, white canvas leaping out in cloud upon cloud—

"*Ah!*"

A gasp from St. Rocher, echoed by a wild, fierce yell from the whole deck. Where her vast spreading foresail had been, was suddenly a limp wreck of fluttering canvas; then, like a child's toy boat, her tophamper doubled forward and was down in wild disarray. St. Rocher clapped O'Brien on the back in mad joy, as he shouted;

"Got her! Weakened her foretop—she's out of if! We're free!"

Aye, free; but at a price. All sound aloft, the *Malouin* had suffered enough below to show what those broadsides would have done to her, had she caught them full on. A dozen men were wounded, eight were dead, from ball and musketry and splinter. The decks were ploughed up, the stern cabins were shattered, there were three heavy shot in her hull.

O'Brien stood on the poop and heard the damage recounted, while Guadeloupe dropped away behind, their crippled enemies hull down. St. Rocher came from investigating the damage aft.

"Making water, my Colonel, but she'll stand momentarily.

Everything's a ruin in the stern; the first bit of heavy weather would put us under."

"Ships are plentiful," said O'Brien, and found Dunker at his elbow. "Well?"

"The prisoner, Captain—-"

"Oh!" O'Brien started, and uttered a short laugh. "Fetch him here. Hobbs! Reeve a block and line at the foreyard. Phelim! Lay aft with six men for a hanging party."

Now there was silence along the decks, and men stared one at another; and St. Rocher stood by the rail with cynical air, watching.

The Marquis de Fleury was dragged in front of O'Brien, and drew himself up to meet those blue eyes, after one glance around him. He was a frightful object; soiled with dirt and blood, clothes half ripped away, shaven pate and flabby cheeks glittering in the sunlight as sweat rolled down. Only his eyes were cool and firm.

"Is there any reason why I shouldn't hang you?" snapped O'Brien, wiping blood from his eyes.

"You might use a bullet," said Fleury. O'Brien laughed savagely.

"Not so. A dog like you is lucky to get off with a rope. Phelim! Take him and hang him and leave his body at the yardarm!"

He watched them with eyes of blue ice as they marched the miserable, flabby figure into the waist, and so forward, binding arms behind back, making ready the line and noose. Here was the culmination of brooding years, in this justice meted out to a wretch who had so fearfully harmed him, who had wrecked his life and love…

He saw them lay the noose about Fleury's neck, saw the man swing on to the line at Phelim's command, saw it draw taut. Then his own voice astounded him. Something broke within him.

"Stop! There'll be no hanging. Phelim, have him locked in a cabin."

O'Brien turned and went below, in savage humor, and into the great cabin where the sunlight streamed in from a great shattered rent in the side.

After a little St. Rocher came in, a queer look in his thin face, and stood looking at his chief with lustrous dark eyes.

"Ye could not do it, my Colonel?" he asked.

"God forgive me, I could not," said O'Brien moodily. "I've waited years for it, I've dreamed of it—and I could not. As you said once, things look different close up."

"And now you will never do it," said Rocher.

Something in the tone, something in the man's face, made O'Brien's eyes lift, brought his head up with a jerk.

"What d'ye mean?"

St. Rocher leaned against the bulkhead and looked down at him coolly.

"He was nerved up to endure it, that's all, and when the rope was taken from his neck, he gave way. The men say he was struck down by the hand of God. He's dead."

And St. Rocher, who had once looked upon such things with a shrug, actually crossed himself.

So closed the past behind Colonel James O'Brien, as the *Malouin* rushed seaward.

II

THE PRINCE OF BARBARY

A Story of O'Brien in the Land of the Moors.

THE THUNDER of the guns had died away long since; the two ships rolled gently side by side to the long Atlantic swell, with the peak of Teneriffe breaking the southern horizon. The Spaniard, a large galleass bound for the Azores, was yielding up the provisions, wine and trade goods of which O'Brien had need, and his buccaneers were plundering her lazaret and cabins.

O'Brien stood at her poop rail; to one side were gathered her officers and passengers, eyeing him half in fear, half in wonder. They had not expected to be set free to go their ways in their own ship, for such was not the wont of buccaneers. They watched this tall, slim figure in its sky-blue velvet and fine Mechlin lace, almost incredulously.

"Colonel O'Brien!" bawled a voice from the waist. "One o' they slaves wants to speak with 'ee!"

"Send him up," said O'Brien curtly.

He looked down at the men there, his own men, who were freeing certain slaves of their irons, sending them aboard his own ship, free men. He who had been a slave himself knew their feelings.

One of them mounted the poop ladder—a slender, tanned figure, moving with graceful agility, handsome head well poised, a short and curly brown beard framing a youthful face. He stood before O'Brien and his quick, sure eyes warmed in a smile.

"Señor, I owe you thanks for my freedom," he said in courteous Spanish.

O'Brien was struck by his aspect—by the look of perfect physical and mental balance shown by perhaps one man in a thousand. He had yet to learn that there was one race of people among whom this frank and open expression was the rule rather than the exception, and that among them it was no index whatever to character.

"Who are you?" he demanded curiously.

"I am named Raschid, and my father is Mulai Ismail, Emperor of Morocco."

O'Brien broke into a laugh.

"And I am the Sultan of Stamboul!" he exclaimed. "Come, my friend, you must try a better one than that to catch this fish."

Raschid gestured with a certain dignity.

"Ask those Spaniards yonder, señor."

O'Brien frowned at him, then approached the Spanish captain.

"Señor," he said, "this man tells me that he is of high birth among his own people. I request you, of your goodness, to tell me what you know of him."

"It is true, señor," said the Spaniard gloomily. "He is Prince Raschid of Barbary, a slave whom we were carrying to the governor of the islands as a gift from Don Hernando de Sol, the governor of Tetuan."

O'Brien rejoined his freedman at the rail and inspected him with curiosity.

"Do you desire to join my crew, then?" he asked. "My lieutenant is a vicomte; I could manage with a prince, mayhap."

Raschid laughed.

"No, señor, I would have you return me to my own country. The pasha at Salé will gladly pay you a ransom—"

"Go aboard my ship," said O'Brien. "We will talk of this later."

Raschid went his way, with a flash of white teeth. Presently the Spanish captain, who was a brave and courteous man, came to O'Brien.

"Señor Capitan," he said, "you have been merciful to us, and I will pay you back with a warning. Beware of that Moor! He was to have been ransomed at Tetuan, but there was some treachery attempted—I know not the exact details. He is a stubborn and a bloody dog of an infidel and has an artful tongue."

O'Brien, who had his own opinion of Spaniards, thanked the captain for his warning, presented him again with his ship and presently turned his men from their task and drove them aboard their own craft. While St. Rocher headed the ship eastward, O'Brien worked over the four wounded men, for he had some surgical skill. Then he went to the cabin and was taking his ease with a long pipe when St. Rocher entered.

"Well, Colonel, better decide upon a course."

St. Rocher, who had known O'Brien in the old days as a colonel of the Irish Brigade, could not forget the fact. Now that both of them were plain piratical buccaneers, with James II reigning at St. Germain and his unlucky Irish gentlemen scattered to the four winds, they were no less "colonel" and "vicomte" to each other. It was the only pretense that O'Brien kept up, this pretense of rank and birth; for, as he truly said, there was need of something to keep them all from going to the devil.

"What matter the course?" said O'Brien. "We're not far from where Sir Richard Grenville went down; I'd like to die as well, under Spanish guns!"

"Devil take Spanish guns," and St. Rocher laughed gaily. "By the way, what's this about a Moorish prince? Is he the young fellow with a beard?"

O'Brien nodded.

"Let's have a glass of wine and have him down. He mentioned a ransom."

So Raschid presently joined them, looking very different in the garments he had taken from Spanish cabins: clean, white skinned, blue of eye.

"I always fancied Moors were dark of skin," said O'Brien bluntly. Raschid laughed.

"We call ourselves Arabs, señor, not Moors. True, my father is somewhat dark, but my mother, Laila Aziz, is an English woman.'"

"Eh?" O'Brien was startled. "English?"

"She is the second wife of Mulai Ismail, señor—stolen from England when she was a girl. She is his favorite wife, and her palace at Meknes is an abode of splendor. Yes, we have many English in our country, both slaves and renegades. You are English?"

"No," snapped O'Brien. "I am Irish, which is another thing entirely. So we can have a ransom for you, can we?"

"A large one," responded Raschid simply. "The Spaniards demanded one, but after it had been paid they sent me away on that ship, by night, and said I had died of the plague. One of my brothers is kaid of Rabat; he will gladly pay a ransom in gold or in slaves."

"How many brothers have you?" demanded St. Rocher, with an eye to the prince's worth.

"Three or four hundred, I think."

"Eh?" O'Brien scowled, for he did not like such jesting. "None of your facetious remarks, now—"

Raschid broke into a laugh.

"Pardon! I forgot you knew nothing of our country. My father has five hundred wives, who are retired to Tarudent at the age of thirty."

That he was entirely serious was evident. St. Rocher whistled and lifted his glass.

"We must drink his health, then—to the father of his country. Ismail! *Salut!*"

O'Brien laughed.

"My faith, I've half a notion to visit this emperor."

"What?" Raschid broke into eager speech. "You would visit our country? Good! Take your ship to Salé or Rabat, which is the same thing but vastly different; obtain my ransom. Send gifts to my father, and he will send you a safe-conduct—he likes to talk with foreigners. You must be an ambassador, of course. My brother at Rabat will shelter you. There are French and Dutch merchants there, and consuls as well, and—"

"And if your pasha did not turn his guns on us, as Christians, then the Christians would have us hung as pirates!" broke in St. Rocher, with grim truth in his jest. "Still, Colonel, we have all that lading we took out of the galleon; and the afterhold is crammed with that mass of trading goods we took off the Portuguese carrack—you had some idea of taking it to New England—"

"Excellent!" approved O'Brien, and looked at Raschid. "Will your people trade for cloth and ironwork and pretty things?"

"Gladly, señor, and at high prices. And if you have jewels to sell, there is no better market in the world."

O'Brien exchanged a glance with his lieutenant. They had jewels to sell, indeed—a whole coffer filled with Spanish loot. So they talked further, and then dismissed the prince, and eyed one another. O'Brien scraped out his pipe, a smile touching his sharp features.

"I see it's got you," said St. Rocher, and he nodded response.

"My faith, but it has! He says this emperor stays a long way inland; I'd have to leave you with the ship."

"Pox on the ship," said St. Rocher, with a shrug. "I see greater things ashore. Let her cruise for a month and then come back after us. Fox is a good man, has been in a King's ship, and understands navigation."

"Get out the charts and let's see where this Salé, or Rabat, is," said O'Brien. "Salee, we called it in English. That's where the Salee rovers hail from, eh? Pirate against pirate."

Thus began an adventure destined to drift into sheer madness—and to carve the name of Colonel James O'Brien deeply in the rocks of Barbary—and beyond.

BY THE time they raised the high cliffs of the Barbary coast, on a warm November day, O'Brien had learned a great deal about the land ahead; and the more he learned, the more his appetite to see it was whetted. But this did not prevent him clearing the ship for action when they sighted a large ship, apparently Dutch, bearing down from the north with a light but steady breeze. As Raschid said, she was more like to be a captured Dutchman used by the corsairs.

Fox had been schooled to his part. He was the one man in this motley crew of Irish, English Jacobite and French who could navigate and command a ship; a lean, dark man, he was very capable when not in liquor.

Since his escape from English and Spanish hands alike, O'Brien had been plying the trade of buccaneer for some ten months, and his present ship, the *Kestrel*, he had taken from a St. Malo corsair, together with some very choice lading still in her hold. The *Kestrel* carried ten heavy guns to a side, a somewhat extraordinary armament to be in private hands; and if the *Malouin* had been able to work his twenty guns as well as St. Rocher worked six, she would never have been taken. What was more to the point, half of the twenty were masked in the 'tween-decks, and ordinarily out of sight, so that if necessity arose the *Kestrel* was as good as any double tiered frigate, while looking like an ordinary trader.

The Dutchman bore down with evident intent to speak, but the flutter of Moslem robes along her decks betrayed her true nature. O'Brien had no mind to waste his men's lives, and hove to, as he could well afford. The Moors came on suspiciously enough, until Raschid leaped into the shrouds with a speaking trumpet and sent a long, musical call across the water. After a brief exchange of shouted words, the Moor came up into the wind and her captain carried on a lengthy dialogue with Raschid.

"Ma foi!" observed St. Rocher, standing beside O'Brien and Fox on the quarterdeck. "We're somewhat in this fellow's hands, my friend!"

"Nothing venture, nothing win," said O'Brien. "There—they've finished."

Raschid approached them, his face beaming.

"That is the chief ship of Salé and Rabat," he exclaimed in Spanish. "They will lead us into the river—we can cross the Bou Rougreg bar. I told them who I was, and that you were ambassadors from the Irish nation come to visit my father. We need fear nothing."

And so, for the moment, it proved. While naturally somewhat off in his longitude, since no system of determining longitude had yet been invented, O'Brien was right enough in his latitude, and the twin corsair cities were not thirty miles distant. In ten minutes both vessels were standing along for the coast.

Although Raschid had been a prisoner in Tetuan for close to a year, he had only recently departed thence, so he knew the exact status of affairs in Morocco, where Ismail sat in Meknes, endlessly building with his sixty thousand slaves and uncounted thousands of conscript laborers, and the great kaids and pashas governed the country in semi-independent state.

His eyes flashing eagerly, he now joined O'Brien and St. Rocher in the cabin at noon meat, and detailed affairs ahead, not for the first time.

"We must have nothing to do with Salé, remember," he said. "It is the new town. Rabat, the old Salé, dominates it. There is Pasha Abdallah, who governs for my brother Yusuf, the kaid of the district. If Yusuf is in Rabat, well and good; he is my friend. If he is away, then I will handle Abdallah. Leave everything to me. What ransom do you ask for me?"

"None," said O'Brien, with the grand air which so became him. "I do not ransom a friend."

"Eh?" Raschid stared blankly. "But that is madness! Collect a ransom—let us say, a thousand pieces of gold. My father is a miser who can well afford to be milked, so do not throw away such a chance. Once ashore, you shall have to wait in Rabat until messengers go to Meknes and return with Ismail's safe-conduct; it will be some weeks. You must have gifts for the pasha, of course, and others for Yusuf if he is there. And be in no haste. We must have Abdallah's permission before any trading can be done. Any ships without a safe-conduct may be plundered, but not this one. I shall see to that."

When the two of them were alone, St. Rocher regarded his friend whimsically.

"Eh, Colonel? Our crow is becoming an eagle. Are you uneasy?"

"If I were a simple trader I'd be devilish uneasy!" And O'Brien's rare smile flashed forth. "Let the boy handle things; why not? We've no other interpreter."

"If anything went wrong, we'd be helpless."

"Before we're helpless," said O'Brien coolly, "somebody will get hurt, my Vicomte!"

And with this St. Rocher had to be content.

It was close to sunset when the Rougreg River mouth opened out ahead—a little stream no larger than the Shannon, where the Roman city of Sala Colonia had stood. Now, on the hill to the north, stood Salé, glittering white; and to the south on the cliff which rose sheer out of the river, the great citadel of Rabat, with the steep hillside beyond it running down to the sea and dotted with stones—-a huge cemetery was here.

Their guide showed them the passage across the bar, and the tide being at flood, the *Kestrel* made it very neatly. At the base of the Rabat cliff was a massive fort commanding the entrance. Beyond this were batteries. In the fairway were two Dutch ships, traders, at anchor, and up beyond in the river itself showed

half a dozen rakish native craft. But the two men on the quarterdeck stared at none of these things, but at something beyond,
straight up the river.

"Do you see it, or do I dream?" said St. Rocher. "It is incredible! It must be all of two miles away, and yet it towers—"

"Exactly like a tower," and O'Brien chuckled. Then he beckoned Raschid, and pointed to the enormous square tower whose
tiles glittered gaudily in the sunset. "What is that thing? Is it
a tower indeed, or part of some building?"

"It is part of the dead city built five hundred years ago—the
Tower of Hassan, all that remains of a great mosque," returned
Raschid, staring at it likewise. "It was built by the architect of
the Giralda at Seville; now it serves as a watch tower, indeed.
Now anchor, quickly."

O'Brien woke up and hurled an order at Fox. The *Kestrel*
came to rest, and when her canvas was furled, her crew crowded
along the rail, staring. Boats were coming out from shore, a
whole swarm of them, bearing fresh fruit of all sorts. The other
ship had cast anchor a cable length distant; her captain was
already speeding ashore in a boat, and he met one coming from
the fort, stopping to make report. Then the other came on
toward the *Kestrel*, where Raschid leaned over the rail and
exchanged rapid talk with the marveling bumboatmen. Provisions came pouring over the rail, and Fox paid as Raschid indicated.

The boat from the fort came alongside, and after a few words
Raschid turned.

"I will go ashore with them, señores! Let no one aboard until
you hear from me."

And, with no more ado, he swarmed down a line into the
boat and was gone.

DARKNESS HAD scarce fallen when there was a soft
hail overside in French, and to the deck mounted a man who
was brought at once to the cabin. He proved to be one Pierre
Santin, a Bordeaux merchant and acting French consul in

Rabat—a position of some account, as the French were high in favor with the emperor at Meknes.

"I am to see the pasha in an hour and give him some account of the Irish nation, messieurs," he said dryly to O'Brien and St. Rocher and Fox. "So I came to discover something about you. What is this farce?"

O'Brien laughed, seated him at the cabin table and passed the wine.

"I am James O'Brien, formerly colonel in the Irish Brigade, and Chevalier of St. Michel. This is M. le Vicomte de St. Rocher. Here is Captain Fox of this vessel. You might tell the pasha that Ireland is a country at the end of the world, whose people believe that hell is a place of snow and ice. M. de St. Rocher and I are curious to visit Meknes, while Captain Fox has some goods of value and some jewels to sell."

"And you have a hundred-odd men aboard, eh?" Santin winked knowingly. "Monsieur, let us be frank. If your trading goods are consigned to me, it will save you trouble, at a small percentage. I'll send a Jew aboard you in the morning to take the jewels off your hands."

"Agreed," said O'Brien promptly. "We anticipate no trouble, having brought Prince Raschid back—"

Santin threw up his hands.

"*Diable!* You do not trust him? He is capable of anything, that young man! You know that the emperor has a bodyguard of fifty thousand black slaves, trained to perfection? Last year this Raschid led five thousand of them against the Beni Zoar, a Berber tribe. He took their chief stronghold and massacred above ten thousand people gathered there, chiefly women and children. That is young Raschid for you! There were piles of Berber heads in every city of Maroc."

O'Brien bent a sharp scrutiny upon him.

"Is this possible? He seemed so mild, so frank and open—"

"Bah! That is the Moor for you—always smiling, always ready to knife you," said Santin. "Look you, now! This Pasha Abdal-

lah is an old wolf, in full charge here, as Kaid Yusuf is somewhere in the hills, hunting. These people understand only one
thing—blood! Abdallah will send men aboard you. He will
demand a deposit of your arms and powder. Then he will loot
the ship and take the men as slaves—all slaves in the country
are the personal property of the mad emperor, you comprehend.
Yield but a little to these people, and they will take everything."

"What do you suggest, then?"

"Me? I suggest nothing, except that your lading be consigned
to me. You two gentlemen, as ambassadors, are safe enough.
The rest of you, and the ship, is as good as lost this moment.
Raschid will betray you without a scruple, unless you hold him
by oaths on the Koran and his father's beard. Remember, you
are Christians, and therefore sent by Allah as the prey of true
believers. And you are under the guns of the fort, while on the
signal platform up above are mounted fifty guns that command
the harbor."

"Guns are no threat," said O'Brien. "It's the gunners that
count. Are they good?"

"Execrable," admitted Santin. "Their powder is no good,
either. Well, I must be off. It is agreed, then. I'll tell his Excellency all manner of stories about Ireland, and if your presents
are worthwhile, ambassadors are safe enough. He'll send tomorrow to land your presents and personal belongings, perhaps to
land you as well. Then he'll open his jaws for the ship, I warn
you. Remember, messieurs, only a strong and bloody hand pre-
vails in Maroc!"

When the consul had departed, St. Rocher grimaced.

"I am beginning to lose interest in this black emperor with
blue eyes," he observed.

"Do you believe in omens?" said O'Brien thoughtfully. "You
heard what that man said at the last. Well, do you know what
the O'Brien motto is? In Irish, it reads: *Lamh laidir an uachtar,*
which is to say, The Strong Hand Above. Now, if that isn't an
omen, what is it?"

"A good epitaph," said St. Rocher, with a laugh.

O'Brien slept little that night. When the sun lifted above the rosy, gleaming Tower of Hassan, he came on deck and summoned Fox, the boatswain, the gunner and a dozen of the chief men about him on the quarterdeck.

"Lads, St. Rocher and I will go ashore today. Now, look yonder!" He pointed upward to the great gun platform and signal station, at the crest of the black cliff above them. "Fifty heavy guns are mounted up there—but they can't be depressed sufficiently to command any ship close in to the cliff. Remember this! As for this fort at the base of the cliff, one double shotted broadside will silence it for a time.

"Now, I don't know what will happen; but you're to let no armed Moors aboard here after we go, without a written order from me. No cargo is to be broken out, without my order likewise. And keep a man posted to watch that platform up above. If you see either me or St. Rocher at the edge of that platform, waving a kerchief, it means to go. Slip your cable then or with the next ebb, pour your shot into the fort and into that ship yonder, and work out close to the cliff. You understand?"

"Aye," said Fox. "But what of you? We'll not leave you—"

"You will if I order it," said O'Brien. "Go your ways and come back here a month from the day you leave, flying a green flag. Either you'll find a welcome and word of me, or you'll be met with cannon—in which case, go and come back in another thirty days. If cannon still meet you, then you'll know that we're done for, and the ship is yours. Understood?"

"Aye," said Fox, with a dour look at the battlements up the river. "But I'd guarantee to land our men and go through that rat nest in an hour's time!"

"So speaks the terrier; but rats can bite," said O'Brien curtly. "Remember your orders."

He was still speaking when a large pinnace was observed coming from the landing upriver, a smaller boat following it closely. The ladder was put down, and in the stern of the pinnace they made out Raschid, now clad in Moorish robes of purest white, and beside him a red bearded Moor in a faded green *djellab*. Once alongside Raschid mounted, and behind him came the other, with a wide grin.

"Buenas dias, señores!" exclaimed Raschid gaily. "This is the Sharif el Benouna, a descendant of the Prophet, on whom be peace! He is the vizier of the pasha and commander of his guards and comes to conduct you and your goods ashore. He will leave a score of his men aboard to guard the ship—"

"He will not," said O'Brien. "No guards come aboard the ship, nor any other armed men, except with a written order from me. After we have talked with the pasha, this may be arranged."

Raschid looked somewhat taken aback, and from this instant O'Brien suspected him. He exchanged a few words with the grinning, red bearded sharif, and then assented.

"Very well, señor. About the ransom, we will talk later; this has been demanded, and will be paid by the pasha. I understand your cargo is consigned to the French consul? Excellent. And here, following, is a Jew come to buy your jewels. He speaks French."

The Jew, one Ben Hassim, came aboard—an old man in black cap and *djellab*. St. Rocher took him down to the cabin, while O'Brien remained to see the packs and cases of goods, all long since made ready and marked, sent over into the pinnace. He eyed Raschid, meantime, and observed that this young man was somewhat changed; a certain imperious, eager air sat upon him, and in his eyes glowed a spark as of hidden fires. Still, it was natural that a prince delivered out of slavery would be a new man.

"Have messengers been sent to Meknes?" O'Brien asked him.

"They departed last night, señor, after the pasha had talked with the French consul." And he laughed. "We have made out a great case for your embassy!"

It occurred to O'Brien that if this man were treacherous he knew far too much.

Presently St. Rocher appeared and drew O'Brien aside. The Jew was taking all the jewels and plate and would smuggle them ashore that night. Did O'Brien want cash or bills of exchange on Meknes or Paris? The amount was large, and O'Brien whistled at the size of it.

"Half in cash, to be paid Fox when the jewels go ashore," he returned. "The remainder in wines and stores of all kinds, to be placed aboard immediately. Arrange prices with him."

He arranged with Fox to divide the money among the men upon its receipt. He was taking with him plenty of Spanish doubloons, and Fox could land at one of the Canaries to give the men a bit of shore play.

The Jew took his departure, his coming and going apparently unseen by the sharif; and the men came crowding around to say goodby to O'Brien and St. Rocher. A last handshake with Fox, and they were over the side. As he came into the pinnace O'Brien unavoidably jostled a Moor, who turned and spat in his face.

O'Brien's fist took him squarely in the mouth and knocked him sprawling, senseless. A welling tide of blood came from his mouth as he lay, and one of his fellows lifted his head, then said something. A burst of laughter came from the others.

"What is it?" O'Brien said to Raschid, and the latter grinned.

"His tongue is bitten through—it saves me the trouble of having it cut off in punishment."

O'Brien began to dislike these laughing bearded men who had peculiar ideas of humor.

THEY CAME ashore at the landing before the river gate of the tremendous battlements, and passed up the hill, along tortuous, narrow streets, the sharif's guards clearing the way with brutal musket butts. As they passed a deeply recessed doorway, Santin appeared and fell in step with O'Brien.

"I have arranged to get the most valuable of your goods from the ship tonight," he said in French. "Anything can be done here, with bribes."

"Then you'll need an order from me," said O'Brien.

"I'll send it for your signature by a slave, before noon."

O'Brien nodded, and the other swung off.

"Don't speak any Spanish," he called back. "There are many renegades hereabouts."

Santin, at least, was a true friend, and stood to profit by his fidelity.

Passing up the Street of the Consuls, where were throngs of wretched Christian slaves of all nations, who pelted them with appeals for help, they came to the entrance of the *kasba*, or citadel, atop the cliff over the river. As they approached it, St. Rocher caught his breath.

"I have seen many marvels," he observed in Spanish, "but never the like of this gate!"

Raschid gave him a look and a smile.

"This is less than nothing," he said. "Wait until you see Meknes, which my father has been building for twenty years!"

O'Brien doubted, and rightly. This tremendous gateway, with its magnificent tiles and sculptures, was in truth a monument to Andalusian-Moorish art; but other marvels lay ahead. Once inside the enormous guardroom, they turned right and glimpsed the crowded warren of low buildings where lived the garrison families, with the great gun platform out beyond; then turned right again and entered the lordly palace of the pasha. As they went, Raschid told how in the old days the corsairs had established a republic of their own, here and at Salé opposite, and how their freedom had been washed out in blood; but O'Brien paid little heed to this history.

Ahead of them appeared fairyland—gardens and pools and fountains, gay tilework, Dutch and French slaves at work among the flowers. All about these gardens were the palace quarters, the machicolated walls rising high above and around, their cannon trained upon the lower town. In one of these three sided rooms, whose arched fourth wall opened upon the gardens, the two ambassadors found themselves quartered. Here were their personal belongings and their gifts for the pasha; the packets destined for Meknes had been taken elsewhere, as Raschid informed them.

"You are free to go about the palace as you will," he said, "but do not pass the gates. The pasha will doubtless send for you this afternoon. *Adios!*"

He departed, and left them besieged by black slaves, who treated them to a bathing and barbering, fetched them sherbets and cakes and great earthen pots of stewed meat and fowl, and who regarded O'Brien's beloved pipes and tobacco with open awe. Refreshed and regaled, they sauntered out into the gardens—and very magnificent figures they made. O'Brien was in his favorite sky-blue velvet, and warm it was, wearing his Spanish rapier with the chased golden hilt, and a jeweled poniard; while the saturnine St. Rocher was in black Genoa cut velvet, with less showy but more serviceable weapons. And each of them, beneath his doublet, carried a brace of fine little brass pistolets, freshly loaded, and loose powder in a pocket for priming.

A great procession cut across a corner of the gardens and, following to the gates, they saw the pasha holding court in the guardroom. Him they could not see, for he sat at the great gate overlooking the town; but the results of his justice appeared in men being flogged on the feet, and two unhappy wretches whose right hands were lopped off.

"I perceive," said St. Rocher, turning away, "that one needs a stout stomach in this land."

A slave sought them out soon after—a black man who spoke French, and who came from Santin with the document to be signed. O'Brien complied, and they returned to their own quarters, for the sun was hot and the stench of the town, even in the garden, was strong. And here, when the heat of the day was past, Raschid sought them out. Slaves fetched fragrant mint tea and left them alone.

"I have news," said Raschid abruptly. "Word has come from my brother Yusuf that he will arrive when he can—which may be tomorrow or next month. Meantime, it will be wise to humor Pasha Abdallah; flatter him, be not brusk or imperative. If he wishes to send men aboard the ship, let him do so. In any case, it will do no good to resist."

"No?" said O'Brien dryly. "We are in no case to resist, my friend."

"That is true," said Raschid, plucking at his beard. "I have prevailed upon the pasha to pay the ransom at once—a thousand pieces of gold, for which he will, of course, draw upon my father's treasury. It might be well for you to give him half of this sum."

"Our little eagle now becomes a vulture," murmured St. Rocher in French.

"By all means," assented O'Brien smoothly. "Your advice is good, Raschid. How do you find it here? You have been welcomed as a prince?"

A peculiar smile twisted the lips of the prince.

"I am well known, of course," he said, his voice silky. "Any son of Ismail, being of the sacred blood of Idris, can do as he will in this land. One of my brothers, indeed, the kaid of Tarudent and Sus, has been in practical rebellion for years—Master of Marrakesh. So long as he is content, my father cares not; revenues come in regularly, and what Ismail chiefly loves is gold."

"You are going to Meknes with us?" asked St. Rocher. The prince hesitated.

"I am not sure," he said slowly. "Things may happen; only God knows the event. You may yet see me enjoying more power than any of us dreamed."

He abruptly rose and departed. St. Rocher gave O'Brien a shrewd look.

"What do you make of it?"

"Treachery," said O'Brien bluntly. "He's a different man."

"Naturally; why not? He said too much in that last remark. Princely brethren are never friends, and unless I miss my guess, the absence of Kaid Yusuf is going to cost him dear."

"Eh?" O'Brien was startled. "You don't think—"

"Why think?" St. Rocher shrugged and yawned. "It's none of my business, but something is going to happen here, mark my word. Are you going to take his advice about the money?"

O'Brien nodded.

"Why not? Most of our goods will come ashore tonight. Temporize!"

In ten minutes an officer came to summon them; his fluent Castilian and his features indicated that he was a renegade, but he refused to answer their questions, and scowled at them with the savage hatred for which his kind were notorious. And so they came to the presence of Pasha Abdallah, a swarthy, bearded man clad all in white, his keen nostriled features proud and handsome, if somewhat vicious.

He sat upon a low leather seat in an alcove luxurious with cushions; two guards stood under the arched entrance, and a secretary sat writing at a desk to one side. This secretary, an old man, was obviously another renegade, as his Spanish testified; he acted as interpreter.

The pasha did not rise or return their greetings, but regarded them with cynical eyes, and his gaze came to rest upon O'Brien's handsome rapier.

"I should like to have that weapon," he said.

"Tell him to go to the devil," said O'Brien promptly. "I'll give him the sword if he can give me a better for it."

The pasha chuckled and clapped his hands. A slave appeared, darted away, came back in a moment with a sword in a shabby leather scabbard, its hilt of plain steel. It was somewhat long, but when O'Brien drew the shining blade from the sheath and read the Latin inscription etched in the steel, he looked up quickly. It was a Ferrara blade made in 1654, and it bent almost double in his hands and sprang back again. A real Ferrara, barely forty years old!

"Does he offer this in trade?"

"Yes," said the secretary.

O'Brien promptly unbuckled his splendid but none too fine rapier and replaced it with the shabby but magnificent Ferrara blade. He was more than delighted with his bargain.

"Now let us talk business," he said. "We have brought gifts for his Excellency."

These had been fetched by slaves, and were brought in. The avid eyes of the pasha gleamed at the sight of them—handsome pistols, a few jewels and trinkets from Spanish loot, a casket of spices, and a huge necklace of red coral. This, as it chanced, was a real treasure in Moorish eyes, Fez being the chief coral mart in northern Africa, and the covetous eyes glittered sharply at sight of it.

Gifts for the two ambassadors—crooked knives of silver, and handsome white woolen *djellaba*, and boots of the finest Marrakesh leather, bright yellow in hue. The secretary explained that yellow boots were compulsory in Morocco by edict of Ismail, to celebrate the expulsion of the English from Tangier and the Spanish from the western ports. He then went on to say that the pasha would send men aboard the ship to guard it.

"Tell him," said O'Brien pleasantly, "that the ship and its contents are our own personal property, and we desire no guards."

The pasha amiably insisted that thieves were numerous and for some minutes the discussion waxed keen, until O'Brien compromised.

"Tell him that our men will allow no one aboard the ship without our orders, but that if he still wishes it in the morning, we may then consider the matter."

The pasha showed his teeth in a snarl and announced that he was master here, whereat O'Brien smiled and looked him in the eye and made no comment. Muttering angrily, Abdallah dismissed his visitors, saying they would settle the matter in the morning.

So their first day in Rabat drew to a close, with Raschid visiting them again in the evening. The ransom had not been paid; that would be arranged on the morrow, he said, and went his way. He wore an air of hurried importance, almost of arrogance.

St. Rocher sauntered out nonchalantly, and O'Brien sat for a while playing with his rapier and testing it. A marvelous weapon, he perceived; too long for general taste, but suiting him the better for this fault, and with a balance that was perfection. St. Rocher was gone a long while and presently returned in high good humor.

"I've been on the battlements," he announced. "To the top of the tower over the gateway. You must visit it sometime. The walls are two feet wide at the top—wide enough for a man to pass along easily. As I thought, the cannon can not be depressed to reach the ship even as she now is. I met the master gunner here; a droll fellow—a Dutch renegade. He was delighted to find that I understood artillery."

O'Brien gave him a sharp glance.

"What are you up to?"

St. Rocher laughed, but made no answer.

Morning found O'Brien waking to a keen zest in this unwonted life—the black eunuchs in the gardens; the thin calls of the muezzin from the *kasba* mosque, answered from the mosques of the town; the ungainly costumes; the strange sights and sounds all around. Then Raschid made his appearance, now with several Moors following him; these waited in the gardens while he came in and talked with the two ambassadors. He was brusk, excited.

"I must warn you," he said hurriedly. "The pasha will summon you shortly to his public audience; he is going to seize your ship at once, and if you object, he intends to have you both flogged. There is no way out of it, though I shall do my best. Also, he is going to pay the ransom. Appease him, for the love of God! I came to warn you. Avoid any trouble—"

One of his followers called sharply from the garden, and Raschid hurried away.

"*Diable!* Something is up, assuredly," exclaimed St. Rocher. "Look! He is talking with the sharif, that red headed chap who brought us ashore. Now they've separated. Well, my friend, this looks serious. What answer have you to our friend the pasha, eh?"

"A pistol in each coat pocket, ready primed—" O'Brien smiled his rare, warm smile—"and you to back me up. What more could any man ask?"

St. Rocher laughed gaily and hummed a tune as he primed the little brass pistolets.

THE MORNING had waxed warm. In the cool shade of the huge guardroom beneath the tower, Pasha Abdallah held audience, while outside that wondrous gate, in the hot sun, the merchants and townsfolk came and went; black capped Jews from the Mellah, swaggering corsairs from the lower town and Salé, scowling renegades who bent black looks upon the Christians, Moors in from the country and even Berbers from the hills, blue eyed, tattooed, fierce and wild.

The pasha sat on a wide divan, placed in the cool depths at the rear of the chamber, facing the entrance gate; on the left was the high arched gate opening on the garrison barracks, with women and children congregated about the well before the mosque, and the fresh sea breeze sifting through. At one side of the pasha sat his secretary, on the other stood Sharif el Benouna, captain of his guard, naked scimitar in hand. Soldiers of the guard stood at the entrances; about stood several *talebs*, or doctors of the law, with stately merchants and officials, interspersed with ragged, filthy holy men such as abounded in Morocco.

Directly behind the pasha was an arched opening into the

second and smaller chamber, whence ran a tunnel-like staircase to the ramparts and roof above.

O'Brien noted all this with a glance as he entered, and saw Santin in the crowd. The Frenchman nodded significantly, and O'Brien knew that all had gone well with the ship's lading during the night. Then, as the ragged holy men spat toward the infidels and muttered curses, the secretary interpreted a swift remark from Pasha Abdallah.

"Señores, it is the custom for all men, particularly Christians, to kneel before his Excellency."

"It is not my custom," said O'Brien, with a short laugh. "In my country, it is the custom for men to kneel to me also, but I do not insist upon it here. Neither let his Excellency insist."

"But he represents Mulai Ismail, the seed of Idris, the chosen of Allah!" exclaimed the secretary, as sharp murmurs began to rise.

"Does he, then, attribute to himself the prerogatives of Mulai Ismail, upon whom be peace?" said O'Brien shrewdly.

This was a trenchant stroke. The secretary had forgotten the usual blessing upon the name of Ismail; and the suggestion that he assumed the jealous emperor's attributes bit deeply. Before the dismayed secretary could collect himself, both ambassadors saluted the pasha with a deep and stately bow, which was compromise enough to be seized upon at once. But the angry face of Abdallah was ominous.

Stuffed leather seats were placed at the right of the pasha. The ambassadors seated themselves, and Abdallah made a lengthy oration, which the secretary shortened a trifle.

"Señores, you have rescued from the accursed Spaniard a prince of the line of Idris, upon whom be blessings, and have returned him to his own land. For this service, no reward would be sufficient; God alone can rightly recompense you. However, on behalf of Mulai Ismail—may his line be multiplied!—his Excellency the Pasha Abdallah is pleased to bestow upon you a ransom of a thousand pieces of gold, which will now be laid at your feet."

There was a stir, and two pairs of black slaves entered, each pair carrying a large open pot, filled to the brim with gold pieces. The throng surged forward, one of the wild holy men haranguing his companions in low, vibrant tones. A figure appeared from the chamber in the rear carrying a silver dish of sherbet, which he set before the pasha. As the slave turned about, his hand shot out, touched O'Brien, and left in his hand a folded paper. Then he was gone again.

"Give him back half for the poor, St. Rocher," muttered O'Brien. "Make a speech of it—I'm busy."

St. Rocher arose, very stately and dignified, and began a flowery address. O'Brien opened the crumpled paper, and to his astonishment beheld English writing, ill spelled but legible. He scanned it swiftly:

> I be Will Dowling, master mariner, slave heer seven year & more. They bee going to kill you bothe. Rashidd planned itt with Benoona ye gard capn. Two curst holy men will atack you to gett ye pasha ye blame. Rashidd has bribbed ye gard & will take ye kasba & town to bee his owne. Gett to ye room behynde & I will meet you. We canot gett away & I will bee glad to dye fyting.

O'Brien crumpled up the paper, his brain working rapidly. No getting away—true enough! But he had his ship and men to think of, besides. So Raschid had formed a grand scheme, eh? Kill the two infidels, blame it on the pasha, seize the town and citadel—true Moorish intrigue. But no time now to think about it. Raschid was not here under the tower, either—

"Diable! Must I talk all day?" came in an aside from St. Rocher.

"Finish," said O'Brien. "Then sit down and listen."

St. Rocher made his final grand bow and sat down. O'Brien spoke rapidly, while the pasha made acceptance of the gift.

"No talk; obey orders. Watch those ragged holy men. Two

will attack; you must take them both. That damned Raschid plotted it. When they jump, shoot."

"Understood," said St. Rocher, and just in time.

Two of the ragged men—men so greatly venerated in Morocco as to be exempt from all law or custom—took a step forward from the crowd, and one of them burst into a wild torrent of words. They were both half naked, unkempt long hair dangling about their lean, scarred cheeks, the light of madness in their eyes. The speaker's voice grew shrill and high; foam gathered on his lips. He was clearly working himself into a frenzy.

O'Brien could not look at St. Rocher—he was watching everything here closely, his eyes on the pasha, on the throng, on the sharif whose naked scimitar was ready to help the two holy men do their work. He quietly got one of his two pistols out, hidden by the lace of his cuff, and pinched fresh powder into the pan. A grim smile touched his lips as he waited, muscles tensed. The strong hand above! Well, with luck he would show these Moors—

Then it came, all in a flash. The shouting holy man, who had gradually worked forward, snatched out a knife and hurled himself at the two ambassadors, followed by his companion.

O'Brien had seen the tensed muscles, and swung around. The Sharif el Benouna, teeth gleaming in his red beard, was swinging back his scimitar. The report of O'Brien's pistolet blended with that of St. Rocher's. From the latter came a second shot.

Dropping his pistol, O'Brien had leaped—he was in the air even before the sharif, shot between the eyes, toppled backwards That swift, sure spring carried him behind the divan of the pasha, into the archway; leaning forward, he caught the pasha by the beard, jerked him backward, and held the Spanish poniard to his throat. Pricked, the hapless Abdallah subsided.

Only then did O'Brien give heed to that was passing before him.

The throng was spellbound, petrified with amazement. One of St. Rocher's bullets had failed to kill; the frothing holy man was dragging himself forward, knife in hand, blood trailing behind. St. Rocher, even as O'Brien looked up, drove his sword through the fanatic. The other lay on his face, dead.

"Will Dowling!"

"Aye, sir." Dowling was waiting in the "room behynde" as he said he would.

A wild burst of voices rose on the air, yet none moved to attack the two Christians, for O'Brien's dagger at the pasha's throat was threat enough, and tacitly eloquent. The half naked figure of Dowling appeared behind O'Brien, wild eyed, unkempt, knife in hand.

"Take my friend out to the gun platform and back," ordered O'Brien. "Tell every one that if you are harmed or if I'm attacked, the pasha dies. Move sharp! St. Rocher, go make the signal to the ship, and quick about it."

The two disappeared, with Dowling excitedly shouting as they ran.

The hubbub of voices was now deafening in the guardroom. A crowd was thronging in by both archways, uttering amazed cries at sight of the bodies, and of the pasha in O'Brien's hands; and yet upon all these men, black, brown and white, had descended a queer hesitation, as though some invisible power held them poised, incapable of action.

Then O'Brien saw the reason, and the peril. Men were talking rapidly to the guards, whispers were growing into full throated voices, and the name of Raschid seemed upon every lip. In the fierce eyes turned upon him O'Brien read gathering menace and peril.

He realized in a flash that his prisoner no longer availed him. The loyalty of the guards had been poisoned by their own commander, the sharif. The two ambassadors were to be cut down, the pasha was to be slain and later given the blame for killing the ambassadors; Raschid was usurping his brother's place, taking over Rabat, leaping into power by force of treachery and blood.

There was a surge forward, the beginning of a rush. Like a flash O'Brien leaped into action.

Abruptly abandoning his prisoner and slipping his dagger into its sheath, he darted upon the open pots of gold. Catching up the fat pieces in both hands, he showered gold upon the crowd, flung it at them and over them in handfuls. There was an instant of astonished silence as the gold fell among them; from outside came yells, a spattering discharge of musketry—then a din of voices burst out, eager and yelping as a wolf bark, and half the throng here began to squabble and fight over the gold. As O'Brien leaped back beside the pasha he sighted Will Dowling and St. Rocher, returning along the narrow street past the mosque at a dead run.

Now came a sudden irruption of men, yelling the name of Raschid. A swirl of fighting figures, broke into the crowd; shots rang out, men shrieked and were cut down. Pasha Abdallah shrilled out frantic orders, but his voice was lost. Will Dowling, now in the inner room behind, panted out sharp English words.

"Back to the stairs, master! The pasha's with us now—let me go to the roof with him! He'll have men on the battlements who may hold true—do you hold the stairs! They'll be at us in a minute—"

True enough. Dowling plucked at the pasha's *djellab*, drew him through the archway. The mad swarm of figures was now sweeping forward. O'Brien drew sword and poniard, sprang back through the archway into the inner chamber. St. Rocher's wild, gay laugh rang out as he led the way to the stairs.

"They saw my signal, *mon ami!* And the tide's at ebb, to judge by her swing on the cable. Trust Fox to do it—Here, this way! Now for work, eh?"

Now for work indeed! Fox had his warning and must save himself. Here was life or death to be met full face.

THE STAIRWAY was like a high roofed, closed tunnel,

running steeply upward. The lower entrance turned at right angles from the guardroom in a high, narrow passage. Halfway up the stairs was another right angled turn. With a bit of crowding, two men might stand abreast on the steps, but not with any comfort for sword play.

O'Brien stood at the entrance, watching the wild figures flooding forward at him, a slight smile touching his lips, his gaze cool and steady. In the outer chamber some were still fighting over the gold, others were pouring toward the stairs.

"Death to the Christians!" roared a voice in Spanish, and O'Brien marked out the renegade—a huge fellow priming a musket as he ran. Apparently nearly all the pasha's guards and followers had been swung into the plot.

As the wave of men and hungry weapons surged forward upon him, O'Brien quietly stepped back into the stairway and up a couple of steps. In a wild mass, the Moors hurled at the entrance, packing themselves about it in a jammed mass, those behind shoving the others on, the foremost wedged there and unable to get ahead. And then began a frightful screaming to Allah and his saints.

For the long Ferrara rapier was running red. Unhurried, deadly, it drove down at the wild faces, bit into man after man, overreaching the curved blades that slashed vainly. A pile of bodies began to block the foot of the stairs. Over them suddenly leaped the tall renegade, slipping in the blood and then flinging up his musket as he regained his balance. O'Brien laughed and drove the point into his throat before he could fire, and he died there.

"Make room for me!" shouted St. Rocher impatiently, from behind O'Brien. The latter drew back and lowered his blade. The enemy had fallen away momentarily.

"Faith, I need all the room myself!" he returned. "They'll be coming again—What's that?"

A roar of cannon shook the air from somewhere outside the tower. After a moment of silence, a second followed. Then single cannon began to speak.

"Fox!" barked St. Rocher excitedly. "The *Kestrel* is going out—they let go one broadside, warped on the cable, let go the other! At the fort! *Diantre!* I'd like to be out there with her!"

"You're not alone in that wish," said O'Brien dryly. "But cheer up, friend. We've no lack of company here to heaven or hell. Lucky that slave gave us warning, eh? Watch out above, now! Here they come—I can hold them well enough—"

He still had one pistol unfired, and now held it primed and ready.

Across the pile of bodies leaped a black man, flinging up a musket. The pistol spoke first, however, and the black choked on his own blood. As the musket fell from his hands, it was discharged; richochetting slugs screamed around O'Brien, but harmed him not. Then came the Moors streaming upward, two by two this time, spears reaching up at the trim, erect figure barring the way.

In this moment O'Brien blessed the Ferrara blade. It sheared through a spear shaft like paper, and the point ripped into the bearer's face. The poniard warded another spear, and the long blade lunged down. Another man sprawled on the stairs. A spear thrust up, but a leap carried O'Brien back beyond reach. A swift glance showed him St. Rocher up above at the sharp angle, talking with two men there.

Now the spears drove upward, and beneath them a bearded black man crawled and suddenly flung forward, crooked blade sweeping out for the knees. O'Brien warded that, and the red Ferrara flicked down and transfixed the black; then came St. Rocher's voice, sharp and urgent:

"Down, O'Brien! Down! *Down!*"

Hearing it, O'Brien flung himself back, so that he lay half supporting himself on his hands. Two of the pasha's guards were behind and above, muskets ready. From the two guns came a thunderous roar; bullets and slugs went shrieking and whistling, drowned in frenzied screams from the Moors choking the entrance below. O'Brien rose to find the stairs cleared and

St. Rocher at his elbow. The two guards were hurriedly reloading their pieces.

"Up with you!" cried St. Rocher. "Things aren't so bad—Abdallah's got three more faithful men up above. These two will hold the stairs. *Faugh!* What a reek of blood and stinking bodies! Come along to the fresh air."

O'Brien mounted, and the two bearded guards grinned cheerfully at him as they took his place to hold the stairs.

Up to the sharp turn, then upward again. All this while had sounded an intermittent discharge of cannon; now there roared another crash of guns in unison, evidently a broadside from the *Kestrel*. O'Brien mounted the last steps and then emerged into the white hot sunlight and stood blinking around, sword in hand.

The top of this immense tower was a platform, broken only by two openings whence smoke might emerge from the fires in the guardroom, fifty feet below. This rectangular platform was connected with the ramparts at three points by walls. Each wall crest was two feet wide, with waist high machicolations. One of these approaches lay at the western angle, whence the rampart ran to a little turret above the sea, and so around the seaward face of the cliff, the other two were at the eastern angles, connecting the platform with the palace and with the ramparts surrounding the gardens.

At a glance O'Brien comprehended the capability of such a place for defense. Half a dozen cannon lined the walls, but with neither powder nor ball at hand. At one side stood Pasha Abdallah, talking with four of his guards and Will Dowling. The barracks and gun platform cloaked from sight all view of the harbor and river and seaward approach, but the whole of the city, with its markets and system of massive walls, lay outspread below, running down to where the marvelous Tower of Hassan bulked up reddish in the sunlight on the lower ground beyond.

Abdallah swung around to meet the two ambassadors, his eyes glittering, rasping words on his lips, curved sword bared in his hand. Will Dowling cackled out a wild laugh.

"He knows now you saved his life, master. He says you be great men and he'll take your orders."

O'Brien nodded.

"Can we get away from here?"

"Nowt hardly, master. That cursed El Benouna must ha' swung over most o' they guards. They have the palace, and there's fighting all over the city."

"Very well. Send one man down to get you a sword from the stairs, and then to keep watch in case our two there are over-powered; we can't afford to be caught in the back."

One of the Moors departed at a run. Two of the others were loading muskets. On the palace ramparts were now gathering masses of men, blazing away with wild bullets at the tower; from here and there about the city, chiefly at the gates, came the sounds of conflict and the hot rising smoke reek of powder.

"St. Rocher," said O'Brien crisply, "take one musket and go down to that seaward turret; you can hold it easily enough. Best hurry—there's a stream of men working around that way."

Dowling translated. One of the guards shouldered his musket, showed his white teeth in a laugh and swung away, following St. Rocher's sinister, tall figure along the rampart to the turret, thirty feet distant. O'Brien strode up to the pasha and clapped him on the shoulder heartily; their eyes met in a momentary exchange, and the Moor smiled and nodded com-prehension. Both men knew there was no escape. Enemies such a little while ago, they were now comrades.

By the two eastern approaches, men were now streaming along the ramparts in single file, weapons glinting in the sun while their fellows still banged away with muskets and pistols. The Moor sent to the stairs returned with a scimitar, gave it to Will Dowling and hastened back.

"Tell the pasha to hold the right hand approach with his two men," said O'Brien. "You and I will take the other."

"Aye, sir. And do 'ee hold back a bit, master—nowt care I what haps, so be I get a crack first at some o' they devils!"

O'Brien scrutinized his unexpected helper for the first time. Dowling was not tall, but was lean and hard, all muscles. His rags showed scars on back and arms. His unkempt, gray streaked hair and beard framed features wild and savage as any Moor's.

Abdallah led his two remaining men to the spot indicated, and O'Brien was somewhat amazed to see him step forward, scimitar in hand, to meet the onrush himself. There was no time to waste in watching, however. Dowling was already bounding toward the other angle, where a number of men were coming rapidly along the rampart, and O'Brien followed with some misgivings, which were all too soon justified. A glance showed him that St. Rocher was already engaged.

The first man to run in upon Dowling was a huge black, swinging a crooked sword. Dowling leaped at him fiercely, and indeed launched a fearful blow which caught the black on the neck and half split him asunder; but the black toppled sidewise over the edge and carried the scimitar with him—all but carried Dowling as well.

Barely in time O'Brien stepped forward, the long Ferrara blade sliding neatly into the next man's throat, bringing him down in a sprawl athwart the narrow way, so that the next must needs step on his body. A pistol blazed, and the ball jerked at O'Brien's beaver, which he had retained throughout the tumult. A step forward, a lunge in tierce, and his man was down.

The pasha, with musket and scimitar at his back, was holding his angle nobly; O'Brien had yet to learn that those who held rank under Ismail must needs be men of their hands. But now some one of the bullets flying so wildly struck Dowling, who spun about and fell quiet. When O'Brien next could glance around, he saw one of the pasha's two Moors at his side, and waved his hand in thanks to the watchful Abdallah.

Now the attack faltered. Faced by a tall, hesitant Moor whose pistol twice missed fire, O'Brien leaped forward at him, thrust him through the hip, and he toppled over as he lost balance. This checked those behind, and they drew back fearfully. Abdallah had won his battle also, but not without loss—his musketeer was stretched out, and the pasha himself was bleeding from a swordcut across the brow. St. Rocher's left arm dangled, and his companion was clear gone from sight; but he waved his blade cheerily at O'Brien, for his attackers had drawn back.

"All well, Colonel?"

"Well enough for this time," called O'Brien grimly. "And you?"

"A scratch, no more." St. Rocher laid aside his weapon, removed his black coat, and set to work binding up his arm with his own torn sleeve. Suddenly a wild yell broke from him. "O'Brien! She's clear! She's clear!"

"Who is?"

"The *Kestrel!* She's in sight below here—" And St. Rocher waved frantically to the ship below, still well out of O'Brien's sight.

So Fox had fought clear! Good!

Dowling came to one elbow, then staggered dazedly to his feet. A bullet, with no great force behind it, had broken the skin of his head, but with no greater damage. Bullets were flying around still. The Moor beside O'Brien gave a sudden cough, clapped a hand to his throat and died with a smile and a gasp to Allah.

"The devil! We're fools to stay here," said O'Brien. "St. Rocher, we'll have to come over to your turret. Can we hold that?"

"Until they turn cannon against us—yes," came the response. O'Brien nodded to Dowling, as the pasha approached them, sopping blood from his forehead. "Call up the three men from the stairs. Tell him to go on to the turret yonder. We'll follow."

Abdallah nodded coolly, took the musket, powderhorn and pouch of his fallen man, and led the way. From the top of the little round turret at the seaward corner of the walls, with only the two approaches along the ramparts, the last defense could be made with some hope. Dowling summoned up the defend-

ers of the stairs, but only one man came. The other two had
been dragged down and slain. Thus, to hold the turret remained
only St. Rocher, O'Brien, Dowling, and the pasha himself, with
the last of the faithful guards. Two men could stand at the
entrance, one facing either approach. As St. Rocher observed,
it was not so bad; but it might be bettered.

From the turret, O'Brien caught his last glimpse of the
Kestrel. With a fair breeze from the south, she had drawn out
of the harbor, and not undamaged either, for her mizzen yard
was down and a heavy shot had knocked a great hole in her
poop. Still, she sailed on, bravely, and swiftly lessened and
headed out westward, and that was the last of her.

WILL DOWLING laughed harshly, as the pasha clapped
him on the shoulder, and turned to O'Brien.

"He's set me free, master—there's a rare jest for 'um! Well,
he's an old warhorse, I've heard tell, and a good fighter. Won't
be long now, eh?"

"Not long," said O'Brien, looking out across the roofs of the
barracks. Men were gathering in the other turrets, crowding
along the walls, spears and muskets in hand; upon the platform
roof of the tower, a scant thirty feet away, were assembling
yelling Moors, preparing for the assault from that angle. Their
muskets were useless, however, so long as the defenders remained inside the round turret.

St. Rocher, who had donned his black coat again, laughed
softly.

"So passes the high embassy to the Emperor of Barbary, eh?"
he observed with faint irony. "Well, whether we go down among
the fishes or leave our heads on Moorish pikes, what matter?
No life endures forever! Still, I'd like to come face to face with
our honest Raschid."

O'Brien nodded.

"Let's hope they attack, then. With nothing to eat or drink,
we'd have a dog's death here, were they wise. Do you know,
comrade, we've spoiled a most excellent plot! Had it come off

aright, Raschid would be a great man. The pasha blamed for
killing us, and slaughtered, and the place in Raschid's hands—
it was a stake worth the gamble!"

"And for us—has it been worth the gamble?"

"Aye!" said O'Brien, and his eyes danced as he met the gaze
of St. Rocher. "I'd do it over again, every bit of it! Well, they're
coming. Who'll take the first round?"

Himself unhurt, he was joined by the Moorish guard, who
had stripped off his *djellab*. Bullets hailed against the turret, as
the lines of attackers advanced along the ramparts; as these
came close, the fire died down. Spears extended, pistols banging
away, the converging lines drew down, and O'Brien stepped
out, the Moor beside him.

For a minute it was mad, fast work, but the long Ferrara
blade and the steel wrist behind it drove home. A spear ripped
O'Brien's coat—two men were down, blocking the narrow
rampart. From the corner of his eye he saw the Moor lock arms
with an antagonist and go hurtling over the edge; Dowling was
in his place instantly, knife driving into the next Moor. Another
yielded to the stabbing blade. Then the knife was gone, and
Dowling was borne back, a spear in his hip.

St. Rocher saved him, neatly spitted the spearman; he stood
cool and imperturbable, his blade dancing in and out, as
Dowling dragged himself back to the turret. Spear and scimitar flashed in against O'Brien, and the Ferrara ran red again—
but a man farther back flung a pistol that had flashed in the
pan, and it struck him over the eyes.

Only the beaver saved him from being brained. He staggered
back, stunned, and came to one knee, clear out of it for the
moment. With a fierce yell, the pasha was past him, flying at
the attackers, crooked sword flashing and driving down. O'Brien
sagged a little, head drooping; but luckily blood was running
from his cut head and his brain cleared.

He lifted his head. A sudden silence had fallen. The attackers were drawing back. O'Brien came upright and leaned on

the rapier, careless that it bent under his weight. Back drew the lines of men. On the tower roof appeared a figure in snowy white, backed by half a dozen guards bearing muskets. It was Raschid, and his voice came in Spanish.

"Señores! Can you hear me?"

"Yes," responded O'Brien.

Pasha Abdallah gave O'Brien a swift glance, nodded, and brushed past him to the turret. His harsh voice sounded in quick dialogue with Will Dowling, who lay there gripping his bleeding thigh; but O'Brien paid them no heed. He looked at Raschid, who had betrayed them all, and his eyes flamed angrily.

"Señores, you have fought well," said Raschid smoothly, "but it is useless, and now you are finished. The palace and *kasba* are mine. The town is in my hands, or soon will be. If you had not been hasty, if you had followed my instructions, you would have been safe and well. But I bear you no grudge, and I am proud of you, my friends! So come and join me, and between us there shall be brotherhood."

"And what of Pasha Abdallah?" said O'Brien.

"That is another matter," responded Raschid. "It is the will of God that he must die."

O'Brien turned and looked at. St. Rocher.

"Well, comrade?" he asked. "What say you?"

St. Rocher inspected his red running rapier critically.

"My dear Colonel," he drawled, "I really perceive no defect in this steel, and I should regret to deem myself unworthy of so good a weapon. Also, it seems to me that we stand in very honorable company here, and could not better it. But make your choice, and I'll abide by it."

O'Brien swung around, and a joyous, hearty laugh rang from his lips.

"Liar and traitor!" he cried out, knowing that many of the Moors understood Spanish. "We trusted you, and you betrayed our trust. No lies will serve you; we know your whole plot. You betrayed those who welcomed you, and your own brother. May the curse of Allah rest upon you! As for us, we find it better to die with this man Abdallah than to live with a coward like you."

Raschid thrust back the hood of his white *djellab*. A spasm of rage contracted his bearded features; shaking his fist wildly, he poured forth a volley of curses.

A musket banged out.

Upon the breast of that snowy *djellab* appeared a stream of scarlet. Raschid was knocked back a step by the impact of the bullet, then fell in a huddled, motionless heap of white. A harsh laugh sounded from Pasha Abdallah.

"Allah Akbar!" he cried loudly. "God is great!"

He had quietly loaded and aimed their one musket, and that shot had come from his hand. One growing, tumultuous yell burst from the watchers as they realized what had happened; then muskets banged forth to right and left, and a hail of bullets spattered about the stones of the turret. O'Brien and St. Rocher drew back to cover, but Pasha Abdallah stood out in the open, shaking his musket at those who had been his own men, his blood spattered face and beard frightful to see. And though bullets tore at his garments, none touched him. A frenzy was upon the man, and as he shook the musket and poured forth a screaming torrent of Arabic, his appearance seemed to hold the Moors spellbound.

"Listen!" St. Rocher touched O'Brien's arm. "What is that sound?"

There was, indeed, a strange sound rising upon the hot, white sunlight—a rattling, rising sound, a pouring thud of unshod hoofs lifting through the air like muttering thunder. The muskets fell silent. Men on the ramparts and about the edge of the great tower looked over and uttered shrill cries. From the turret, nothing of the street or town below could be seen, for the tower blocked the view, but of a sudden arose a fierce wild yell from hundreds of throats.

"Yusuf! Mulai Yusuf!"

The tide of men along the ramparts ebbed quickly; they fled, running, breaking up into groups. From below came a spatter of shots, then shout upon shout.

"Allah! Yusuf!"

Pasha Abdallah wiped the blood from his fierce eyes and swung about, and laughed.

Yet, for all his exultant laugh, O'Brien saw that his face was gray with fear.

Into the city and into the *kasba* rode Kaid Yusuf, followed by a horde of wild riders whose robes were spattered with blood; and now he sat among his chief men on the bloody divan in the guardroom and dispensed justice that was swift and terrible. Outside, in the fly swarming hot sunlight, grew a pile of heads.

O'Brien was led in, with St. Rocher at his side, and doffed hat in a low and sweeping bow, while Pasha Abdallah saluted the kaid with a kiss on the shoulder, as became the blood of Idris. O'Brien noted that Yusuf was a man of very dark complexion, obviously of negroid blood, with bloodshot eyes and an air of fiercely eager cruelty. He spoke briefly, and the pasha nodded.

"Mektub!" he replied. "It is written."

So saying, Abdallah strode from the guardroom with two huge black guards beside him.

Yusuf looked at the two ambassadors, while the pasha's old secretary addressed him rapidly, and Pierre Santin, behind him, put in a word or two. He beckoned, and they came forward, and a hard, glittering smile touched the dark Moor's features. He spoke, and the secretary translated.

"Señores, you are valiant men, and it is evident that you are under the protection of Allah. You will resume your quarters in the palace until word arrives from Mulai Ismail, upon whom be peace, respecting you. Whatever you may desire is yours. It is the command of Kaid Yusuf ben Ismail that each of you express a wish, that in honoring you he may honor Allah."

O'Brien gestured slightly, and St. Rocher made answer first.

"Tell Kaid Yusuf that we would have the company of an English slave who fought beside us, and who indeed warned us of this plot. Pasha Abdallah freed him; let this freedom be confirmed."

Upon hearing this, Yusuf fastened his gaze upon O'Brien. The latter smiled.

"Say to Kaid Yusuf," he responded in stately Spanish phrases, "that while it is true that Allah has protected us, this was to be expected, inasmuch as we are ambassadors to him whom you call the Sword of Allah." At this reference to the emperor, there was a quick hum of approval. "However," went on O'Brien, "a brave man fought with us, the Pasha Abdallah. It is my request that no blame and no harm come to him."

Upon hearing this, Yusuf gave a sharp order. Into the room was brought a blood soaked *djellab*, bundled up, and laid before him. A guard unfolded it, and laid bare the grinning head of Prince Raschid. With the head was a right hand, but not the hand of Raschid, for it was dark.

Yusuf looked down at the head, then spoke slowly; the secretary translated.

"Señores, your requests are both granted. The slave will be brought to your quarters and given freedom under the seal of the pasha and the Kaid. As for Abdallah, he remains unharmed; but, since his hand slew one of the sacred blood of Idris, that hand has already been removed from him. Go in peace, and may you be brought from the darkness of infidelity to perceive the light of the true faith!"

Such was the tale, and the end, of Raschid ben Ismail, Prince of Barbary.

III

THE SEAL OF ISMAEL

An Irish Buccaneer among the Moors.

UPON THE *bled,* the rolling upland of Morocco, the sun beat down white hot, blinding, although it was the season of rain. The brown plateau would break suddenly into green, deep ravines; the brown hills would open into unexpected cañons where thatched mud houses were set among fruit trees.

Here, where the slow party of horsemen and wagons wound toward the hills, following a mere track along an ancient valley, there was no life. In the van rode a dozen horsemen—as their scarlet trappings signified, they belonged to the black bodyguard of the Emperor himself; that famous guard of fifty thousand trained black slaves. Behind them rode O'Brien, alone. In the wagon behind followed St. Rocher, racked with fever, attended by Will Dowling—the English seaman whom they had freed from slavery at Rabat.

Rabat lay behind, and the sea. As O'Brien rode, alone, his laughing, proud eyes were gloomy and his browned features were set hard as steel. Proclaiming themselves ambassadors from Ireland, he and St. Rocher had abandoned their buccaneering venture and set off inland to visit the wild, savage emperor of whom they had heard so much. It had seemed a mad, glorious enterprise, but now things looked different. Ismail, the emperor, had sent letters of safe conduct and a dozen of his guard to fetch the ambassadors to Meknez, and after two weeks of slow travel, O'Brien began to doubt if Meknez existed.

Fortified farms, barren hills, dirt and cruelty—and the escort!
Their commander was a Dutch renegade, named Akbar, a sullen
giant who was a prey to strange moods, and hated all Christians.
He got on badly with O'Brien. And now St. Rocher was
down—

O'Brien's head lifted suddenly. Ahead opened a gully, and
from this broke half a dozen men, spurring away, mounting and
riding fast, fleeing out across the brown plain. Where they had
been, remained a naked, filthy, bleeding figure. O'Brien joined
the escort as they drew rein and dismounted beside the renegade.

"Berbers," said Akbar. "Down from the hills on a raid. They
caught this fellow."

O'Brien had heard much of the Berbers, savage hillmen who
had resisted all Ismail's efforts to convert them to Islam, even
catching him with sixty thousand men in one trap from which
he barely escaped with two thousand survivors. And this bleeding thing on the ground—

"Bah!" said Akbar callously. "He's some villager, better off
dead. Let him be."

The eyes of the bleeding thing burned up savagely. He was near dead, his tongue half cut away, knife cuts all over his body, but he was conscious. O'Brien stooped; the other tried to spit upon the infidel, only to fall back in a faint.

"Pick him up and care for him," said O'Brien. Akbar surveyed him insolently.

"Are we dogs or soldiers? We escort you; we do not obey you!"

O'Brien had had enough of this renegade's insolence. His fist lashed out; the blow lifted Akbar from his feet, stretched him senseless. The black men caught at their weapons, but here came Will Dowling, running, from the halted wagon.

"Tell these men," ordered O'Brien, "to put this poor devil in the wagon, You take care of his wounds."

"But, master!" stammered the former slave. "You have struck Akbar. For a Christian to do this—"

"Devil take you! Obey me!" snapped O'Brien, and Will Dowling translated.

The blacks sullenly decided to obey, and it was done as O'Brien ordered. Then Dowling turned to O'Brien.

"We must have rest and water, Cap'n," he said. "We are close to Mulai Idris, the holy city of pilgrimage, but no Christians are allowed there. Still, they say we may stop by the old Roman city, a league distant. We can find water there."

"Have it as you will," said O'Brien.

"And, for heaven's love," pleaded the ragged bearded Dowling anxiously, "stay your hot hand! It be bad enough for Christians, as I know to my cost, but if they lift hand against any of Ismail's men, naught can save them! Not even Moors dare strike his guards—"

O'Brien's eyes smote upon him stormily.

"Do you expect to live forever? Fool, it is better to die like a man than live like a dog."

Will Dowling shrugged.

"All right, Cap'n, I be willing to stand by 'un! Lord knows they'll never ha' me alive again for torturing."

He went back to the wagon, and O'Brien stood over Akbar as the renegade struggled up.

"Look you, Dutchman!" said O'Brien harshly, holding out the letter bearing the golden seal of Ismail. "Obey me, do you understand? I will answer to your master—and by Allah, you will answer to him likewise if you do not obey!"

Akbar met his gaze with furious eyes.

"We shall see, infidel," he answered. They both spoke Spanish. "Ambassadors, indeed! Do you think we are fools, here in Morocco? Do we not know that there is no such nation as your Ireland? Bah!"

O'Brien rode on again, but the storm had passed from his eyes, and a laugh touched his lips; for his fingers were itching after the rapier by his side, and he knew that ahead lay the death of men, and perhaps his own, and therein was the great gamble of this venture. If he won, he won greatly. And he was not in love with life.

So they wound under the high hilltop where the sacred city of Mulai Idris lay sprawled over the hill in the shape of a five-pointed star, and presently they halted among Roman streets and arches and ruins, above a gully where ran clear cold water. And much was to happen, here in this dead city whose streets had once been tramped by a British legion, and whose name had been Volubilis.

It was the close of the year 1690—the twentieth of the reign of Ismail, whom men called the Sword of Allah.

FOR WEEKS O'Brien had been hearing about Ismail's barbaric cruelty, his manner of rule, his astounding ways of living and acting. Now, as he stood between two Roman pillars and suveyed his camp, he thought little about Ismail and much about O'Brien.

Akbar and his command were camped to one side. The two wagons, with the slaves provided to care for the ambassadors, were under the orders of Will Dowling. The latter, who had acquired some skill in leechcraft, announced that St. Rocher was deep in stupor and would come out of it sometime during the day, either dead or back to life. As for the wounded Moor they had picked up, he was like a savage beast, too hardy to die of his wounds.

So O'Brien found himself alone, on this day after reaching Volubilis. Akbar refused any speech with him, but he had learned that Meknez was only a day's ride away—two days' travel for their slow party. And Mulai Idris sprawled like a starfish over its mountain crest, a league distant; the holy city where lay buried Idris, founder of this Moroccan realm.

O'Brien had discarded his travel stained clothes, and this morning wore a very elegant suit of cut Genoa velvet, all green and gold, with his plain rapier won at Rabat. Will Dowling came up to him with eloquent protests; green was the sacred color of Islam and he must not wear it.

"Stow your jaw!" cried O'Brien fiercely. "You prate eternally of what I must not and must do, and I am sick of it! Give me no more advice, honest Will. Faith, I intend to live and die myself, and devil take all else. And what does this renegade dog want now?"

Akbar was swaggering toward them, followed by a pair of the black guards. He came to a halt before O'Brien, hand on hilt of his scimitar.

"Well, Christian!" he exclaimed. "Last night you dared to strike me, and now you must kneel to me in apology, or else my men will take you in chains before the emperor. Choose!"

O'Brien looked at him and laughed a little, but the blue eyes were very sharp.

"So!" said O'Brien quietly. "You renegade, who have denied your people and race and faith, would have an apology?"

"And at once," blustered the other arrogantly. "Here you are in my country; you are an infidel dog, and if you forget the fact, a flogging is the least you may expect."

"True," said O'Brien. "Well, since you demand it, I will apologize. Tell your men that they may comprehend what is being done and may be witnesses."

"Gladly."

With a laugh, the renegade turned and spoke to his two guards, who showed their teeth and guffawed. He swung around again, and this was his last laugh on earth, for O'Brien's rapier slid from its sheath and drove into his throat, so that he coughed and clutched and sank down, gripping at the yellow earth.

Seeing that the two blacks stood staring, dumbfounded, O'Brien took out the letter of safe conduct, opened it to show the golden seal of Ismail, and then stooped. He plucked forth Akbar's dagger and drove it through the letter into the dead man's breast, and so left it. The two guards looked one at the other, then they turned and ran toward their comrades, shouting. In five minutes all of them had saddled and were spurring away toward Mulai Idris.

Will Dowling came from the wagon, heard what had passed, and muttered in his beard.

"They will bring fanatics from that city and murder us all by torture," he said. "But no matter! Call me when they come, ye mad Irishman!"

So O'Brien was left there alone, and very cheerful about it he was, humming a merry tune as he wiped his rapier clean and loaded his pistols. He was a little sorry for St. Rocher, because the vicomte would detest being killed in his sleep, but this could not be helped.

For James O'Brien, late colonel of the Irish Brigade, late slave in the Virginia plantations and buccaneer and sea rover, and self-appointed ambassador from Ireland to Emperor Ismail, felt that he had come to the end of the trail. He had seen how Christians acted in this land, how the consuls and traders and priests permitted here, allowed themselves to be treated, and for himself he could not stomach it.

Perhaps the stark sunlight of the land had smitten him; but

as he sat here on a broken column and looked at the hills and plain, and shook the sun bleached hair out of his eyes, he smiled again at the thought of it all. He was here, alone, against an empire of blood and cruelty, and he was a little tired of struggling, and very lonely. He rather thought St. Rocher was dying and, with St. Rocher gone, all the zest of the game was lost. So, as the morning wore on and he saw the dust clouds rise and caught the glitter of arms pouring down from the mountain slopes, he laughed again and swept a bow to the sacred city on its peak.

"Greetings, Mulai Idris!" he exclaimed. "You who came here, eight hundred years ago, a wandering adventurer—receive my salute! We'll talk it over together tonight."

He did not call Will Dowling, but strode out among the ruins to the head of the path that mounted from the arroyo below and stood there, waiting, while doom came rushing on.

He could see them plainly now, sweeping down across the long level ground that reaches toward the Roman city, that level stretch where the Berber tribes took the Arabian Idris for their saint and lord. Behind the men of his escort came a wild throng, horsemen and men on mules, and behind these straggled a crowd on foot. Here and there in other directions rose more dust clouds, betokening a gathering eager to shed infidel blood. O'Brien smiled again and looked down at the deep arroyo, and the little path mounting to where he stood. Romans had died here, as he would die here—but a few others would pass first down the ways of hell.

The foremost came on, flooding down into the arroyo, leaving their beasts there and pressing up the path afoot. They were yelling madly at sight of him, weapons glittering in the sunlight; not all were Arabs, for he caught shouts in French, and one voice in English.

"Back, ye ruddy fool! Don't you know they're for killing you?"

O'Brien stuck the rapier into the ground before him and lifted his pistols. At this the foremost halted abruptly, but those behind shoved them on. A pistol banged and the ball sang overhead.

Calmly enough O'Brien aimed and fired, and again. Two of the foremost Moors went down, and the swelling tide broke back. Yells arose in a furious outcry and, glancing around, O'Brien saw Will Dowling just behind him, dragging the body of Akbar. As he looked, Dowling set up the body in a sitting posture against a rock, pointed to the glittering golden seal, and yelled at the men below. Shouts of execration answered him.

"I threatened 'un with Ismail's wrath," said he, grinning shaggily at O'Brien. "Cap'n, we be done for sure enough. They mean business. That fellow we picked up has crawled out of the wagon and be a-settin' in the sun. A wild 'un, he be."

"Go back and watch over St. Rocher," said O'Brien.

"Safe enough; still asleep, but sweat's beginning. He'll live, I think."

"Not long." O'Brien laughed harshly. He was busy reloading his pistols. "Back with him."

Will Dowling obeyed, leaving O'Brien there beside the dead Akbar in the sunlight.

Across the plain swept the dust clouds; more and more men came straggling to join the crowd choking the ravine below; wild yells assailed the man who looked down calmly upon the milling scores. An occasional shot rang out. Fierce bearded faces looked up, black and white and brown, curved swords glinted, the name of Allah reechoed from the sides of the arroyo.

Then, with a surge, the crowd came on at the slope, led by a red bearded Berber.

The Berber and a black man were in the lead. O'Brien stood watching calmly, unmoving, until they were twenty feet below; then he fired his two shots. The Berber clutched at his throat and fell. The negro screamed and slid down under the feet of those behind. These, trampling forward, came into the path, rushing upward in single file as they needs must.

The long rapier glittering, O'Brien faced the curved blades

sweeping up at him. The first man thrust upward a small round hide shield and slashed under it at the legs, but O'Brien leaped in the air and thrust down above the shield, and the man shrieked as the glittering point drove in through his eye. The little shield fell from his grasp, and O'Brien swooped upon it and then drew back a pace until he had gripped the handle. It just saved him from a thrusting lance—then he was leaping down at them all, the rapier darting and licking out like a tongue of death.

In this place, which for long afterward was known in the Arab tongue as the Ravine of Blood, now befell a curious grim game wherein life was staked upon agility and effort. White and brown and black men, pressing upward, trampled down those who fell, and a rivulet of scarlet was presently running down the sticky yellow mud to those below. The little hide buckler served O'Brien well, fending off the darting lances while the long rapier drove into those who scrambled up at him, so that man after man went screaming or choking to death while no blade touched him.

"Get a horse and run for it!" shouted the English voice of some renegade amid the crowd. "Before they think to take you in rear!"

"Thanks, friend," returned O'Brien amid a momentary lull as they drew back. "But here is the seal of Ismail for safe conduct, so why fear?"

"Art mad!" came the response.

O'Brien shook the sweaty hair from his eyes and laughed, then they yelled and surged upward anew.

Now the dust borne on the wind came from the plain and hung in the air above the ravine, so that those who fought upward against the one man had no sight of what passed elsewhere. They came in a crowd, clawing at the yellow earth, slipping in the blood, and one or two gained footing outside the path. A scimitar swept away half the hide shield, but the man who smote that blow did not live to boast of it; the rapier darted in and out, and again the knees of men were loosened in death, and blood ran down the yellow slope. The bodies of those who died, however, made footing for those who lived, and O'Brien saw that the end was close upon him, as the living trampled the fallen and surged forward. Dust hung like a haze in the air, and the odor of blood was rank. O'Brien was tiring now, and lances were reaching forward after him. He paused to drive down the rapier through a brown throat, and then leaped backward a few paces for the last stand, behind the body of Akbar.

They surged forward like a bursting wave to finish him.

O'BRIEN STOOD by the broken Roman walls and saw a strange thing come to pass below.

From beneath the dust, across the ravine came shrill bursting yells that halted the onrush of men. He could see figures of horsemen moving there among the hindmost, and thought they were laying about with whips. A spreading cry of affright rose up from all those crowded fanatics, and the surging tide broke and dissipated up and down the ravine, and back upon the plain.

Only the dead and hurt remained, and the green clad figure above them.

Looking out across, as the dust lifted, O'Brien saw a great company of horsemen who had come up—Arabs in gay, fluttering robes, most of them armed with fusils, and in their midst a yellow robed figure sitting a magnificent white barb. O'Brien wiped his rapier upon the kaftan of the dead Akbar, and rested. He saw numbers of the dismounted Arabs talking with those who had just ridden up, and presently one of these last dismounted and crossed the ravine, and called to him from below in good clear English—

"I am a friend!"

O'Brien stared, frowning, for the man was a black Moor and no renegade. With a friendly grin the man mounted and stood before him, gazing curiously.

"Is it true that you are one of the ambassadors from Ireland?"

"Aye," said O'Brien, amazed. "Where learned you English?"

"In Tangier—was I not interpreter to the Earl of Teviot before he was slain there?" and the black man laughed, amused. "Yonder is my master, El Husenin, chief architect to Mulai Ismail, whom God protect! He is a man of great power, and desires to judge this matter."

O'Brien smiled.

"There is naught to judge. Bid him lead his men forward and end it."

"*Sidi,* speak not thus," said the other earnestly. "That were your death; El Husenin is lord of all this region—"

"Fool, does it seem to you that I fear death?" said O'Brien harshly, and pointed to dead Akbar. "There is the safe conduct of your emperor, and there is the knave who refused to honor it. Go tell your master what you have seen."

The black man perceived the golden seal and prostrated himself before it, then rose.

"It is the order of El Husenin that you go back to your camp," he said. "He will come and talk with you, for he loves to talk with Christians. I warn you, as a friend, anger him not, for in wrath he is terrible, as you may yet see."

"Very well," said O'Brien. "Let him judge the matter; and if I like not his justice, he will be the first to die."

"You must indeed be mad," said the other, looking curiously at him. "Why do you wear the sacred color of the Prophet, whose name be blessed? Know you not that in our country it is worn only by those descended from Muhammad? For others to wear it is death."

O'Brien laughed and said a wild and bitter thing whose sense the other man quite misunderstood.

"It is the color of my country, Ireland, therefore I wear it. All the greatest men in the world came from Ireland—even the ancestors of your prophet. That is why it is his sacred hue. Tell that to your chief architect."

The other man bowed, apparently in blank wonder.

"I shall tell him, *sidi.* And I warn you, in speaking with him do not try evasion, for he can read the thoughts of men. I shall interpret and must hold strictly to what is said."

"Bah!" said O'Brien, with a wave of his hand. "Go your ways, for I am weary of your words. And here—take this to your master."

He stooped, jerked loose the blood spattered safe conduct, and thrust it at the Moor, who took it with reverence and departed.

For a moment O'Brien stood looking out at the horsemen opposite, then he sheathed his rapier and strode back among the ruins of the Roman city.

When he regained the wagons he found that the Arab teamsters had fled. The horses had disappeared, with the mules. Seated at one side, in the sunlight, was the native they had picked up on the previous day; his face was swathed in bandages from which his eyes glared out at O'Brien like the eyes of a wild animal. None else was in sight.

"Dowling! Will Dowling! Fetch me water or wine."

"Aye, Cap'n," came response from the covered wagon where St. Rocher lay.

O'Brien flung himself down wearily, and presently the ex-slave came with wine and water and bread, to stare at him amazedly.

"Not dead?"

"Do I look it?" O'Brien drank deeply and thirstily, then recounted what had taken place. Will Dowling plucked at his ragged beard, and his sunken eyes were filled with astonishment. Then swift and sudden terror leaped in his face.

"El Husenin! The chief architect—God ha' mercy!" he exclaimed jerkily. "Did he ride a white horse? How was he clad?"

"In yellow." O'Brien looked at him. "You know the man?"

A groan burst from Will Dowling.

"Aye! And when he wears yellow, all men flee from him, Master O'Brien. That signifies he is in bloody mood. Chief architect—Ismail is his own architect, they say, and El Husenin is one of his names. That man is the emperor himself, Cap'n!

And tonight will see us crucified on a mud wall, or impaled on the highway."

O'BRIEN STOOD looking grimly at the approaching cavalcade. Will Dowling sat to one side in speechless terror, near the bandaged native.

Half a dozen of El Husenin's men dismounted and came forward, then paused, matches alight, their fusils trained upon O'Brien. Behind, the others dismounted, but stood at a distance. Among them were five of the late escort, Akbar's men. These approached and squatted down at a little distance, glaring at O'Brien and fingering their weapons.

El Husenin—unless it were the emperor himself, as Will Dowling thought—left his white steed and strode forward. His yellow robes were spotted with blood. About his waist was girded a scimitar; a glorious weapon whose sheath of gold was set with diamonds and emeralds; but he bore no other mark of rank. The black Tangier interpreter walked beside him.

O'Brien inspected the man with open curiosity. He saw that El Husenin was quite black in the face; a man of medium height, with long and spare countenance terminating in a forked black beard. Two distinguishing traits marked those features. One was a white spot on his cheek near the nose. The second was the quality of the eyes—fierce, penetrating, seeming to flash fire. When they fell upon O'Brien he felt as though a physical blow had been struck him.

El Husenin looked him up and down, and O'Brien gave him look for look, meeting the appalling force of that savage gaze with calm hauteur. Then the black man spoke curtly in a strong, deep voice, and the Moor beside him translated.

"Why have you dared to kill true believers?"

O'Brien could well believe that this man might read his very thoughts. He felt a curious mental conflict as he met those implacable eyes, sensed that they were probing into him, dragging at his very brain. A slight smile touched his lips as he made response.

"It was not I who killed," he said proudly. "It was the will of Allah."

The effect of these words was tremendous. The translator faltered upon them; El Husenin started visibly. All unawares, O'Brien had chanced upon the exact phrase which Mulai Ismail invariably used after his insensate killings—that sanest of madmen who in his twenty years of rule had slain above twenty thousand men with his own hand.

"Dog of a Christian," said El Husenin, "explain that saying."

"Easily," said O'Brien with an air of disdain. "I bore a safe conduct under the seal of your emperor himself, who is the elect of Allah. Certain men violated that safe conduct. If they died, how does that concern me? Let your emperor look to it."

"You speak not as a man, but as a king," said El Husenin, his eyes flashing.

"Before Muhammad, upon whom be peace, was born, my ancestors were kings," said O'Brien.

A grim smile came to the black face of El Husenin.

"You are a Christian—good! In my army yonder are many former Christians who have seen the light of the true faith. Acknowledge that Muhammad the blessed is the Prophet of God, and I will make you a leader of ten thousand men, and a kaid with a province to rule."

In the man's face O'Brien read an absolute sincerity behind these words.

"When you, El Husenin, renounce your faith, then will I consider your offer," he said.

For an instant the Moor's face darkened as an angry rush of blood suffused the dark skin to a deeper hue; then the threat passed in swift admiration, and he broke into a laugh.

"Time to talk of this matter again," he said. "You have come to this land to see the elect of Allah? What have you heard of this Mulai Ismail—may his line increase! Speak!"

"Much that is evil," said O'Brien. "And much that is good. He is said to be ruled by two passions; by religion and by greed."

El Husenin seemed amused by this.

"Well for you that he came not against you this day with arms, infidel! Do you know that no man can stand before him in battle?"

"Perhaps it is well for him that he did not," said O'Brien. "Certainly none of his men have stood before me. But are you here to bandy words or to give justice?"

"By Allah, that you shall see," was the answer.

El Husenin whirled, gave a sharp order, and the five men of the emperor's bodyguard came forward. He shot questions at them, and they made answer, one of them pointing at the bandaged native. It was clear that they were telling how the ill feeling between Akbar and O'Brien had come to a head. And it was also clear that they were suddenly frightened. When El Husenin produced the safe conduct and held it up, they stood staring, all a-tremble.

Then, quicker than eye could follow, El Husenin dropped the vellum and his scimitar came out. With incredible swiftness, he leaped. That leap was like the dart of a hawk. Five times the steel circled in the air, and at each blow a black neck was severed neatly.

O'Brien stood absolutely stupefied. El Husenin thrust the blade into its gem blazing scabbard and swung back to face him, eyes bloodshot with rage.

"That is my justice, infidel," rang out his deep voice. "But you have lifted your hand against true believers—and you shall not escape. First, however, do you think that men of El Maghrib are fools? You came hither as an ambassador from Ireland. Where is your nation? Where is your king? Where are your letters such as all ambassadors carry?"

With an effort O'Brien fronted this savage beast, held his own eyes cool beneath the gaze that made his brain reel, gave the Moor a slow and arrogant look.

"I take it, El Husenin, that you are a great lord, in the confidence of your master?"

"Yes," barked the other curtly.

"Then I shall speak frankly with you, and; you may set my errand before him. My master, King James of England and Ireland, is at the court of France; we, his people, are fugitives in other lands. My fellow ambassador, Vicomte de St. Rocher, is a nobleman of France. At sea, we make war upon the English, and Spaniards, from whom we haw taken much gold and goods. Now, let me tell you that your master is something of a fool."

The terror struck translator fumbled this out. El Husenin, who had been studying O'Brien, only returned one word—

"Explain."

"I brought great store of valuable goods to Rabat and sold them there," said O'Brien coolly. "Did your master see any of it? No. It was smuggled ashore by night; those who serve Mulai Ismail there are unworthy of trust. He lost greatly by the evasion of his tax."

Anger flamed in El Husenin and his face darkened again.

"Infidel," he said, "you are a bold man to say these things!"

"Talk not like a child," said O'Brien disdainfully.

Somewhat of his own force flamed out in his eyes and struck suddenly at the Moor; his slim, soldierly figure, so different from the *djellab* shrouded shapes around, seemed a thing of slender steel.

"You," he went on calmly, "are used to servile men around you; slaves; men who fear for their lives. I fear for nothing, and I go on my knees to no man. Now, listen to me. I seek your master to obtain letters from him. With theses I and my companions may bring Spanish and English plunder to Rabat and sell it there—to the advantage of your master. The gifts I bring are rich."

"I desire to see those gifts," said El Husenin, with a glance at the wagons.

"They are not for your eyes," said O'Brien coolly, "but for those of your master. I offer you no bribe, El Husenin, so seek none from me."

The other was stung by his tone, and regarded him with a gaze that struggled betwixt swift fury and a grudging admiration.

"Infidel," said El Husenin, "do you know that to me and to my master belong all things in this land—all men, all property? If it is my wish to strike the head from a man, he yields. None dares to gainsay me. As Allah liveth, no man has spoken to my face as you speak."

"If you fear the truth, so much the worse for you," replied O'Brien.

El Husenin regarded him for a long moment; shrewdly.

"I did not know there were Christians like you," he said. "I shall take you to Meknez and my master will crucify you, because you have dared to lift hand against true believers."

"He will not," said O'Brien. "He is not a coward, unless rumor speaks falsely."

El Husenin laughed at this and pointed to the green velvet suit.

"You wear the forbidden color, you break our laws and customs, and you expect to escape punishment?"

"Laws are made for slaves," said O'Brien, and at this the dark eyes flashed suddenly.

"True, by Allah! Yet you shall be crucified. But my master will desire to speak with you, for it may be truth that Muhammad—whose name be exalted—was of ancient kinship with your people. Regarding this we must ask the doctors off the law."

"Nay, ask your master," said O'Brien, "for I hear that he himself is a taleb and knows more about your religion than all your wise men."

El Husenin laughed a little, then turned and called to his waiting men. A number of these came forward, leading his white horse and another with it. One of them pointed to the sun, and El Husenin nodded and strode a little apart and knelt.

So did they all, save those who bent their fusils upon O'Brien, watching him lest he make some hostile move. El Husenin and all his men bowed, with their faces toward Mulai Idris, and a slave brought the leader water in a small ewer for the prescribed ablutions. When the prayer was completed, El Husenin turned and spoke to O'Brien,

"Here is a horse, a gift from the stables of the emperor. You shall ride with me, for I have business in haste. Your companions will be brought to Meknez. You will come before Mulai Ismail—may he be blessed!—and he will crucify you! I tell you this frankly, for only the hand of Allah can save you from his wrath."

O'Brien smiled.

"Do you think Allah has no power, then?"

El Husenin laughed suddenly and strode forward, and caught O'Brien by the arm. His fingers were like steel.

"Good Christian!" he exclaimed. "You are a man; I like you. But you shall be crucified."

O'Brien turned his face toward Will Dowling.

"Did this translator give his words aright, Will?"

"Aye, Cap'n," came the response.

"Good. Then I'll ride with him. Make him promise safe conduct to the emperor."

When El Husenin understood this, he nodded quickly. Then he turned to his white horse. One man held its reins, another held the stirrup for him. With a movement of the utmost agility, El Husenin swung upward to the saddle. In the same motion, too swiftly for the eye to follow, he drew his scimitar, and as he came into the saddle, his. blade flashed down. The one stroke, an outlet for his frustrated anger, severed the head of the man at his stirrup.

So O'Brien rode away from the Ravine of Blood and the Roman Walls, a plain white *djellab* covering him from the sunlight; and little dreamed the horror toward which he was spurring.

O'BRIEN WAS given in charge of the Tangier interpreter, who remained with him constantly.

Late that same night, riding hard, El Husenin and his array came to a spot called the Oued Beht, eight leagues from Meknez. Above a rushing mountain torrent was a level plain, where two thousand men were encamped, all blacks of the bodyguard. In their midst was a huge copper kettle such as was used in Martinique for boiling sugar. It had been taken from some captured French vessel in times past. About it, and about the wagon which had brought it here from Meknez, were twenty Christian slaves who had it in charge.

Why they had come here O'Brien did not know, and the interpreter would tell him nothing. All next day he rested or wandered about the camp, seeing nothing of El Husenin. Toward evening, however, men rode in with shouts, guns were fired, and the black soldiery were drawn up in ranks. O'Brien perceived that they were trained to high precision, well drilled.

To the Oued Beht and into the camp rode five hundred wild southern Moors, bearing in their midst a tall and handsome man who wore golden fetters. El Husenin kept his tent. The commander of the guards showed the prisoner to a tent, and O'Brien turned to his companion as the men fell out of ranks.

"Who is that prisoner?" he asked curiously.

"Muhammad," responded the Moor, frowning. "The favorite son of our emperor, king of Tarudent, for three years past in rebellion. He was captured by treachery and brought here. All men love him. May Allah help him now!"

O'Brien wakened next morning to an idle camp. The day drew on, and nothing happened. In the afternoon, early, appeared his own two wagons with their escort, and he delightedly greeted Will Dowling. Five minutes later he was gripping hands with St. Rocher—pale and wasted, but rid of the fever and promising to .be soon upon his feet again. As they talked, a great shout and scattering shots drew O'Brien from the wagon, and he found the Tangier Moor awaiting him.

"Come!" said the Moor excitedly. "Mulai Ismail is about to meet his son. Come!"

O'Brien followed him, and behind them trailed the bandaged native whom they had found beside the road, his wild eyes glittering through his dirty bindings. They passed amid the drawn up ranks, until the Moor halted near the wagon. Here a fire had been built by the slaves under the copper kettle, into which they were dumping oil and pitch; the wagon was drawn up beside it, so that a man standing on the wagon was on a level with the top of the great kettle.

The doorway of a tent close by was open, and between guards O'Brien saw El Husenin sitting there, still wearing his blood spattered yellow robes. The interpreter pointed.

"There sits Mulai Ismail—you recognize him, *sidi?* And here, by Allah—here comes the lord Muhammad!"

In his golden fetters, looking very proud and handsome, was led the captive prince; but when he stood before his father, the pride fled out of him and he prostrated himself. Ismail caught up a lance and held the point at his throat, and the prince cried out in fear.

"For the love of Allah, for the love of the holy Muhammad, pardon me!"

As the Moor murmured the translation, O'Brien saw Ismail throw the lance aside and make a gesture to two men beside his tent—butchers, brought from Meknez. A number of the guards seized upon Muhammad, lifted him to the wagon, and stretched out his right arm, holding it there across the edge of the copper kettle. Ismail angrily beckoned one of the butchers and motioned. The man drew back, stammering something.

In a passion, Ismail swept out his golden scimitar, and the man's head fell. The other butcher leaped for the wagon, his heavy knife upraised. The blade fell, and the hand of Muhammad fell into the kettle, the guards plunging the stump into the boiling oil and pitch.

No sound came from the tortured prince; but a long, deep

mutter came from the watching blacks. Ismail looked on, implacable; then gave a fresh order. The right foot of the prince was held across the kettle rim. It was lopped off like the hand. As though his tension were snapped, Ismail uttered a wild, bestial scream.

"Now do you know your father?" he yelled. "Heretofore you seem to have been ignorant of it!"

With the words, he snatched a fusil from the nearest guard, applied the match, and shot down the butcher who had done the work. Muhammad, looking down from the wagon, uttered a horrible, strangled laugh.

"Here is a valiant man!" came his mocking, panting voice. "Look at his bravery! He kills the one who obeys and the one who disobeys. All that he does is vain. Allah is just, Allah is great!"

With this, he fell senseless, and was carried away to a tent.

O'Brien stood staring, stupefied with the horror of the scene. Ismail glared around, and men shrank from his look, knowing him to be in one of his insensate rages; his bloodshot eyes fell upon the two men, and he strode up to O'Brien, snarling. The Moor translated hastily.

"Now you know with whom you have talked. What have you to say?"

O'Brien looked into those mad, powerful eyes, and smiled.

"I knew from the first with whom I talked. Are there two such men as you in this land?"

Ismail growled, and his hands clenched and unclenched.

"Christian dog! Now let Allah save you if that be possible! You shall be placed upon a stake at the gate of Meknez—aye, ere tomorrow's sun be set! Do you understand?"

O'Brien gazed steadily into those flashing eyes and gathered his muscles. Rapier against scimitar—why not?

As his hand moved, however, something came between the two of them—a bandaged figure, whose hand caught at the robe of Ismail and rent it away. The emperor drew back a step.

The native plucked the bandages from his face, making strange noises with his mutilated tongue, and from Ismail broke a cry of recognition, of astonishment. He caught the filthy figure in his arms, kissed the man's shoulder. To the amazement of O'Brien, he almost prostrated himself before this naked, maimed, unwashed savage.

Forgotten, O'Brien drew back and touched the arm of the interpreter.

"Who is this fellow?" he demanded. The Moor gave him a sharp glance.

"Know you not? The man whom you rescued. He is a very holy man, of the blood of Idris, so holy that Ismail gives him free entrance of the palace, refuses him nothing; he is what you Christians call a saint—what the French call a santon. We call him a marabout. He is the most holy man in all our country. Look! He can not talk; he is writing—"

The maimed man, indeed, was tracing in the dust with his finger, and Ismail stooped to read the words. He straightened up, summoned men who led away the filthy holy man, and then turned to O'Brien. The fury was gone out of his face, replaced by a wondering awe; and of a sudden O'Brien realized that he was a man sorely smitten by a great grief and remorse.

"Christian, you have conquered, and I am glad," said the black emperor. "This man has told me to pardon you and take you for friend; Allah speaks through him, and I obey. Great is God! Allah, and Allah, and Allah! Muhammad—"

With a choked cry, Ismail turned and rushed to the white horse beside the tent. One leap and he was in the saddle. He spurred like a madman away from this place toward Meknez, and after him spurred his black troops, riding away in a whirl of dust and a thunder of clattering unshod hooves.

O'Brien stood looking after them in the sunset glare, and wondered at the ways of Allah.

IV

THE STRONG HAND ABOVE

*A Novelette of Colonel O'Brien
and the Barbary Pirates.*

A T T H E opening of the year 1693 a naked, filthy slave was laboring with fifty thousand others, building the walls of Meknez, when he saw a group of men passing below. As a result of this glimpse came the temptation and endurance of one man, the resurrection of another, and the death of many.

The staring slave had been pounding down the mastic of which the huge walls were built. Now he dropped his pounder and rushed to the side of the Spanish renegade who, whip in hand, directed this particular gang.

"Look!" he cried, pointing at the group, still visible. "Do you see that tall man in front? Tell me who he is, and we may both profit by it."

So wild, so distraught was the slave's look, that the renegade peered to see who had gone by below,

"That is an ambassador lately arrived from Ireland, they say, or the Irish king. He stands high in favor with Mulai Ismail, and goes to the palace every day. You know him?"

"Aye." The slave glanced around. "I'll write a letter tonight. You get the ear of Abraham Maimoran, the royal treasurer, and if this ambassador gets the letter, there'll be a hundred gold pieces for you and Maimoran to share."

"Eh? You are in earnest?"

A flame danced in the blue eyes of the gaunt, scarred slave. "That I am! If we—"

The renegade overseer was absorbed in what the slave pro-

posed; the slave himself was deaf to all around. Neither of them
caught the muttered warnings from the other slaves, or saw the
approaching figures—until too late.

Half a dozen of the black palace guards, fusils in hand,
matches alight, came up the ramp. Ahead of them ran a spare
black figure clad in yellow robes, which were spotted with fresh
blood. Wild fury twisted his aquiline features. Just as the two
caught sight of him, he lifted his lance and drove it forward; it
transfixed the renegade through the body. As the man fell, the
emperor uttered a wild cry. For this man, black of features with
a white spot by his nostril, was Mulai Ismail, Lord of Morocco.

"Bring the Alcaide Melek here!" he commanded, and then
turned upon a group of Arabs and renegades who followed his
bodyguard—the overseers of this portion of the work. "Dogs!"
he cried out. "So this is how you work when you think I am
not watching, is it? By Allah, you shall learn from me—"

He whipped out his gold hilted scimitar, whose diamonds
and emeralds flashed in the white sunlight, and sprang upon
the group. In a frothing rage he cut down man after man. None
dared to resist, nor indeed could any man in Morocco stand
before this spare, lean warrior. When five of the overseers lay
dead, he whirled about and faced the panting Alcaide—one of
the highest of the court officials, who had in charge all this
section of the work.

"Give him the bastinado!" he ordered. "And after it, five
hundred lashes, that he may teach his underlings how to work."

He laughed cruelly and glanced around, meeting the eye of

the gaunt slave. Now, Ismail was not the homicidal maniac he appeared, by a good deal. He survived by making men fear him, but also by a shrewd craft which backed up his physical prowess. Every slave in Morocco was his personal property—and so was every other person and all personal property his. He rarely harmed his Christian slaves, for they were his expert workmen.

"So, infidel dog, you dare to stand there idle?" he said softly. To the utter amazement of all who watched, the slave did not fall upon his knees, but gave a wild laugh.

"Aye, beloved of Allah!" he rejoined. "How better to draw the attention of Ismail than to stand idle?"

"So you desire the attention of Ismail?" The emperor smiled thinly.

"Aye. To tell him that I have a brother who just passed this way," said the slave boldly. "His name is O'Brien, and he is ambassador to your court from our country; I am his brother, whom he has long thought dead. Give me grace and pardon, beloved of Allah!"

Bold as was this demand, it was the only possible way of salvation. Ismail, who feared nothing on earth himself, hated men who cringed, but listened to those who bearded him. In all his reign of nearly sixty years, he was only known to spare one man; but this man met him with a laugh and a shrewd trick, and Ismail admired him. Now he eyed the slave keenly, and wiped a splotch of blood from his long forked beard.

"Confess that Mohammed is the Prophet of God, and you are free," he said.

The slave laughed and pointed to his white scars.

"These scars and twelve years of slavery are the answer, son of Idris!"

Ismail eyed him and smiled to himself, then beckoned one of his guards. The slave was led away—to be impaled, as all men thought. Ismail beckoned another of his Sudanese, and pointed to the bodies of those whom he had slain.

"Go to the homes of these men. Say that it was the will of Allah that they should die, and bring to me their slaves and possessions and all that they owned."

The guard departed, and there was nothing strange in this errand, since one of Ismail's black guards had more power than all the Arabs in Morocco, and who touched him died terribly. As for the bodies of the dead, they were pitched into the molds of the rising walls and pounded down into mastic, to lie with thousands of other such.

For in this manner were the walls of Meknez built.

COLONEL JAMES O'BRIEN, late of the Jacobite service, the French and Swedish service, and the high seas generally, said nothing of the note that had been thrust into his hand as he entered the palace. Staggered as he was by the news, he thrust it resolutely from his mind. His ability to deal with one thing at a time was a factor in his success.

With his buccaneering lieutenant, Vicomte de St. Rocher, he had invented an embassy from Ireland and had come to Meknez—only to find that these Arabs were not to be fooled. A chance meeting with Mulai Ismail let O'Brien save himself by proposing that Salé be opened to buccaneers. Further, it placed him in the emperor's favor, even to an embarrassing extent, as he found on reaching Meknez. Ismail had a passion for converting ambassadors to Islam.

St. Rocher was down with fever, a gaunt, pain racked shadow of himself. Each morning O'Brien was ordered to the palace, to remain until noon in the company of Ismail. And each morning, as he came, fresh amazement surged upon him at this place, this incredible place of which Ismail was the builder and architect. To any sane man, indeed, it was a city not only of blood uncounted but of wonders hard for the European brain to grasp.

Now, as he felt the note rustle in his pocket, O'Brien swaggered on past the two pashas holding court at the gate—the black pasha who judged the black folk, the white pasha whose tribunal was for the Arabs. The guards saluted him and the big Sudanese of the bodyguard who was his escort, and he went on.

Here, for miles across the hills, were enormous crenelated walls; his city done, Ismail was building full fifty palaces for his chief sons, each palace with its own grounds and enclosures. The work cost him nothing. He had close to thirty thousand Christian slaves, as many criminals of his own people, and he drew savagely upon all the Moroccan towns and tribes for enforced labor and for building materials.

The note burned in O'Brien's pocket. St. Rocher must know nothing of it; that hardy, generous comrade was in no shape for work—and this meant more than work. Thus resolved, O'Brien turned a corner of the walls and came upon Ismail sitting in an archway, beside him a dish of dried peas; the emperor was a frugal liver. About were his retinue, and before him, out in the sun, were drawn up some seventy Berbers, who took turns in haranguing Ismail.

O'Brien, saluting the emperor, turned into the shade beside a Dutch renegade who was waiting to have some building plans approved, and spoke to him softly.

"What is going on?"

The renegade laughed.

"These are a deputation of chiefs from the Zgoul Berbers, who have never accepted the true religion. They have come to argue religion with Ismail, and have been presenting their arguments all morning. Our lord wears a green vest, therefore he is in merciful mood—ah!"

Ismail cut short the harangue and uttered a few words. The seventy Berbers, lordly hillmen, rose. The Dutchman's eyes glittered.

"He says their arguments are good, but he has a better one. Watch!"

A trumpet blew. Into the courtyard marched a company of the black guards, surrounding the Berbers. Next instant the curved swords were at work. Five minutes later, the seventy heads were being piled before Ismail, who ordered them placed at the city gates, and the bodies sent to feed his lions and leopards and wolves, kept in the gardens. This detail finished, he glanced around and beckoned O'Brien.

The latter stood before him, an interpreter at his elbow.

"Infidel," said the emperor, stroking his forked beard and meeting the bright blue eyes of O'Brien with a slight smile, "your master King James is a fugitive at the court of the French king, who is my friend and brother. He is a fool, this king of yours, who knows not how to rule; nonetheless, I love him, because his brother Charles was the first to call me emperor and make treaties with me. Therefore I am resolved to set him back upon his throne."

Amazed as he was, O'Brien merely bowed.

"You have just seen," continued Ismail, "how the will of Allah works with those who refuse the light of the true faith. Now, you are a man whom I like. I desire that you shall become a convert to Islam. When this is done, I will make you commander of my bodyguard, the first man in El Magrib. You accept?"

Those who heard stared in astonishment. So did O'Brien, knowing what this meant. The Sudanese, whose numbers ranged from fifty thousand to three times that number, had a separate city outside the walls. It was the blacks who garrisoned the seventy forts which held all the country in subjection. Their children were brought up with special training to follow in their profession. Pitilessly drilled, they were Praetorians whom all men feared bitterly, save Ismail alone. They feared him, to the very marrow.

"Son of Idris," said O'Brien easily, "you are a taleb, a doctor of the law. You preach in the mosques. You know how Mohammed, may his name be blessed, ordained that no infidel be brought to the faith except of his own will, voluntarily."

"That is true," said Ismail, with a gratified nod. "The will of men may be prevailed upon, however."

"That depends upon the man," said O'Brien, and a smile lightened the grave, hard lines of his features.

"Accept," said Ismail, "and whatever you ask of me, that I will grant."

The note burned again in O'Brien's pocket, but he only shook his head.

"There is nothing I would have of you, son of Idris."

Ismail, knowing that O'Brien had received and read the note, regarded him curiously, then made a gesture of dismissal.

"When you change your mind, infidel, come to me, wherever I may be," he said. "Now go your ways, for I have sent gifts to your house, and my own physician to visit your friend. Come to me this afternoon at the stables."

O'Brien bowed deeply to him and returned from the palace to the city as he had come, the Sudanese at his side.

He saw the great gangs of slaves at work, and upon the hillside opposite rose the smoke of the lime kilns, where more than a few of them were burned alive. He saw the clouds of dust arising down the valley, where caravans of slaves and plunder, of building materials, came pouring in endlessly from every quarter of Morocco. He was saluted by a few renegades, and met glares from others; rich men, these, for the entire province of the Dra with its farms and towns had been made over to the English and Spaniards and French and Dutch who became converts; and these handled the artillery trains of Ismail.

So presently he came to the house, close by the convent of Spanish friars, which had been given his embassy, so called, as a dwelling place. The black remained at the door, and O'Brien went in to find the emperor's physician, Abd el Melek, treating St. Rocher. A dozen slaves had brought gifts, but O'Brien ignored these and went to his friend's bedside, when he had greeted the Arab healer.

"How goes it?"

"Well enough, Jack," said St. Rocher. "But this cursed weakness! If I could but see the ocean and sniff the salt sea wind, it would put me on my feet again."

O'Brien turned to the physician, who spoke excellent Spanish.

"Abd el Melek," he said frankly, "my friend must get back to the coast. This matter lies in your hands. Arrange it with your master. Have him sent at once with an escort to Salé, and five hundred pieces of gold shall be your reward."

"As Allah liveth!" gasped Abd el Melek, and his eyes glittered. "It shall be done, señor, depend upon it. Have him ready to depart this very day. I shall manage it."

He took his leave in haste. St. Rocher broke into protests, but O'Brien stilled them.

"Listen, St. Rocher—here you can help me. I must get out of this country or we both are lost, you comprehend? Our ship will be back at Salé in another three weeks, unless she has been sunk or taken by the Spaniards, and you must be there to meet her and go aboard. Take charge. Be ready to meet me—"

"Are you mad?" St. Rocher, pale as death, came to one elbow. "That is impossible—"

"Nothing is impossible," and O'Brien laughed gaily as he patted the gaunt hand. "Look you! I shall reach Salé a week after you—too late to meet the ship, unless you go ahead and take charge of her. She would not return for another month, you know. Meet her and set sail. After a week, remain off the coast—there'll be no bad weather this season; we must chance that. I'll come in a small craft from Salé, heading east by south. Hang off and on, a day's sail from the port. Simple enough."

"Diantre!" swore St. Rocher. "And if the Moors attack?"

"You have Ismail's letters. I have his safe conduct, freshly indited and sealed. We're safe enough from attack. Bah, old friend! No more protests. Boldness does it every time."

He went to his own room, a pleasant chamber opening on a court whose fountain splashed sweetly, and there drew out the note again. It was short.

> Jack: I saw you passing. I have been a slave here twelve years, since they captured my ship on the way to Rome. Ask Maimoran, the treasurer. He'll get you speech with me.
> —PHELIM.

O'Brien's tanned features worked strangely. Phelim O'Brien, his own brother, accounted dead these long years—a slave here! Well, please God, it would not be much longer for poor Phelim.

Little did O'Brien realize that Mulai Ismail had read that note and laughed softly over it, before allowing it to reach him.

WITHIN TWO hours Abd el Melek had earned his five hundred gold pieces, and O'Brien paid them with a glad heart, as St. Rocher and his escort departed. With St. Rocher went the English slave redeemed at Salé, Will Dowling by name; a faithful heart but no lion.

Thus, when the siesta hour was done, O'Brien found himself alone, with the half dozen black slaves provided to serve him, and the Sudanese guard. He was dressing to go to the palace as Ismail had ordered, when Abraham Maimoran arrived.

This man, whose father had elevated Ismail to the throne, was the chief of all the Jews in Morocco, and Ismail's treasurer. Each day he brought to O'Brien, as to the five hundred women of the seraglio and other pensioners, the exact measures of grain and food meted out by the emperor. Barbarically splendid as Ismail could be, he was also the most stingy of men, and himself kept the keys of his storehouses and granaries. Maimoran was a man of forty, bearded and extremely ugly, wearing black Jewish hat and *djellab;* he was very crafty and avaricious. Like most of the Jews and nearly all the Arabs, he spoke Spanish fluently, and greeted O'Brien with great courtesy. When the receipt for the day's supplies was signed, he came to business.

"Señor Don," he said thoughtfully, "I am your friend, and shall prove it. Mulai Ismail is resolved that you shall become a convert to Islam; you are in great danger. His second wife is English—you have seen her palace? Good. She sent word to me that tomorrow you are to be killed, unless God intervenes or you accept Islam."

O'Brien smiled.

"Perhaps," he responded cheerfully, "I will myself intervene."

"That is what I wanted to suggest," said Maimoran, eying him. "I am going to the palace with you; we shall find Ismail at the stables. Take this—" he produced a lump of brown sugar wrapped in cloth. "Ismail will show you a white horse of Arab strain. Let the horse find this sugar in your hand."

"Eh?" Puzzled, O'Brien put the little roll into his pocket. "I do not understand."

"This horse, Achmet, has made the pilgrimage to Mecca," said Maimoran, with a faintly ironic smile. "Ismail venerates him, or affects to do so; takes all care of him with his own hands. Any criminal who touches that horse—which is difficult—receives pardon. Now do you comprehend?"

"Oh! Perfectly." O'Brien nodded eagerly. "My thanks, señor. And there is another matter in which you can aid me. I have just learned that a brother of mine—"

Maimoran intervened.

"I know; he spoke to me yesterday," he rejoined. "But I regret to say that Ismail has learned of the matter, and has placed him in charge of the lion pit, a most dangerous occupation. My master is a crafty man, señor, and without mercy. He himself has taken charge of your brother, I find, and means to witness your meeting."

"Think you he will ransom my brother?" asked O'Brien bluntly.

The other shrugged.

"Who can predict what that man will do, señor? I think not, however."

O'Brien took from his pocket certain papers, and selected one. It was a bill of exchange given by a Jewish merchant at Salé for certain loot purchased from O'Brien.

"Do you know this merchant?" he asked, handing over the bill.

"For five hundred Louis d'or!" Maimoran's eyes widened. "Certainly; Ben Hattar's name is good here, or in France or Italy. You wish me to cash this?"

"I wish you to keep it," said O'Brien, regarding him keenly. "And to earn it."

"Oh! That is another matter, señor. How?"

"You know the cemetery outside the Bab Mellah, at the end of the Street of Goldsmiths?"

Maimoran nodded, since the *mellah*, or Jewish quarter, was his birthplace.

"On next Friday noon," said O'Brien, "I want to find two good horses awaiting me there."

"What? You are mad!" The other started as though stung. "Señor, where would I obtain horses? And on Friday the cemeteries are thronged with visiting crowds, and Ismail preaches in the chief mosque—"

"Exactly," said O'Brien, smiling a little. "And there is another bill of exchange, of equal amount, to be placed to your credit with Ben Hattar—when I reach Salé. Friday is six days away; you have time for anything. Halfway on the road to Salé, at whatever place you may designate, I want two fresh horses awaiting me. That is all. Is it yes or no?"

Maimoran breathed quickly, plucked at his beard, eyed the floor. At last he shrugged.

"Agreed," he said and, tucking away the signed paper, rose. "Are you ready? I dare not keep Ismail waiting."

They departed together, O'Brien very slim and straight in his plain black velvet, the guards preceding them with whips and clearing the way to the palace gates.

Well did O'Brien know that he was not apt to live until the next Friday, unless he used hand and brain. When Ismail became obsessed with an idea, all else yielded to it. Strongest of his ruling notions was a fanatical desire to convert Christians. And O'Brien was such a magnificent one!

"There's no trusting Maimoran, either," thought O'Brien, as he swaggered along, giving the renegades eye for eye, and affecting not to hear the piteous calls that the naked slaves on the walls sent after him. "He'll help, because I've assured him a staggering sum; but the knave would betray me in a moment if it were worth his while. Whether I can get to those horses on Friday, or can use them, I don't know—but what matter? We'll gamble largely, and trust to fate for the rest! So Ismail wants to see my meeting with Phelim, eh? Devil take him, he's planning some deep game, depend on it."

Passing the palace mosque, they went on by the enormous vaulted granary, so large as to contain the entire yearly crop tax of all Morocco, and on toward the gardens and stables, whose astonishing aspect greeted them from across a deep ravine. To the left was the palace of the English sultana, and everywhere ran walls—enormous walls, mile after mile of them, enclosing gardens, barracks, the city of the Sudanese, mosques, orchards and olive groves.

"Ismail has passed this way," said Maimoran grimly, but softly, and pointed to the bridge ahead, spanning the ravine.

A number of slaves were working at new foundations, and two of them, just freed from their chains, were dead. Their bleeding corpses were picked up and tossed in between the molds, and more mastic dumped in to be pounded down.

"Well, that be freedom for poor Tom, anyhow," said an English voice as O'Brien passed by.

They went on toward the stables—no mere sheds, but an

entire city, complete to its mosque. Maimoran told his companion of the twelve thousand horses here, of the white dromedaries, and pointed to the garden spaces allotted to the lions and leopards and wolves. As they neared the enormous vaulted structures through which ran streams of living water, Maimoran indicated the granaries and saddle rooms—huge separate buildings at the side.

A thunder of hoofs; into the open burst Ismail and his following of kaids. Ismail brandished a lance in one hand, and in the other upheld one of his favorite sons, a child of two years, while riding at full speed; then, dropping the child into the arms of a slave, he whirled his horse and led his luckless followers straight for the gate of the lion garden. It was flung back as he thundered down, and he went at full career in among the trees, where half a dozen lions paced about. One of them halted facing him, with a snarling defiance. Ismail hurled his lance, leaped from the saddle and, scimitar in hand, hurled himself upon the transfixed beast. One blow, and the lion stretched out, quivering. One of the frightened keepers, a huge black, was edging away from two of the lions. With a spring, Ismail was at his side and hurled him at the beasts, who clawed him down instantly. A leap into the saddle, and the emperor was spurring out of the garden again toward the new arrivals.

"God save us all this day!" said Maimoran composedly. "Remember the sugar!"

Ismail drew rein before them, laughing eagerly.

"Allah upon you, Jew!" he cried. "Tell this unbelieving dog to look into the eyes of a horse that has made the pilgrimage, one of the Beni Adair strain! Quickly! Tell him to give look for look with a sacred creature that has more brains than most men!"

Maimoran translated. O'Brien, smiling, went up to the glorious white horse, an animal whose eye was wild as that of its master, still quivering from the proximity of the lions. The animal flung up its head with teeth bared, then scented the sugar in the closed hand, and the long slender muzzle came down to caress O'Brien, who stroked it and crooned softly. To all appearance the two were old friends, and Ismail stared down in open amazement. Then O'Brien flung one arm about the neck of the horse, and looked up into the savage face, and his eyes laughed.

"Allah wills that this horse is a friend, beloved of Allah!" he said. "Therefore grant me one favor."

"It is granted," said Ismail, frowning angrily, for it was his invariable custom to so do when any man gained the shadow of this horse. "What is it?"

"The life and freedom of one of your slaves, who is my brother."

"His life, gladly," said the crafty Ismail. "But his freedom I can not give, for that is in the hand of Allah alone. I know the man. Come! Bring him, Maimoran, for now I must rub down this delicate beauty of Arabia."

He whirled the horse and rode off, the kaids and guards after him. Maimoran chuckled and led O'Brien toward the buildings, and translated these last words.

"Well done, señor, well done! Now he is in good humor, for when he rubs down his horse, his mind is at ease. Come!"

So it was presently the privilege of O'Brien to see Ismail remove his saddle, mounted with gold and diamonds, and rub down the sleek Arab carefully. Into the distance, beneath the vaulted roof, stretched the long double row of . stalls, running water in between, with every luxury the insensate imperial brain could imagine for these horses which he loved madly. When he had finished the task, Ismail seized a tomato from a basket borne by a slave, refreshed himself with the juicy fruit, then beckoned Maimoran.

"Tell the infidel to follow."

O'Brien strode along, openly astonished at all he saw, until he came to an alcove where Ismail halted. There upon a marble bench sat a man in Arab costume, but the hood of the white *djellab* was flung back, to reveal a gaunt face in which blue eyes blazed.

"Shamus!" he cried out loudly at sight of O'Brien. "Jack, old lad—God love you!"

O'Brien sprang forward, and then perceived how his brother Phelim was chained.

A CROWD had gathered about the spot, renegades and guards and court officials. O'Brien took his brother into his arms, and thought no shame of the swift tears; then he heard the voice of the gaunt Phelim, breathing soft words at his ear.

"Careful, for the love o' God! Watch your words. They know English. The devil means to do for you, Jack—"

O'Brien stepped back, and swung around to face Ismail, who was smiling strangely. He had felt the manacles and chains that held Phelim to the marble seat, and waited for Ismail to speak. He had not long to wait.

"Will you take his place, infidel, and let him go free?"

"No," said O'Brien, when Maimoran translated. Ismail looked taken aback at this reply. "But I will buy his freedom, if you will ransom him."

A sudden passion shook Ismail. He bared his white teeth in a snarl.

"I will not! Infidel, you have defied me enough—aye, the two of you! If it is the will of Allah, you shall die in two days."

And, without giving O'Brien any chance to reply, he beckoned to Maimoran and strode away. O'Brien, left alone with his escort, turned to Phelim, but the latter warned him.

"Get away with you, Shamus, quickly! He's seeking an excuse—get out of here!"

"Then God bless you for this time; I have plans afoot," said O'Brien, and so turned away and started back to the city with his escort.

He knew this advice was wisdom; Ismail was not in one of his homicidal rages, but was in a crafty and deadly mood, fit for anything. And in these moments Ismail was more deadly than in his worst rages—which were more than half assumed to inspire fear in those around him.

Leaving the far spread palace, O'Brien came back to his own place again without further incident; he knew only that within two days something definite would take place. Ismail had some deep scheme in mind. And now, with St. Rocher gone and sunset at hand, for the first time a dreadful oppression seized upon him, and a sort of despairing madness.

Wine and brandy, made by the slaves for their own use by special permission of Ismail and sold surreptitiously to others, was at hand in plenty. O'Brien drank deep, in morose and gloomy mood, but the liquor brought him no cheer. He realized now how utterly alone he was, sitting in this house with only the black slaves around him. What had begun as a mad and gaily reckless adventure, was now sicklied over with the pale cast of reflection and circumstance.

Doom was gathering about him and upon him; he felt it, sensed it, and for once found himself well nigh helpless. He knew not what to do, which way to turn. Despite his boldness, his laughing defiance of Ismail which had first won that proud warrior's liking, he now saw himself lost beyond hope—because of Phelim. Somehow, Ismail was turned against him, no doubt by some court official who feared this infidel; yet the man was made up of whimsies and queer moods, like all despots. His actions could not be foretold from one day to the next.

"If I could get away with Phelim," mused O'Brien despondently. "But I can not. Horses are the means alone—there is no way of doing it, of getting that far. This accursed country, this devil of an emperor, have closed me in with insuperable barriers like their own gigantic walls; cruelty, lust, savagery all around—"

He staggered to the window and, flinging back the curtains, came close to the wooden bars across the opening. A sound fell upon his ears, and he stared at the blank dark walls close by; it came again, and he trembled, caught at the bars, wondering if he were mad or drunk, that he should hear it. But no; his brain was clear enough. Voices of men singing, chanting. Not the wild, mad Berber singing, nor the harsher Arab music, but chants that he recognized at once, swelling softly, sweetly, faintly as fairy music drifting to him from Ireland and the long ago.

Then he remembered what this house was, next to his own, and with a shaky laugh he wiped the sweat from his forehead and listened again. Yes, the Spanish monks were singing in their chapel, chanting their vespers with soft chiming of bells and an organ—these friars whom Ismail permitted here in the heart of his power, because they doctored his ill and disabled Christian slaves back to life and labor again. A practical man, Ismail, with shrewd wisdom behind his madness.

O'Brien flung himself down on his couch, and the chanting voices sent him into peaceful slumber. And, if there were a prayer on his lips, that was nobody's affair.

That sound of voices in the night, amid such surroundings, effected a singular change in him when he wakened and went about his morning's business. There was a smile on his lips, a gay laugh in his blue eyes. This hard man, whose keen wits and sharp sword had won him through wars and slavery, the trample of armies and the rush of buccaneers, looked out upon the city of the savage Arabs and Berbers, and his lips curled as he sharpened the long rapier which had served him so well.

"The will of Allah!" he murmured, with disdain. "Very well, Ismail; let that come to serve me as well. I'll set my God against your Allah. If it be so ordained, we'll win back to the clean sea yet, Phelim and I—and then, glory be, I'll stick to the sea! And now it's all clear enough."

Clear enough—aye! He had forgotten the O'Brien clarion; here amid all Ismail's power, he had been impressed by everything around, had sunk to mere loneliness. *Lamh laidir an uachtar!* The Strong Hand Above! Well, he would stick to it, a very madman if need be; and why not? No sane logic could avail him in this place. The Strong Hand Above....

The words were upon his lips when men arrived seeking him—a number of palace guards, with a kaid who spoke Spanish and summoned him instantly to the palace. Ismail desired speech with him immediately. Beyond this the kaid would say nothing at all.

O'Brien buckled on the rapier and started forth. An insolent Arab pressed close to him and spat upon him; like a flash O'Brien buffeted the man to the ground. A yelling crowd began to surge in, and O'Brien whirled upon the kaid, his eyes flashing.

"You misbegotten dog!" he snarled, hand on rapier. "Call your guards around, whip off these curs—or I'll drive the life out of you and drag your body before Ismail! Quick!"

Startled, frightened, infuriated by these insults, the kaid nonetheless obeyed, stung into action. The guards closed in. A whip or two bit out, and the crowd shrank back. O'Brien strode along humming a gay tune; and if he went to death, he meant to go not alone. In this mood of reckless abandon, he came into the palace and found Ismail sitting, as was his wont, in a cool alcove while scribes and doctors of the law sat around. To his amazement, Ismail greeted him with friendly courtesy and ordered him to be seated, then extended a folded document bearing the golden seal of the emperor.

"Here," said Ismail abruptly, "is a letter to your master King James of England, now in exile. I shall confide it to your care, and I am also sending with it gifts for him, that he may know me for no mean person."

"Son of Idris, I am honored by this mission," said O'Brien.

"The throne of your master depends upon it," said Ismail, with a fierce intensity. "Now listen, infidel! I am offering to restore your master to the throne of England. My ships shall be gathered, ships from France will join us to carry my army. Your master is to come to Lisbon, where my fleet will meet him and take him to England. Think you this plan will succeed?"

O'Brien's head reeled at this fantastic scheme, worthy of such a man.

"Beloved of Allah," he said, "who can stand against your might? How can my master King James repay you for your kindness and friendship?"

"By listening to the arguments in that letter," responded Ismail, eagerly. "I have set forth to him the excellence of the true faith and have bidden him acknowledge the Prophet, whose name be exalted! He will see that my arguments can not be answered. Return to me with his answer in due time. Be prepared to leave here in ten days."

O'Brien found himself dismissed, and went back to his own house, somewhat in a daze. Yet, upon thinking over the matter; upon recollecting the eager intensity of Ismail, he saw that the man had been in deadly earnest, had forgotten momentarily everything else. Upon the morrow his mood would undoubtedly have changed.

When O'Brien would have gone out that afternoon, he found guards at his door with orders that he was to remain in the house, until next day. The walls were closing in upon him.

But, that night, came word from Phelim.

BRIBERY HAD done it, of course. One of the black slaves, serving O'Brien's dinner, laid a walnut beside the dish, touched his arm, and departed. O'Brien crushed the shell and found a roll of thin paper. It held writing in French, obviously written by another slave for Phelim.

> Tomorrow afternoon they arrive, the champions. You must provoke the fight your own way, lest Ismail pit you against them all at once. There is no escape. Beware Le Borgne, an expert fencer. The Englishman has no skill. I am at the lion pit beside the Canot.
>
> —P. O'B.

The Canot, as O'Brien knew, was a great building in the center of the town, not far from his own quarters, where the slaves were housed under guard. Beside its wall was the wide pit where lions were kept—beasts destined to be pitted against dogs or naked men in fight. But what was this about champions?

O'Brien shrugged the matter away, as he tore up the note. No use looking for any reason in all this affair. Ismail was capable of giving him a letter to King James one day, and killing him the next. What could be afoot, he had no idea, except that it was evidently a question of fighting.

Maimoran arrived that morning with the daily rations. When he handed over the receipt to be signed, he slipped into O'Brien's hand a brass Spanish cuarto.

"Show this coin to the man holding the horses, and again to the second man. He will wait at the ford of the Oued Tiflet. That is more than halfway, but is the best I can do."

"Good," said O'Brien.

"And, señor, the other five hundred—"

"In the hands of Ben Hattar if I get through."

Maimoran departed. To O'Brien's questions of what Ismail intended, he had professed complete ignorance, but did not fool O'Brien. The man knew something, but would not talk; a bad omen. He was cautious, too, in choosing for token a mere brass coin which would not incriminate him.

Still prevented from leaving the house, O'Brien mounted to the roof and spent most of the morning there, furbishing his rapier and watching Meknez in enforced idleness. Ceaseless caravans, files of men both troops and slaves, all raised a thin cloud of dust which settled and hung over olive groves and city in the windless air; rain was long due, but had not come, and the country was suffering.

A cracking of whips, a scattering of the throngs in the street, and past the house up the hill went two mules, driven hard; behind each of them trailed a screaming thing, drawn by the feet, hands clutching vainly at the stones. Again, later, came three creaking wagons piled high with human heads—tribute taken by the sword from a Berber tribe. O'Brien looked down at the crowds, and a thin smile curved his lips. He saw now what he must do; the only thing he could do.

"Not a soul dares brave the wrath of Ismail or his guards," he murmured thoughtfully. "In all this land, there is no one who is not cowed and prostrate. Well, then—the Strong Hand Above! If I can live until Friday, which is only two days away, well and good."

He must depend upon Maimoran, he perceived, upon the horses being ready, upon St. Rocher reaching Salé and meeting the ship—he must depend upon half a dozen things, any one of which might go wrong and ruin everything. The one quality lacking in Meknez was boldness; therefore audacity might well win everything for him, if he dared play the card. So he sat and smiled over Meknez, and laid his plans craftily, while the razor keen blue steel brightened under his hand.

The noon meal over, O'Brien was making ready for his siesta when a Dutch renegade who was emplacing guns on the walls came swaggering in with a message.

"Señor Ambassador! In an hour's time my master commands your presence in the gardens. I will come for you with an escort."

"You seem amused," said O'Brien, looking keenly at the man. "What is forward!"

"Nay, señor, that is the will of Allah, and how should I know?" And, laughing, the fellow departed.

An hour later he returned with six Sudanese guards and O'Brien accompanied them forth.

Warned as he was, and with a grim prescience of what lay ahead, O'Brien wore only cotton shirt and loose trousers, with the rapier girded on, and over them a loose *djellab* of fine white wool, one of the gifts sent by Ismail. The Dutchman chaffed him on this costume and on the heavy boots beneath so different from the universal yellow slippers of the Arabs, but O'Brien only gave him a chill smile and answered nothing.

They came to the gardens behind the huge granary, those same gardens where Ismail had cut off the breasts of a favorite concubine because she plucked an orange without his leave; and here O'Brien beheld a real assemblage. The eighty per-

sonal guards of Ismail were grouped around an awning spread
to shade him, and on either hand were the two hundred kaids
and sharifs, or descendants of the Prophet, who made up his
usual entourage. Besides these, again, were other Sudanese
guards in rank about an open space, in the center of which was
a gaunt naked figure lashed to a post with cords. This was
Phelim O'Brien, as yet unhurt.

O'Brien threw back the hood of his *djellab* and saluted Ismail,
who beckoned to him with an affable smile and, taking a rich
pomegranate from a pannier of fruit, thrust it upon him.

"Sit, infidel; sit and talk!" he commanded. The Dutch renegade acting as interpreter, translated. "I know that you can fight.
You are a good Christian. You cannot prevail against the will
of Allah, however. You must become one of the Enlightened."

O'Brien met the savage dark eyes, smiled and put the yellow
hair out of his eyes. Standing at one side, he saw three men,
richly armed; one of them had but one eye, and he knew this
must be Le Borgne. The other two were doubtless his companion champions.

"Beloved of Allah," responded O'Brien easily, with a merry
smile, "that is not like to come about this day. Now I see yonder,
bound to a post, my brother, whose life you gave me."

"You have good eyes, Christian," and Ismail chuckled. "But
they do not see far enough. I gave you that man's life, true, but
who am I to fight against the will of Allah? And Allah has
willed that unless you call upon Mohammed, whose name be
blessed, that man yonder will be impaled."

"His fate has nothing to do with me," said O'Brien, with
affected carelessness. Here was the moment; he must attack,
before Ismail did so. "Allah forbid that I become as one of those
accursed weaklings who serve you, men who deny their race
and faith. I see three of them there, unless I mistake—very dogs
of the gutter. Would you have me to become like them?"

From some who understood his Spanish, came snickers as
the words were translated. Le Borgne glared at him balefully;
the Englishman and the Italian with him scowled at O'Brien.

Truth it was that these three men, hastily summoned to Meknez, were the chief swordsmen of Ismail's forces and were drill masters of his troops; they were famed as invincible; chiefly Le Borgne, who held to a straight rapier instead of the scimitar.

Just what fine scheme Ismail had in mind, O'Brien never knew, for Ismail did not voice it. Before any reply could come to his speech, O'Brien split open the pomegranate, took a mouthful of the fruit, and spat forth seeds and pulp—full upon the three renegades. He broke into a sharp laugh, and his gaze gripped that of Le Borgne.

"*Canaille!*" he said in French. "This day you die, so play your part well for the last time!"

LE BORGNE snarled and started forward, but his companions checked him. Ismail was rising to his feet, for all this had taken place very swiftly, when O'Brien swung around to him with a great cry that checked his unspoken words.

"Beloved of Allah! I will make a wager with you! Let these three miscreant dogs come against me with weapons, and for each of them that is slain, give my brother yonder one day's reprieve from the stake! Thus shall the will of Allah be made manifest in this matter!"

When he had heard the translation Ismail smiled cruelly.

"So let it be, infidel," he ordained. "Take place there before your brother, and if these three can come past you, let them slay him. One at a time. You first, Ali!"

This was the Moslem name of the one eyed Frenchman.

O'Brien saluted the emperor gaily, and a shout burst forth from all around, as Ismail settled down on his cushions, eager to watch the swordplay. Turning, O'Brien strode out to the stake, and met the gaze of his brother Phelim, and heard the latter's fierce greeting.

"Hail and farewell, Shamus! Let me have that scoundrel of an Englishman to play with before I die, for he's a cruel devil to all of us."

"Not dead yet, Phelim," said O'Brien, and slipped out of the white *djellab*. His rapier flashed from the scabbard, and he leaned forward quickly and slit the bonds that held Phelim to the stake. "Bide you, now, and get the blood into your arms—you shall have him and full welcome, if the chance comes!"

There were no formalities, no delays. Le Borgne was already striding forward, his *djellab* flung off to display splendid garments beneath; O'Brien looked very slender there in the white sun, very boyish. Voices rose in swift, frenzied betting, the name of Ali predominating. Then the Frenchman, with a bitter oath, lifted his rapier and the blades clashed and clung.

Almost with the first touch, O'Brien knew that here was a master of fence indeed, but he laughed suddenly in the renegade's face and taunted him with low and barbed words.

"A good thrust, honest Moslem! How does the French tongue sound to you, good brave soul? You who denied your faith—on *tierce*, now; thrust inside, swiftly! That's the way, and here's the wrist in *carte*—"

Le Borgne disengaged, blood springing from his shoulder, a flame of hot anger in his eyes at the taunting words. He poured a flood of oaths at O'Brien and leaped in with a furious, driving blade; the hot sun, the dust, the fierce yells of the watchers, closed in the two men.

"The dogs are loosed, Shamus!" came the voice of Phelim in urgent warning.

From the corner of his eye O'Brien saw the other two renegades springing forward. No fair play here, but bloodlust in hot savagery clamoring for the kill! He was in *carte*, and forced suddenly, obliging the Frenchman to throw *carte* over the arm. Parrying *tierce* with a swift, strong blade, O'Brien made a lightning return in *seconde*.

The return was deadly. Le Borgne staggered back and flung out his arms, just as the other two came up with whirling scimitars and hurled themselves upon O'Brien. With one agile leap he was away from them, and his point drove lightly into the flanks of the Dutchman, who roared with pain and rage.

A rush and flurry of dust—then the Dutchman was roaring again, this time in a new voice, as the gaunt, naked shape of Phelim hurtled upon him barehanded. O'Brien had no time to give aid; the Englishman was upon him with a cut for the knees, and only a leap evaded it—a leap and a thrust forward, the long rapier scraping the brown throat.

"Close, Englishman!" gasped O'Brien. "Come, Sassenach—Moslem blade against Christian sword, eh? Here's for you—"

A clash, and the stout rapier parried the sweeping blow, licked in, a hot blue tongue, with hot blue eyes driving behind. The Englishman backed away, and that was fatal for him, since the long arm of O'Brien reached in and in, and the rapier touched him on the hip. He lost his head there and swung up for a mad wild blow that never fell. Straight through his throat tore the blue steel; he stumbled back two steps, and went down on his face, dead.

Panting, O'Brien saw Phelim rise up out of the dust, blood upon his face but the Dutch renegade's sword in his hand. O'Brien looked at him and laughed, while yells resounded.

"Fair enough, Phelim! Sorry I could not leave you the Englishman—quick, lad! Can you leave your prison?"

"Aye, if I have anywhere to go," said Phelim, coughing with the dust. "But not at night, for there's a guard at the gate."

"What gate?" snapped O'Brien, wiping the sweat from his eyes.

"Next the Canot or Bitte. A lantern burns over the gate all night; the guard remains just inside."

"Tomorrow night, then. Sometime after midnight. Be ready."

The throng was closing in upon them. With an appearance of unconcern, O'Brien put up his rapier and donned his white *djellab*. Phelim dropped his weapon. The guards hemmed them in and Ismail stood before O'Brien, dark eyes ablaze.

"*Insh'allah!* That was well done, infidel!" he exclaimed loudly. "But you slew only two of them—therefore this slave shall live for two days, and on Friday at noon he shall sit upon a stake before your doorway, as punishment for having lifted hand against a true believer."

Ere this was translated, Phelim was led away. And now chanced a curious thing, for it was all silent, all unknown to those around, and yet plain as a bell to the two men concerned.

As O'Brien looked into the eyes of Ismail, temptation seized upon him. This man before him was the first swordsman, the first athlete, in Morocco; a man to whom no feat of arms or of physique was impossible. Yet O'Brien knew instinctively that he could draw blade and thrust home a split second before Ismail could whip out his scimitar. His fingers itched for the brain impulse—and in the eyes of Ismail he read that his thought was known to the other man.

For a long instant the two of them stood there motionless, and a slight smile came to the lips of Ismail; who was, in fact, said to read the thoughts of those with whom he talked. He waited, himself utterly without fear, to see whether O'Brien's brain would send the order to hand and arm; and in his eyes, O'Brien saw that he knew.

Then it was past and gone; the chance lost. Laughing, Ismail turned away, and O'Brien drew a deep breath. The Dutch artillerist came swaggering up to him with unexpected warmth.

"Señor, that was a noble feat of arms! I am glad you slew Le Borgne; I hated that man. For that, I love you. You are placed in my charge until Friday, when our lord speaks again with you. Until then you are to remain in your house."

So O'Brien strode away with the renegade, certain guards clearing the way. As they came into the high walled road piercing midway through the palace grounds, a building ahead of them discharged from doorways a great, endless swarm of children, all boys. To his astonishment O'Brien perceived that there must be from three to four hundred, jamming the whole roadway, their shouts and yells deafening. He turned to the renegade.

"What are those boys? Who are they? From the town?"

The other laughed amusedly as he replied:

"Nay, from the loins of Ismail, señor! You know there are five hundred women in his seraglio? That is true. Girl children are killed at birth; these are sharifs, of the blood of Idris, future sultans of this land, if it be the will of Allah! See that you jostle none of them; to lay hand on them is death."

O'Brien continued his way, and stopped at a bazaar to buy a short, curved dagger. The renegade aided in the purchase, and O'Brien smiled grimly at this.

O'BRIEN WAS feared; this was very evident. He found himself under a strict guard as though he were an actual prisoner. When Maimoran arrived next morning, the Jew explained this very suavely as being for his own good; the troops were incensed against the infidel who had slain their champions, he said. O'Brien merely looked him in the eyes, and he faltered in the lie. Then, with a swift glance to make sure none was within hearing:

"Señor, you can not get away. It is madness."

"Madness is needed," said O'Brien. "The horses?"

"Will be walked up and down, as for sale. The spot is not far from the animal bazaar. From seven o'clock onwards."

"I shall want them about eight," said O'Brien. "If I want them at all."

Maimoran shrugged as the Dutch renegade sauntered into the room, got his signed receipt, and so departed. To get away from the eternal surveillance, O'Brien went up to the flat roof and sat by the parapet, watching the city below. The day was cloudy and a drizzle of rain began to fall, lending this city of blood a dreary and dismal aspect.

O'Brien perceived very clearly that he had passed all limits. Beyond doubt, palace intrigues were at work to insure his death; the renegades, strong in influence, and many of the Arab kaids, were certainly working on Ismail, with whose suspicious nature a word or a look could be more potent than any sane reason. With the morrow, Ismail would be preaching in the chief mosque; his fanaticism would be inflamed and anything might result.

"This mad venture," reflected O'Brien, "has cost a huge sum and has brought in nothing except a few cheap gifts from Ismail. If Phelim gets away, then it's well worth it all; but it seems a pity not to make this devil Ismail contribute to the O'Brien fortunes. Faith, they're in a devilish bad way at present!"

He had brought a supply of tobacco from the ship, and sat there sucking at his broken pipe and using the last of his tobacco, when a tumult in the street below drew his attention. Ismail and his retinue were wending into the city, and O'Brien watched the procession of riders and guards with frowning intentness as they drew past and out of his sight. He felt thankful that Phelim was not confined in the palace. Behind those triple walls, with their hundreds of guards, his brother would have been far beyond reach.

And yet, with the moment close at hand, O'Brien knew that his simple plan of getting Phelim and riding for Salé was sheer madness. In vain did his mind cast about for any better scheme; there was none, and the time was growing shorter with each hour. Hearing a step, he glanced around and saw the Dutch renegade.

"News, señor!" The man was laughing heartily as he spoke. "My comrade Ahmed has just arrived to relieve me until midnight, and is taking you this afternoon to the palace by special command. You will like Ahmed; he was a Greek once, but Mulai Ismail turned him into a eunuch and now he is in charge of the seraglio guards. The seraglio means to have a look at you, so brush up, señor, and don your best!"

"Is this some jest?" queried O'Brien coldly.

"Devil take me, señor, if it is! Lalla Aisha, the giant negress who is first lady of the seraglio and who rules Ismail with a rod of iron, has commanded your presence in the gardens."

At this junction Ahmed arrived, puffing. A fat, unhealthy man, splendidly attired and armed, who addressed O'Brien with a servile air, in good Spanish. A fawning, craven fellow, this Greek, but one who could be insolent and bold enough with those under him. O'Brien got rid of him curtly, promising to be ready after the siesta. What this summons might hold remained to be seen; he doubted whether Ismail had anything to do with it, knowing that Lalla Aisha did indeed rule Ismail, or rather was one with him in his rule, for she was his one and only confidante and held his implicit trust in all things.

So it was with curiosity rather than apprehension that O'Brien set forth with the Greek and four Sudanese, after the siesta. About his neck, beneath the *djellab* in native style, was slung the silver hilted dagger he had purchased that morning. The Greek was fawning and obsequious, and when O'Brien roughly commanded his silence, he swaggered along sulkily.

Entering the palace precincts, they did not seek the vast expanse of gardens behind the granary, but turned instead off to the left, into a portion of the triple walled grounds that was new to O'Brien. The Sudanese guards were replaced by two huge black eunuchs armed with whips, and presently O'Brien was ushered alone into a small garden surrounded with high walls where were latticed balconies. The Greek plucked at his arm.

"Go forward, señor. Seem to see and hear nothing. We await you here. Return in half an hour."

The doors closed behind him.

O'Brien sauntered among small orange trees toward a tiled fountain in the midst of the court. Around this, on all four sides, ran an arched colonnade. No one was visible. He was to all appearance entirely alone, yet he felt at once that unseen eyes were watching him; behind the lattice work of the balconies he caught a movement of robes.

Anger seized upon him, for he comprehended that he had been fetched here merely as a sight to amuse the women of the seraglio. He circled about the fountain, then flung back the hood of his white *djellab*, and his blue eyes struck around here and there. He had not taken note of the entrance, and now could not see by which door he had entered—all four sides of the alcoved quadrangle looked exactly alike. As he hesitated, a soft voice floated to him, a woman's voice, and to his amazement the words were in English: yet nothing could now amaze him in this city.

"The door under the green arch, and quickly! Lose not a moment!"

O'Brien glanced around, and perceived a green tiled arch to his left; beneath it was a door, one of the many opening off the colonnades. A sense of urgency was upon him, perhaps from the inflection of that woman's soft voice; through his confusion, his bewilderment, pierced a sharp note of warning, of peril close upon him.

Trap or not, he dared not hesitate. Turning, he strode quickly to the arches, but not directly to the green one. Once beneath them, he turned again and an instant later was at the door indicated; rather, the double door, set upon pivots in the native style and opening toward him. He caught a large iron ring in the door, and one side swung outward, showing a tiny tiled passage within. It was empty.

O'Brien stepped forward, and as he did so caught at the dagger beneath his *djellab*, and plucked it out. The corridor in which he stood was very narrow, but high, and light came from windows twenty feet above him. Next instant came a step, and a single figure in light fluttering robes, hand extended. A woman, young, golden haired, gray eyes wide with eagerness and swift excitement.

"Come!" It was the same voice that had floated to him, a rough and impulsive voice now, and he perceived that if she were indeed English, she could have been no lady of quality. "A murrain on ye—art struck dumb? Come! D'ye not know it was all a trick, that Ismail planned to find you in the seraglio that he might kill you?"

"Nonsense, mistress," said O'Brien calmly. "I have his own safe conduct—"

She laughed, bitterly enough.

"Aye, and therefore he must seek means to break his word openly to all men. He had ye brought here, and who would believe it as the truth? But come! I can take care of you; Lord knows I care not for these black devils—come! Y'have not a moment to lose gawking!"

Somewhat stupefied by all this, O'Brien found himself accompanying her, at so rapid a pace he must needs run to keep up. He had not the slightest idea whither they went; now along narrow corridors, then for a moment out in the open, flitting across the top of the enormous walls, only to duck swiftly into narrow doorways beyond.

They crossed one great tiled room where fountains plashed from the walls, climbed long stairs, and after what seemed miles, came into a little bare quadrangle enclosed by blank walls. The woman pointed to flat stones upon the ground, at the farther end.

"There lie the daughters of Ismail—damn his black skin! Hurry on—almost there now."

She was panting, and color flamed in her cheeks; a handsome wench enough, thought O'Brien, as he followed into another doorway and narrow corridor beyond. Then she paused abruptly at a door, took out a huge key, unlocked it swiftly, and flung it open.

"Inside—quick! Guards are close—"

O'Brien entered; she closed the door behind them both, turned the key again, and stood breathing rapidly, but he paid her no heed, for he was staring at this place, like none he had seen or would ever see again. Her laugh sounded at his ear, low and wild.

"Art safe enough here, my handsome soldier! None but Ismail himself dares to touch that door or enter this room."

He could well believe it.

A huge room was this, high ceiled, with one small high window to give light and air, but across it was a heavy grille of iron bars. One end of the room was piled high with great chests, and others stood about the walls. Deep shelves held smaller boxes and hide packets; rolls wrapped in silk and linen, boxes large and small, made up the helter-skelter contents of the place.

"I stole the key from Lalla Aisha today," said the woman exultantly. "I knew where she keeps it hidden; she will not discover the loss until tomorrow."

"And just what is this place?" queried O'Brien.

"The miser's treasury!" Her voice rose in shrill delight. "His storehouse of wealth, of riches plundered from all Maroc! Those chests hold coin and gold dust; here are gifts brought to him, jewels from all the world; seek for yourself, take what you will! There is no haste. Fill your pockets, handsome soldier! Then we'll talk, you and I."

O'Brien perceived that she must be speaking the truth, yet could scare credit it. He went to one of the chests and flung back the lid, to find it filled with Berber jewelry of silver and raw gold. One side of the room was heaped with arms—fusils, swords, spears, all of the richest workmanship, most of them studded with coral, inlaid with ivory, sparkling with gems.

The smaller chests and boxes were given over to jewels of every sort, good and bad, mounted and unset. O'Brien rummaged among the whole, but his thoughts were rather with this wretched Englishwoman than with the stuff before him. Thanks to her, he was temporarily escaped from the trap Ismail had set for him, yet there must come a reckoning. It was a curious twist of human nature which bade Ismail lay such a trap, when he could have flung his guards on this man at any moment; still, history was replete with instances of this exact trait, and it might be that Ismail's worst nature was seeking a specious pretext for the murder of O'Brien.

No man, however, could entirely disdain this enormous mass of wealth, gathered during thirty years or more, the loot of all Morocco and the lands beyond. A box opening to his hand was heaped to the brim with gems wrenched from their mounts, to many still clinging fragments of gold; here were the white blaze of diamonds, the rich luster of rubies and emeralds, the soft sheen of pearls, all flung together in one mass.

O'Brien dipped into the casket deliberately, stuffed jewels by the handful into his inner pockets, then turned away and halted before an open Buhl secretaire, doubtless a gift from the French monarch. Upon it were sheets of vellum, reed pens and brushes, ink pots, and an open leather case in which was a huge seal of solid gold, with vials of liquid and sheets of gold leaf close by. He saw at a glance that this must be the sacred seal itself.

The woman was speaking, but O'Brien ignored her. He leaned over, seized upon a sheet of vellum, and fell to work. She joined him, watching him awhile at the business, and uttered a sniff of disdain.

"Handsome soldier, is this a time to play?"

"This is play well worth while," he rejoined, and straightened up. "There! Let it dry, and we'll add the writing above it, when—"

He turned from the vellum, upon which now glittered the golden seal that was revered throughout Morocco, as she caught his arm and drew him around.

"Look at me, handsome soldier!" she exclaimed, her eyes a-glitter. "Now it be my turn, since naught else interests you here."

And O'Brien knew suddenly that here was a new peril, which most men would have welcomed gladly enough.

"I HAVE seen you before today," she said, her hand caressing his shoulder as she spoke. "And now, what matter? Here we be alone, you and I; and see, I have a knife ready if they take us. Do you know how Ismail kills his women? He makes them kneel before one o' those iron chests, with their breasts over the edge, and has two slaves slam down the lid. Would like to see this body o' mine so treated, handsome soldier?"

"Peace, woman, peace!" said O'Brien, and put her hand away,

frowning. "This is no time to be love making, and I have no mind to it. By now they'll be searching the city for me."

"Like enough," she said, with a shrug. "But I know one way out of here, if you can kill the black who guards the little gate. Wilt take me with you?"

"Peace!" commanded O'Brien. "Peace, for God's sake, and let me think!"

Time had passed. In this silent room, with all the noises of the palace shut away, the little high window was darkening.

O'Brien had no mind for the woman, even as he said. Yet he was no fool, and he knew that without her help he could never be drawn from the trap into which he had fallen. There in the city, Phelim awaited him this night, and with morning would be two horses ready.

Where could a third enter into the matter?

This woman, taken two years ago aboard a ship bound for the plantations, begged him to rescue her from this living hell of slavery. She had done her part, too, had acted with a courage and audacity few men would have equalled. Beyond shame or pride, she besought his love with ardent words, tempted him into a madness that could end only in ruin. The thought of Phelim steadied him, held him upright.

Presently he turned to her, caught her hand in his; a desperate resolution was in his voice as he spoke to her, quietly, patting her broad, roughened fingers.

"Hark'ee, mistress; I must speak plainly to you. Heaven knows I'm grateful to you for what you've done, but seek no love of me, now or later. That's final."

She drew away her hand, snatched at her knife. Even in the gathering darkness he could see the hot flame of her eyes.

"Disdain me, would you!" she cried out. "Because I've belonged to the Moors—"

"Stop your nonsense," and his harsh voice silenced her. "Nothing of that sort, mistress. I'm sorry for you, I owe you much, and I'll do my best to pay it, in my own way. If we can get you out of here, well and good; your life will be your own again. But I've a brother who's a slave in the town yonder. Tonight I've arranged to help him away. You shall have a share in it and somehow we'll manage the job, since we must. Does that suit you?"

He heard her quick, hard breathing at his side.

"I'll be true to you, handsome soldier, I'll be your slave and—"

"You fool, put your mind to the right things!" snapped O'Brien angrily. "Talk about love later on, if you will. Now we must think about life itself. All Meknez will be scoured for me this night, and I've plenty to do besides dilly-dallying. Put your thoughts on escape, mistress, for that's more the point just now."

She fell to weeping softly, and O'Brien drew away from her and stretched out on a pile of soft silks. After a little he heard her voice.

"Be not angry, handsome soldier," she said. "We must bide here a bit, till midnight, then we can get away—"

Darkness had come now, and with the darkness came the faint, distant shrieks of a man that after awhile became silent. Although O'Brien knew it not, these shrieks came from the Greek renegade, who had been crucified against a mud wall for having lost his prisoner. And the Greek had not died alone.

O'Brien was relaxed, dozing quietly to pass the time, when there came a flurry of movement, and he found the woman at his side, gripping him hard, her voice low and tense.

"I took the key from the door—"

"Eh? What the devil is it?" he exclaimed, sitting up.

"Quiet, quiet!" A sudden agony of terror was in her voice. "I heard steps—they're at the door! It must be the black devil himself; none else would come; he has his own keys—"

O'Brien stiffened. He, too, heard a thin scrape of feet, and heard something at the door, a key feeling for the hole, doubtless. Then he was on his feet, pressing the woman down, flinging the piled silks over her. His rapier came out, for he had put aside his *djellab* because of the heat, and with one swift step he was at the door, behind it, so that it would open against him.

The massive portal swung a little, and he heard the voice of Ismail giving some order, and the response of a slave. Then the door opened wider. A beam of light penetrated into the treasure room and Ismail entered alone, holding a silver lantern over his head. The emperor set the lantern on the floor and swung the door shut again with a crash.

Then he saw O'Brien, saw the rapier point licking out and touching his side.

For a long, long moment there was dead silence, tension gathering swiftly upon both men, the lanternlight striking up full at them. Immobile, rigid, O'Brien stood like a statue, his rapier piercing Ismail's robe, touching the hard muscled body within. He was tempted still to drive home the thrust—he had fully intended doing so—but Ismail's steady gaze held him.

In that savage gaze was no fear whatever, but a calm acceptance, a sure understanding. The eyes of the two men held in a level and unfaltering gaze, and grudging admiration swept into O'Brien's heart. Then, unexpectedly, came a sweep and flurry, and the woman was on her feet, plunging forward with knife upraised.

"Stop!" O'Brien's voice checked her. "Stop!"

Ismail glanced around, and for an instant wild fury contorted his features, but only for an instant. She halted the thrust, her eyes flaming on O'Brien.

"Art a fool?" she rasped.

"Not such a fool as to kill him, when he can serve us," said O'Brien, and this drove into her wild brain. "Tell him that he'll die if he cries out. Not otherwise."

She snarled at Ismail, but repeated the threat, and a proud smile touched the bearded lips as he responded. She spat an oath at him.

"He says he'll die if it be the will of Allah, and not otherwise.

Let me kill the black devil, d'ye hear?" she panted, with a volley of hot oaths. "If you'd seen what I have—"

"Silence, woman. Tell him that I am the will of Allah just now."

Ismail heard this and, watching O'Brien's eyes, laughed suddenly.

"Bon Cristiano!" he exclaimed. The two words held a wealth of meaning. And O'Brien, meeting that calm gaze, knew that despite all blood and cruelty and despotism, here stood a man before him, the same fearless man who had hurled himself upon the lion. He, too, broke into a short laugh, and in this moment arose a singular kinship and comprehension between the two of them—though it was short lived.

"Take his arms," said O'Brien.

The woman obeyed, stripping Ismail of two daggers and his magnificent diamond studded scimitar. As her hands passed over him, Ismail ground his teeth in a spasm of sheer rage; it passed swiftly. O'Brien's cool gaze perceived that the woman was shivering now, trembling violently, exactly like the horse forced into proximity with the lion.

"Pick up the lantern," he ordered, "and hold it to light the desk yonder. Tell him to sit down and write a free passage for us, in his own hand."

"He—he can not write," she answered, with a frightened glance. "He can read, but has never learned to write. It is well known."

"The devil!" said O'Brien, and regarded his captive thoughtfully. Then he pointed to the gold circlet on Ismail's hand, a ring which he had seen kissed in veneration by many; a plain gold ring graven with the name of Ismail.

The other understood his look and gesture, and burst into swift passionate speech. In a flash his self-control was swept away; Ismail flew into a spasm of wild ferocity, real or assumed, so that the woman shrank back and clutched her knife. O'Brien laughed and thrust a little, sending the rapier point under Ismail's skin.

"That's better!" he observed. "Faith, the scoundrel near had me, if he'd kept up his royal dignity! But now he's no better than a madman. Quick, mistress! Something with which to tie him up."

Under the sting of the steel, Ismail flinched not. Instead, he was working himself into a raging fury, regardless of any threat; his voice swelled loud and louder, and in another moment he would be screaming out curses and shouting for aid—but this moment never came. O'Brien shifted his weight, let the rapier fall from his hand; swift as light, he lashed in one short, hard blow with his body behind it. Straight to the angle of that cruel jaw drove his fist, and Ismail toppled backward, knocked senseless. O'Brien chuckled as he surveyed the prostrate man—then leaped forward barely in time to check the woman's knife from slitting the brown throat. He flung her away, roughly.

"Fool, fool!" she babbled at him. "If ye do not—"

"Silence!" snapped O'Brien, and his voice was like a whip, so that she cowered suddenly and fearfully. "Put up that knife. Get me strips of cloth, and quickly! They know he's here, and we've got one chance, and one only. Do as I say!"

He slipped the ring from Ismail's hand, stripped off the jeweled turban and the yellow cloak, then took the strips she handed him and made shift to tie Ismail hand and foot, and to bind up his mouth and jaw so that he could not shout. He could not blame the woman for her lust to kill Ismail, but he rose and restrained her less roughly.

"Look you, mistress, our hope lies ahead, not here. If we kill him, he'll be found soon enough; horsemen will go out, couriers to every city in Morocco, with the news, and we'll have no earthly chance to get clear. But let him be found thus, and his own pride will keep it quiet. Also, he'll think we're somewhere in the city. It'll be morning before they dare to seek him, so we'll have a good chance. Will there be a guard outside? What did he say when he entered?"

"He bade the guard wait," said she, in sullen humor.

"Look out, then, and see. If there's but one guard, bid him enter," said O'Brien grimly. "You'll have your fill of blood before this night's out, I promise."

She opened the door cautiously, peered out into the corridor, then spoke, lowering her voice to a crude imitation of Ismail's tones. O'Brien caught up his rapier and stood ready. A Sudanese, one of Ismail's personal bodyguard, came into the room—and the rapier point went through his throat.

"That's better," said O'Brien coolly, and put up his weapon. "Blood or no blood, get you into his clothes, and pull up the hood of the *djellab*. I'll don those of Ismail, and we may have a chance to get out of here alive. Move fast, woman! Life hangs on it now!"

WHEN THE palace guards changed at midnight, a Sudanese took his station at the little gate beside the seraglio mosque, which Ismail habitually used when unattended. As the emperor was likely to come or go at any hour, there was no danger of the Sudanese relaxing his vigilance.

Barely had the man settled down to his watch, indeed, when the door opened abruptly and two figures appeared, one of them carrying a lantern; its rays fell upon the diamond studded scimitar of Ismail, and the black leaped to attention. The two were about to pass when a low ejaculation broke from him, and he leaned forward; the hand that held the lantern was not black but white! He stooped to peer suspiciously at the two figures, but that was his bane, for a curved blade was plunged into his throat, and he became a huddle on the stones.

The lantern was extinguished. The two figures moved out from the walls and were gone in the direction of the city beyond.

Exultation filled O'Brien as the palace fell into the darkness behind. The impossible had been accomplished, but perils enough remained ahead. He dared not seek his own quarters, for these would certainly be watched. What had just chanced, showed that Ismail's ring and cloak were not sufficient to get them past danger; nor was the folded vellum in his pocket, bearing the golden seal, for it was still blank.

"Whither now?" said the soft, husky voice at his side.

"To get my brother. Near the Canot or Bitte."

"No getting out of the city before the gates are opened at sunrise."

"No need," replied O'Brien. "Horses will be waiting outside."

He still wondered about the third horse; this, he reflected, could be somehow managed.

Twice they encountered parties of the night watch, but these were seen afar because of their lanterns, and the two hid themselves in side streets on each occasion. Presently loomed ahead of them the huge building that housed the Christian slaves each night, lanterns burning outside its entrance. Following the directions of Phelim, O'Brien turned the narrow street beyond, and sighted a light over a small doorway. Beneath the light lounged a black soldier, one of the ordinary troops, in a tattered *djellab*, spear in hand.

As the two figures came up the lonely, deserted hillside street, the black caught sight of them, recognized the robe of Ismail, and affrightedly leaped to attention. O'Brien held his dagger ready—there could be no mercy, no faint heart, at this crisis! As they came within the circle of light, however, the alert black perceived the imposture. He leaned over to peer into their faces, and some animal sense warned him of peril. As O'Brien moved, he twisted himself aside, and a cry came from his lips.

Too late! O'Brien leaped, and the steel drove out. Here was no craven, however, but a fighting man; hurt though he was, the black got his back to the wall, whipped out a knife in his left hand, stabbed desperately with spear and blade as O'Brien gripped his throat. A third body hurtled in upon them—the woman, stabbing savagely, plunging her knife repeatedly into the black body with a vicious and ferocious hatred.

The soldier went limp. The hurried panting and the stamp of feet quieted as O'Brien half hurled, half dragged the man's body back into the archway. Before him was blackness.

"Phelim!" he exclaimed guardedly.

"You, Shamus? God be praised!" came the response. "I'm alone here—"

O'Brien reached up to the lantern and got it off the hook, and its rays showed a deep and narrow chamber, where a mat served Phelim for bed. The gaunt man came to him eagerly, clung to him; there the two men, so long apart, embraced with the vague light of freedom on their horizon.

It was some time before O'Brien could quiet the sobbing man, for in this moment Phelim quite gave way to emotion. Then he recollected the woman, and gently parted the arms that hung about him.

"I'm not alone, Phelim—faith, man, will ye give me air? And glory be, but I've a present for you, a little remembrance from Ismail himself to be putting heart into your body." And with a laugh, he turned toward the entrance. "In with you, mistress! And bring the scimitar that we—What the devil!"

He stepped back hastily across the black's body. The woman had not followed him in, but was half leaning against the side of the arch in a despondent attitude. She put out a hand, and O'Brien caught her as she slumped forward.

The knife of the black man was buried to the hilt in her side.

"Phelim! Lend a hand here. Devil take it, wake up, man!"

Between them they lifted her inside, shrouded the lantern, fell to work. In another moment they found it was hopeless; Phelim, amazed as he was at sight of her bared woman's body, asked no questions but shook his head.

"The life's ebbing out of her, Shamus."

"Aye, poor thing! Best let the knife be. Lord, but she looks peaceful! Say a prayer for her, Phelim—it's long since I was praying."

"More shame to you," said Phelim, and fell to saying a prayer.

Midway of his muttering, the woman's eyes opened and she looked up at O'Brien. Peaceful she looked, indeed, and a smile touched her lips.

"Handsome soldier!" she murmured, so that Phelim's jaw fell at hearing the English words. "I'll be all right in—in a minute. La, but I be tired! Will ye not gi' me one kiss, my handsome soldier?"

"That I will, heart of gold," said O'Brien, and stooped so that for a moment his lips lay upon hers.

When he lifted his head, her eyes had closed again and her lips were smiling; she lay there dead, more happily than she had lived. Phelim touched her face and crossed himself.

"Well, Shamus lad—and what does it all mean?"

O'Brien extinguished the light and then settled down, and the two of them fell to talking.

There were long years to be bridged, and Phelim, although two years the junior, looked now a man of sixty. The present was more important than the past, however, and when O'Brien had sketched the night's happenings, Phelim fingered the diamond studded scimitar and growled an oath.

"Look you, Shamus! With the blank sealed vellum, we'd have a chance to get out the gates this night, before Ismail is found and starts the hounds after us. That is, if I had aught to write with. I know the cursed language, can read and write it well, can pass for a Moor if need be. All we need is to get past the gates, but there's the rub."

O'Brien laughed gaily.

"Cheer up, old heart! I'm stuffed like a sausage—here's brush and ink cube, so fall to work. Mayhap you're right about passing the gates, for they'll be tight guarded after Ismail gets loose, sure enough. All my plans have gone amiss now, and it's devil take the hindmost. Can we wait in that cemetery for the horses which will be coming?"

"Aye," growled Phelim, searching the dead guard for flint and tinder to relight the lantern. "You take this man's clothes,

I'll take my own. With sunrise, the folk will be flooding out into the cemeteries; hillmen are encamped now outside the walls by the hundred. Best go out by the north gate and work our way around, eh? That'll throw them off the trail later, when they get after us. Ah, here's the cursed pouch! Now for a light."

"How have you lived so long in this land, Phelim?" asked O'Brien curiously, while the other scraped with the flint and steel. "A man such as you—"

Phelim uttered a low, harsh laugh.

"How? Because, praise be, I'd learned fortification. I've planned the seventy-odd forts Ismail has scattered all over the country—I've shown him the use o' bastions and the like. I've guided his building from here to Tangier. I made myself too useful to kill, and when a pinch came, as it did once or twice, I took up the study of their dog religion and they had hopes of converting me. But it's been hell, Shamus, hell! Now give me the writing stuff, and we'll get the job done while you change clothes."

The lantern caught and flickered up. Phelim spat on the ink, took brush and reed pen and fell to work scrawling Arabic above the seal of Ismail. O'Brien set to stripping the dead black, with a grimace of distaste, and moved the woman's body gently away.

"Poor soul!" he said. "Well, she had her day, and Ismail knows it was her hand that betrayed him."

"Bah!" said Phelim callously. "Women are less than dogs in this land. She served her turn and died well; let me have as good an ending when the time comes! It's done. Leave that blade of Ismail's here. I dare not carry it—too well known. Put it in her hands, if you like. I'll take the black's weapons and do the talking. You carry the lantern. Where's that letter you spoke of—the one to King James?"

"Here," said O'Brien.

"Show the seal if need be. Pull the hood well over your head. We have renegades to deal with at the gates, so mind your tongue. Now for it—ready?"

O'Brien caught up the lantern, cast a glance at the smiling face of the woman; and next moment the two brothers were on their way.

THE GATE was passed without a question, and the lantern was handed over to the guards with a coarse jest from Phelim that drew a roar of laughter.

In silence, now, the two followed the road that skirted the walls, those enormous battlements rising huge and menacing off to their left, with only a light here and there showing. No stars were out, for rain clouds still clung low to the hills, but Berber camp-fires glimmered down in the valley.

O'Brien's heart was high as he strode along, and he hummed a lilting Irish marching song until Phelim abruptly bade him be silent, and pointed to lights ahead.

"The Bab Berdain—the Gate of Victory. Smell the heads on the night wind? Faugh! The cemeteries lie beyond, and we'll cross them; tomorrow they'll have dances there, and snake charmers and magicians. Making ready the pits for the fire walkers now. No more noise! Devil take you, have ye no sense?"

O'Brien laughed softly and followed in his brother's steps.

Now they were in among the tombs and stone slabs, following one of the many trails, and so came to a walled tomb with a great dancing platform beyond it. Phelim turned in at the lighted entrance, and the two of them slipped into a dark corner. One or two Arabs were at prayer, several others were chatting in low tones.

"Sleep here till sunrise," grunted Phelim.

And so they did, the strangest sleeping place O'Brien had ever known, with the drift of songs coming from the Berber camps, the singsong chants of the night watch along the great walls above, the taint of corpses on the wind— and Morocco, vast and arid and terrible, running out to the horizon on every side. Small wonder, he thought, that few slaves ever escaped from this city. For beyond the rugged land was the barrier of the sea. Yet he laughed a little at thought of how men must have been seeking him, and how they would be seeking him on the morrow, and so fell upon sleep beside the snoring Phelim.

When he wakened, dawn was coming up, and hunger was gnawing at him, for he had not eaten since the previous noon. He found the tomb empty except for two sprawled sleepers.

"Art a-hungered?" growled Phelim as they rose and left. "So am I. By the saints, you little know what hunger means till you've been a slave in this land, where a crust of bread will get a man slain. We can not seek food at the camps here, for I cannot speak the Chleu tongue and these Berbers mock all Moors."

"Starve for it, then," said O'Brien with a shrug. "Wait; I have some silver pieces—take them and buy something to eat, eh?"

Phelim nodded, took the money and went striding away across the graves, toward the lower ground. O'Brien sat down to wait, and the day broadened overhead. Presently Phelim came back and rejoined him, bearing a great pouch of dates, a round loaf of bread, and a leathern water bottle.

"Did you pay for them, then?"

"Aye," said Phelim, with a grim look, but O'Brien saw the splotch of fresh blood on his tattered robe and asked no more questions.

They ate in silence, washed down the meal with water, and presently sauntered on toward the gate of the *mellah*, as the Jewish quarter was known. The gates had already been opened, country folk were entering, and those of the city were already coming out to the cemeteries. The two fell in among the throngs and then sat down by the side of the road, O'Brien keeping up the hood of his *djellab;* the rapier hampered him, but he made the best of it, and they were inconspicuous among the crowd coming and going. When sellers of sweetmeats or water approached, Phelim gruffly sent them on their way.

They both knew that now all depended on Maimoran, and O'Brien had the brass cuarto ready.

After a little there was great disturbance around the gate,

whose massive portal was piled with pyramids of Berber heads. Soldiers appeared, then a company of horsemen came trotting out, spurred to a gallop, and went off down the road in a cloud of dust.

"Ismail's out," said O'Brien, and laughed softly.

"And the roads are stopped," added Phelim, significantly, squinting keen eyed at the lessening cloud of dust. "Pray heaven it rains today, for dust will betray us as we ride."

"You're a good mediator with heaven," and O'Brien turned over his hand to show the spatter of a drop. In ten minutes a fine drizzle of rain was coming down.

Now the morning life was taken up full swing, wagons coming up to the gates, throngs pouring out to the cemeteries and to the animal bazaar down the road, great crowds of women flocking forth on their one day of freedom to visit their dead, white clad save for the one little eye hole. Donkeys crowded the road, laden with firewood and vegetables; lumbering camels swung along; gangs of slaves and criminals marched past to the eternal labor of building. And of a sudden O'Brien came to his feet.

"Ready, Phelim! Here's our man."

He was approaching, indeed—a Jew, as his black cap and cloak testified, leading two saddled horses, apparently superb beasts, loudly bawling them for sale. Jests flew at him from every side; let Ismail or one of the kaids see these horses, and he would quickly get rid of them, and have a bastinado into the bargain! And since when had Jews owned horses, when all such animals in the land were the private property of Ismail?

"By Allah, I will buy your horses!" cried out Phelim. "Ho, Jew! Let us try them out to test their gait! I'll buy them, Allah upon you!"

There was a huge guffaw at this, and men looked to see whether the Jew were simple minded enough to let himself be bilked. O'Brien came close to the man and thrust the brass cuarto at him, then pocketed it quickly and took one of the bridles. Apparently overborne, the Jew broke into loud protests; Phelim drew knife and threatened to slit his belly, and leaped into the saddle. Next instant the two were spurring away down the road amid roars of laughter, while the Jew hastened to get himself out of sight inside the walls of his own *mellah*.

"Faith, that was a pretty play," cried O'Brien. "Would that I understood it all. Free, Phelim! Free and away despite everything!"

Phelim laughed harshly.

"I never thought to see the day when I'd bless a Jew, but this is it. Let me take the lead, and hide your face lest you be recognized."

So they rode, thundering along past the animal bazaar and out on the long road to the west, with none following that they could see. Past the olive groves and grazing flocks they flew, until presently they were riding out across the open, with the walls of Meknez fallen away into the distance and drowned by the rolling ground. Then Phelim drew rein.

"Between forty and fifty leagues lie ahead of us, Shamus," he exclaimed. "Best save the horses now, against need. At most, we can not cover more than half the distance today; we must take a hill track that I know to avoid the sacred city of Mulai Idris."

"And there are men ahead of us," said O'Brien.

"Safe enough," said Phelim. "On, then, at a good stout clip—push hard before the heat of the day, then rest an hour or so. What's that ahead?"

"Horsemen, and the ones we wot of. We've overtaken them."

"Then on, and get it done with," exclaimed Phelim. "Gallop when I give the word, and keep your face down."

They pressed on, rapidly overtaking a clump of horsemen ahead, the same troop they had seen leaving Meknez. Aware of the two riders, these halted and blocked the road, but Phelim urged his horse into a gallop and drove straight at them, screaming hoarsely and holding aloft the vellum with the golden seal of Ismail. The troop parted hastily, opened the way for the supposed messengers, let them through and on their way. Phelim laughed wildly and kept up his mad pace until a turn of the road shut them from sight, and reined in with an exultant look.

"Now we're free indeed, Shamus—and scarce a blow struck. So on with you, and sing your heart out if ye will!"

Once away from the city, they met few or none upon the road, and those few hurriedly fled from the sight of them. Men who rode horses were too apt to be emissaries of Ismail, who seized whatever they desired in all directions; and the Arabs had long since learned to dread the black man who oppressed them so savagely with his black legions.

So the long leagues fell behind, hour after hour, with the thatched huts and the little walled farms, fortified against Berber raids, and ever closer drew the sea with its blessed promise of friends and safety. Noon came and passed, and they rested the horses for an hour by a bubbling brook in a deep ravine, then took up the road again with Mulai Idris well behind them and the *bled,* the upland farming country, stretching away ahead to the hills and the forest of Marmora's giant oaks. In this journeying they learned each of the other's life during the past years, bridging the deep gulf that lay between as best they might.

A wild and fierce exultation filled O'Brien as he rode, with only the memory of the smiling face of the unknown woman to dim his exhilaration. Ahead lay action, prompt and sharp, at Salé; thanks to Phelim's knowledge of Arabic and the seal of Ismail, they could pass all barriers unhindered, obtain a sloop, sail out and meet the *Kestrel* and St. Rocher. The evil land lay behind them, the open sea ahead....

"Shamus!" It was an hour yet to sunset when the voice of Phelim cut in upon his musings. "Three men riding toward us—mules, not horses. I see the glitter of arms."

O'Brien could see it also, for the sun had banished the rain clouds long since and now hung hot and red in the western sky.

Three riders, no more, and a glitter of steel on the road. Phelim, who had an eagle's eye, soon discerned more.

"Two of them garrison Spahis—from Rabat or Salé, no doubt. But the third—"

"Lord save us!" exclaimed O'Brien, staring. "I know that figure, lad—aye, no doubt of it. The man I told you of—the slave, Will Dowling. He went to Salé with St. Rocher; what the devil is he doing here?"

"Heading back for Meknez, by the looks of it. Do you speak with him, while I talk with the Spahis."

The riders met. The two Spahis, both black men, gaped at sight of Ismail's seal, then kissed it reverently, held it to their foreheads, and fell into talk with Phelim. O'Brien pushed on past them to where Will Dowling waited—a shaggy man, still in Moorish garb, a slave here for seven years ere O'Brien won his freedom.

"Well," said O'Brien softly. "Ye know me not, Will Dowling?"

The other started violently, blinked at him, then checked wild words that came to his lips. He glanced at the two Spahis, and fumbled in his breast.

"You, master!" he rejoined. "Here, St. Rocher sent me wi' this writing for ye, and a happy man I am it's no return to Meknez for me! There's the devil's own news—but read it for yourself."

O'Brien took the folded paper, opened it, read St. Rocher's neat French script. For a moment his head drooped; the bitterness of utter despair, dismay, hopelessness, smote him like a sword and weighed him down. Then he found Phelim gripping his arm and pointing as he spoke.

"Shamus!" As O'Brien turned, the two Spahis whirled their horses about and set off at a gallop the way they had come. "Hark, Shamus! There's a kaid and fifty horsemen back on the road half a league—I've sent those two Spahis to order them to join us. They take me for a special messenger of Ismail, d'ye mind? I've ordered 'em to ride on with us to Salé—faith, we'll reach there like princes!"

"Little good it'll do us," said O'Brien, and held out the paper. "Read this—from St. Rochenr."

But Phelim refused the message.

"I've forgot English writing—what does it say?"

O'Brien read it, and his voice all but faltered with bitterness on the words that sealed their doom.

> "Jack:
>
> I send our friend to warn you. The *Kestrel* was brought in to Salé today by two galleys; they caught her unawares. Half our men are dead. They say the others will be chained as rowers on the big galley here, which leaves in a few days on cruise. I can do nothing. The Moors laugh at me and are stripping the ship clean as I write. Am near rid of the fever—"

The other two stared at him, and under their gaze his head came up, and the shadow of his old gay smile twisted his lips.

"When all's lost, there's but one thing to do, lads. So let's get about doing it at once."

"Aye, all's lost," said Will Dowling dejectedly. "The ship taken, the men gone, no way of getting clear o' this cursed land. And the Moors at Salé ha' turned against us, too. Then what's the one thing to do, master?"

O'Brien laughed, leaned over in the saddle, and clapped him lustily on the shoulder.

"Fight like the devil!"

THE TWIN cities of Rabat and Salé, homes of the Barbary rovers, were in the full blast of activity, for April was drawing near and it was the harvest season. When the Moors were expelled from Spain in 1609, men from the town of Hornachos had settled here, and ever since had wreaked a dire vengeance on Christians.

Now the shipyards were emptied, women and old men manned the walls, and the galleys of the corsairs combed the seas to the coasts of Europe and Newfoundland. Within the space of three weeks, above twenty English ships alone had been brought in; captive ships crowded the length of the Rougreg River, others were anchored inside the bar or had been hauled ashore. Droves of Christian slaves had been dispatched to Meknez. Merchants had flocked here from every part of Morocco, and the great open space within the Rabat walls was crowded with tents and bazaars, while others had been set up outside the walls.

St. Rocher, whose title of ambassador gained him fair treatment, was walking the high battlements of the *kasba,* a prey to sharp anxiety. He had heard nothing from O'Brien. Down below him lay the *Kestrel,* a sorry ruin, stripped of gear, her guns being hauled ashore on the Salé side. Almost beside her lay the greater of the two galleys which had brought her in—the only corsair ship now in harbor, held here for certain repairs. The crew of the *Kestrel* had been shifted into her bodily, what remained of them, to replace her dead rowers; two days more and she would be plying forth again to quest new prey.

Departing to Meknez, St. Rocher and O'Brien had left friends here; now these were gone. In the interval of slow travel and fever, heads had fallen. The new pasha was a Spanish renegade, admiral of the corsair fleet, and St. Rocher found his own position a parlous one, despite his letters from Ismail.

A stir in the long, straight Street of the Consuls below drew his attention. This street ran the full length of the wall beside the river to the eastern gate, and up its paved slope rode a troop of horsemen shouting the name of Ismail and plying relentless whips to clear the way. St. Rocher gazed down as they came to the wide space before the Gate of the Oudaiah, below him, and left their sweat-white horses; but a better eye than his would have failed to recognize any one he knew beneath those baggy, travel stained *djellaba.* He turned away and sought his own quarters off the citadel gardens, with heavy heart.

Some few moments later the renegade commanding his guard sauntered in—a fawning, cowardly fellow, a Tuscan slave formerly.

"Señor, you are wanted in audience by the pasha," he said, and grinned. "His Excellency is in trouble, and because of you. And if you have a gold piece, señor, I have something to trade for it."

"Yes?" St. Rocher gave him a look, decided to risk the gold piece, and in exchange received a folded paper, which he opened eagerly. Upon it were four Irish words written in English script:

Lamh laidir an uachtar

"O'Brien's motto—The Strong Hand Above!" A sudden laugh came to the saturnine lips of St. Rocher. Instantly he was transformed, and with a dancing flame in his dark eyes, he flung a second gold piece at the renegade and caught up his sword belt. "Ready, then?"

In the huge open chamber beneath the glorious Merinide gateway, the pasha held audience, and his dark, passionate features were uneasy. His guards stood around him, but facing him were the three men who had just arrived with a troop of horse for escort, with the ring of Ismail for token, with letters bearing Ismail's golden seal for authority. To those letters the pasha bowed, while the leader of the three addressed him in sonorous Arabic. St. Rocher, entering, met the flashing glance of O'Brien under the *djellab* hood, and stood tense, while an interpreter murmured what was passing before his eyes.

"Pasha Abdallah, Slave of God!" cried Phelim. "I am named Ali, and I bear the greetings of Ismail, the Sword of Allah; may his name be exalted among the faithful! It has come to the ears of the master of the world, who knows all things, that you have taken a ship of the infidels and that instead of sending her crew to Meknez as is commanded, you have placed them aboard one of your galleys. If this be true, you shall answer for it. Know you not that all infidel slaves are the property of the seed of Idris?"

"By the beard of the Prophet, whose name be blessed!" returned the pasha. "What is done, is done, and if there be liars in the world, what is that to me? It is true that a ship was taken, and as is the custom, I have put her men aboard a galley to replace those who were slain at the oars. To this end I hold the authority of our Lord Ismail himself."

"That may be," said Phelim, with a harsh, sardonic laugh. "But this ship belonged to ambassadors and held the safe conduct of the sharif."

"That is not so at all," said the pasha bluntly.

Phelim held up his vellum bearing the seal of Ismail.

"Look you, Abdallah ben Aisha!" he exclaimed angrily. "Here is my authority, and it goes far. We go aboard this galley to question these men, and I desire this Christian ambassador to accompany us, that we may have his testimony, for full report on this matter must be sent to Meknez before set of sun. Hear and obey!"

"I hear and obey," murmured the pasha dutifully. "As Allah liveth, who am I but the slave of Idris? An escort shall be ready in half an hour, and boats prepared to take you aboard. Meantime, refresh yourselves and rest."

"Gladly," said Phelim. "And while we wait, give orders that those slaves aboard the galley be released from their irons to await us and to be numbered, for such is the will of Ismail, of the seed of Idris!"

The pasha gave the order, and meditated what bribe to offer this gaunt, harsh man, who was apparently a renegade like himself.

St. Rocher quietly moved about, humming a little under his breath, and presently found himself at the elbow of O'Brien. The latter spoke softly, while Phelim held the pasha in talk and slaves served sherbet and cakes.

"It's nip and tuck, comrade; all hell's loose behind us. When we get aboard that galley, we must clear her and go, or we're lost."

"Good," said St. Rocher. "But it can't be done, Jack. She's under the fort's guns and has men quartered aboard. If we could wait until night—"

"Can't wait an hour, man! Even this delay may pinch us. There, Phelim's hurrying him up—my brother, Jack. Faith, you should have seen Ismail when I knocked him asprawl! Watch yourself, now; be ready."

Phelim played his part well, and if Will Dowling were recognized as St. Rocher's companion, and given blame for bearing the news to Meknez, little honest Will cared. The pasha bade his unwelcome guests Godspeed and sent them down to the water gate with an escort, and there boats were ready to take them out to the galley. Now Phelim's part was done, and the rest was in the hand of O'Brien, to win or lose.

Yet, as they drew out toward the galley, O'Brien perceived how desperate was their hope, how all but impossible. The galley lay anchored inside the bar, under the guns of the little fort on the rocks, with the great gun platform directly above her. Alongside her were swarms of small craft, for she was of large size, with high poop and two furled lateen sails, one to a mast, and carried six small guns, three to a side.

Aboard her was a great crowd of Arabs and Moors, soldiers and ship's complement and outfitters. In her waist were some forty of O'Brien's crew, their irons being knocked off; not a few of them were hurt or wounded. What this handful of naked, unarmed men could do against five times their number, was doubtful.

"Thank heaven the tide's on the ebb," murmured O'Brien, and touched Phelim's arm. "Your task is to cut the for'ard cable as soon as may be. Will Dowling, slash through the after hawser. Lose no time, either of you."

Next moment, they were at her ladder in the waist.

Her captain, a swarthy Portuguese renegade, waited to receive them; and as he came to the deck, O'Brien saw that the least delay or suspicion would be fatal. The only chance of success was to strike like a thunderbolt. He flung back the hood of his *djellab*, then shook off the clumsy garment completely. His gathered men had sighted St. Rocher, and now a low growl arose from them as they saw his face. O'Brien caught at his rapier.

"Up and at 'em, lads!" he called sharply, and drove the long blade through the Portuguese.

St. Rocher's sword flickered out, and there was a moment of utter, stark madness as steel snicked home and men died, and those two naked blades ran red. The Arabs, indeed, thought they had to deal with very madmen, and gave back in sharp terror from the two. Then the cowed, naked slaves wakened into life, and went leaping and bursting out among the Moors, snatching at weapons, smiting with fists, bringing men down here and there. Some of them met death, but more gained weapons and fell to work with them.

"*Allah! Allah akbar!*" rose the yell, and in upon the press drove a mass of the corsair's crew, as O'Brien's voice gathered his men to meet them.

Here was the instant of crisis. Overboard had dived the outfitters and workers in hasty panic; some score of the Arab crew, hard fighting men all, swept down upon O'Brien to end the matter swiftly while others gathered behind them; from the walls and battlements above rose a swelling uproar of yells and shouts.

O'Brien was laughing as he fought, meeting the onrush with steady rapier, while St. Rocher stood beside him with deadly steel playing in and out. The rush broke against them, and then man after man of the buccaneers smashed headlong into the fight with knife and scimitar, ax and hammer, Irish yelps and English cheers echoing up together. The mêlée became stubborn, unyielding. The yellow hair of O'Brien had vanished now; he was down, with St. Rocher plying desperate steel above him—then up again, blood streaking his face, the rapier lunging like a tongue of death. Back they were driven, their naked men forced into a mass.

"Treachery!" The wild Arab yell shrilled up from poop and stem. "Treachery! By Allah, we are betrayed! We are adrift!"

It was the voice of Phelim, and to it Will Dowling added his roar. O'Brien knew not what was said, but its effect was instant. The corsairs broke ranks, stared about, saw that the galley was indeed cut loose.

"Strike 'em!" blared O'Brien, and flung forward. "St. Rocher! Get the canvas out!"

A blast from the poop—Phelim had found a swivel gun there, loaded, and held a coal to it from a charcoal brazier heating a tar bucket. The load of slugs tore through the mass of Arabs, broke them. The naked slaves, with weapons to spare now, hurled themselves on the dark men, scattered them, drove them to bow and poop—and on the poop was Phelim with a crimsoned blade, taking the vengeance that had bided twelve long years, and roaring Arabic curses on them so that they knew not which was friend or foe.

Now it was no longer a battle, but a slaughter of those who stood, until figures went plunging overboard, swimming for the shore and the drifting small craft, and O'Brien cleared the last of them from the bow. Already the naked men were swarming aloft, unfurling the two sails to catch the offshore wind, sending the galley out toward the bar.

A crash and thunder of guns, and she shook from stem to stern as the great shot from above ripped into her, hulled her in poop and waist, ploughed up her deck. A splinter knocked O'Brien, headlong, ripped his arm from shoulder to elbow. He staggered up and made his way aft, his voice rallying the men to the forgotten oars. These were put out, and as he came to the poop, with Will Dowling wrapping a cloth about his hurt, came a second discharge of guns above. This time the shot passed overhead, but the rigging was spared.

Not a cable's length from the little fort below the great rock, now—and smoke spurted from the five culverins there, and again the galley reeled, but her masts held, and the canvas was bellying out. A scrape, a shudder, and she was across the bar, with O'Brien aiding Phelim at the helm.

"Down, all hands!" Well O'Brien guessed what was coming now, and there was no evading it. His voice rose in a shrill yell. "Down! Down! Down with ye, Phelim—"

Phelim grunted scornfully. O'Brien tripped him, sent him sprawling, held the helm with his one good arm—and then it came. The guns up above on the great platform vomited flame and smoke in a roaring thunder of brazen throat. Grape and bullets and slugs came down upon the galley in a blast of death, ripping through the canvas, peppering her decks, striking down man after man.

Standing there at the helm, O'Brien shook the hair and blood out of his eyes, lifted his crimsoned arm, shook his fist back at the guns above.

"The Strong Hand Above!" he shouted exultantly.

And she heeled over a little and ran out to the westward and the sword rim of the ocean that lay across the horizon—a riven, splintered thing, wounded and sore hurt, but peopled by men who babbled laughter over their wounds and counted freedom from Ismail well won at the price.

For such, indeed, was the will of Allah.

V

FOR GLORY AND THE MAIN

A Story of O'Brien, Buccaneer.

THEIR MAJESTIES' ship *Bristol,* decidedly in a bad way. She was fourth rate, forty-two guns, was by no means new, for she had been launched at Portsmouth under Cromwell in 1653, and was now forty years old almost to a day, as proved by the Navy List.

The morning had broken in warm splendor, as it is so apt to do between the Canaries and the African coast, but it found Captain the Hon. Sir Philip Boteler in a devilish bad humor on his wakening. A heavyset and somewhat nearsighted man who loved the bottle and a good horse rather than the sea, Sir Philip was hugely disgusted with the alleged life of glory that had beckoned when, on a drunken wager, influence at court appointed him to a good ship and he set forth to better the exploits of Clowdisley Shovell in six months' time.

He had every right to be disgusted on this sunny morning. Only the previous afternoon he had come up with two French privateers who refused to run or even to strike, as he had a right to exact of all who met the blue flag. Against the urging of his officers, Sir Philip started to give the "mounseers" a hot lesson—with the result foreseen by his officers, who were well aware what would happen when forty-two culverins tried distance against a dozen twenty-four-pound guns, ably manned by Malouins who knew their business. Luckily for Sir Philip, a black squall broke about sunset and saved him from disgrace, but it also settled his ship, and sent him to bed a most seasick gentleman.

He arose to a warm and sunny morning, quaffed his pint of Canary and ordered his officers admitted to his presence. His manservant, after adjusting his wig properly, informed him that there were no officers except Lieutenant Houghton, in the sickbay with a smashed leg, but the master gunner was waiting.

"Sink me!" exclaimed Sir Philip in dismay. "Have him in, have him in! Good morning, Master Gunner. What's this I hear, man? No officers?"

"True enough, Sir Philip," said the brawny, dour officer. "None but me and Lieutenant Houghton, your Worship. The master was swept off the for'ard deck when the squall hit us, and the chaplain was hit at the last broadside—"

"Damme and sink me!" said Sir Philip. "They're lucky. What a night I've had! Never so devilish sick in my life. Sick, d'ye hear? Not ill—sick. What's that paper ye have there?"

"Casualty list, your Worship," said the master gunner. "Out of a hundred and twenty fit men, we've not forty left. Near as we can reckon, there were some two score killed during the fighting, but the storm was worse. Half of them that are left be talking mutiny. They're out o' that pressed lot we took aboard—"

"Good!" said Sir Philip with energy. "Pick out the chief men and have them triced up at the capstan and given thirty lashes. Damme and sink me! I'll teach these dogs the meaning of discipline!"

"Who's to do it, sir?" said the master gunner bluntly. "Besides, there's no capstan. The bosun's dead, and his mate missing. The men do say there's been too much tricing up already, your Worship. Since that foul mouthed boy was doused from the yardarm and took by a shark, they've been muttering a great deal. But I came to tell ye, sir, there's a ship in sight."

"Signal her, then," ordered Sir Philip. "Damme, must I do everything aboard this ship?"

"She's a Sallee rover, sir, by the cut of her jib," said the other dourly. "We're in a dead calm, and she be coming up with her sweeps, but slow."

Sir Philip bounced out of bed. The wine had gone to his empty stomach.

"So that's her game, eh?" he roared. "Damme! Strike the wounded lion, will she? I'll teach the cursed heathen what a king's ship is like! Sallee rover, is she? Muster all hands and double-shot the guns—"

"Your Worship," said the other desperately, "there's eight foot of water in the hold, the rigging is gone, and half the guns are out o' service. We've no powder. We had to flood the powder room, you remember, when fire broke out—"

Sir Philip reached for his breeches.

"Muskets and cold steel, then!" he shouted. "Get to work, ye damned runagate! I'll be up in two minutes, and let me find things in order or I'll know the reason why!"

The master gunner retired, talking to himself in no pious fashion.

Sir Philip, ever the neatest of men, arrayed himself carefully. He had the Garter, which neither Princess Anne nor hard fighting could get for Marlborough, and he adjusted the gemmed star carefully. After cuffing his manservant well for not putting fresh lace at his wrists, he buckled on his sword and sallied forth, breathing valiant scorn of all Barbary rovers.

When he stepped into the warm sunlight on deck, a glass beneath his arm, he came to a stupefied halt. It is true that he had drunk well the previous afternoon, and had been very sick all the night; now he saw for the first time what Frenchmen and squall could do to a fine king's frigate, and the sight simply paralyzed him.

Not a scrap of canvas or rigging was left to greet his eyes. The topmasts were gone, and so were the main and foremasts, close to the deck. The gilded superstructure above the poop was gone. The bulwarks were a mass of shattered splinters, to which a few scraps of the waistcloths still clung. Guns were made fast any way, in and out of ports—where any ports remained. The men, half naked, sprawled about in the sunlight, insolently disregarding the splendid apparition on the quarterdeck.

Sir Philip focused his glass as the master gunner came up to him.

"So that's a Barbary galley, is it?" he asked.

"A half galley, your Worship," said the one remaining officer. "A galley has three masts. She has but two—and has been knocked about herself, lately."

True enough. The galley was creeping down the bowl of the sea like a wounded thing, her half dozen sweeps glittering in the sunlight. There was a slow, heavy swell running, but not a breath of wind. The master gunner spoke suddenly, his voice sharp.

"Look! God's love, sir—look to the east'ard!"

Sir Philip knew the sun rose in the east, and turned in that direction. Against the sun dazzle he could see nothing.

"Well? What is it?" he demanded testily.

"Two ships." The gunner spoke hoarsely, and snatched the glass from him; having been at work all that night, the man showed slight respect. "We're done, sir. Yonder be two more o' them damned rovers, and one a big ship, too."

Sir Philip licked his lips and, not knowing what to say or do, kept quiet. He fingered his lip uneasily, thinking of the precious freight he had taken aboard at the Gambia River fort—the gold dust and ivory for London.

"Now we be all slaves and that's the end on it," said the master gunner.

"Slaves?" said Sir Philip, blinking at the word.

"Aye." The other faced him bitterly. "Slaves to the heathen Moors, all of us; slaves, to be pulling sweeps or sweating blood under the lash!"

"Why, damme!" exclaimed Sir Philip in astonishment. "Ye talk as if 'twere my fault. Mind your respect, my man. Nay, at worst we'll buy our safety with the Guinea freight."

The other laughed harshly.

"Buy? They'll take that and all else."

Turning, the master gunner descended to the waist and assembled the scowling men. He pointed out the threatening dangers, lashed them with his tongue, received sullen oaths and shrill laughs for response. One and all had the same answer, with cutlasses in hand to enforce the word.

"What use fighting? We be done for, one and all, wi' that swine on the quarterdeck. To hell with him and you too. No slavery among the Moors is worse than slavery here."

When Sir Philip comprehended the situation and began to rage among them, one man laughed and knocked the little sword out of his hand, and buffeted him across the face. Sir Philip went back to his quarterdeck, and did well to save his neck from these men who hated him for what he was and what he was not; which, in all truth, was a great deal.

Meantime, the half-galley had crawled up close, and a man stood up to hail them in the bow—a man with graying yellow hair, and sharp blue eyes, and his left arm in a sling. That blue seaman's eye of his needed no recounting of the *Bristol's* story.

"Ahoy, there!" came the English words, so that Sir Philip and all his men leaped to the sound of, them. "Lay out your fenders! I'm coming alongside. Stand by to catch a line."

HE STEPPED to the shattered frigate's deck, a man slender, straight as the rapier at his side, and when his gaze fell upon the wondering, mutinous men around, they fell back hastily and gave Sir Philip passage.

"What's this, what's this? You're no Barbary pirate?" cried Sir Philip hastily. The other broke into a laugh.

"So my rig deceived you, eh? Small wonder. I'm James O'Brien, late of the Irish Brigade and elsewhere; Colonel James O'Brien, at your service. The Moors took my ship, so I took one of theirs and got away from Sallee."

"I'm glad to have the honor, sir," said Sir Philip with dignity. "I am Captain the Honorable Sir Philip Boteler. If you'll descend to the cabin and enjoy a glass of wine—"

"Faith, we'll be descending to hell if we stand on ceremony!" cut in O'Brien sharply. "You see those craft coming up? Boteler, eh? You're from that branch of the Ormond Butlers that went over to the Dutchman—aye, I remember. Well, are you ready to fight?"

"Fight?" gasped Sir Philip, and his jaw sagged. "I—we've nothing to fight with!" he said querulously. "Our men gone, only these mutinous dogs remaining. Guns out of service. A wreck. And I've got gold dust and ivory below, from the Guinea forts."

O'Brien whistled at this, sized up the man swiftly, and nodded. He looked at the master gunner, who stood by.

"Your rank?"

"Master gunner, sir."

O'Brien glanced at the men, who had crowded about to hear, and ignored Sir Philip.

"Listen, all of you," he said curtly. "I've thirty men aboard there, plenty of powder and shot, nothing but small guns; my galley is knocked about, but her rigging's sound. We've just one chance, my lads—and that's to fight. Yonder's a half-galley like mine, and a fine large galley, the best in their fleet, probably full of plunder and slaves, for they're just in from cruising. What d'ye say? Sling a dozen of these culverins aboard my galley, with shot to match. Pile aboard and lend my men a hand. If ye'd seen the slaves in Barbary as I have, ye'd fight a way through hell to avoid being taken."

"One moment, sir!" Stepping forward, Sir Philip faced O'Brien angrily. "I don't know who ye may be," he said, "but a Jacobite by your own word. You'll kindly remember this is a royal ship of their Majesties, and you can not order my men and guns—"

O'Brien looked him in the eyes.

"By your own name," he said, "you're one of a scoundrel family that deserted their own king and took money from the Dutchman. And you'll kindly remember that we're all Christian men here, in bad straits, and should stand together."

Sir Philip purpled with rage.

"Damme and sink me, sir! You're a rogue and a vagabond, a rascally Jacobite, and if there are orders to be given here, I'll give them, d'ye understand! You're standing on my deck, I'd have you know."

O'Brien bowed to him, with a laughing grace that angered him the more, and then turned. Over the broken rail had come half a dozen more men from the galley, led by a tall, saturnine man in black velvet. O'Brien beckoned this latter.

"M. le Vicomte de St. Rocher," he said, languidly, "I'd have you meet the captain of this vessel, no less than the Honorable Sir Philip Boteler." A note of steel leaped suddenly in his voice. "Take him, men!"

Two of his men darted forward, and next instant Boteler was gripped by each arm and held fast. He swore at his own ir-resolute men, at his gunner, at the laughing St. Rocher and O'Brien; then the last named shrugged disdainfully and swung about.

"This is now my ship, lads!" he cried. "You're done wi' the king's service; you've taken service with me! Master Gunner, will ye take my orders in this pinch?"

"Aye, sir," said the master gunner stoutly. "But I'll ship with no buccaneer, if that's your meaning."

O'Brien clapped him on the shoulder.

"Good man! True man! I'll have none that's false to his oath, egad! Get to work and rig shears; sling a dozen culverins aboard me. St. Rocher, back with you and dump overboard some of those useless old guns of ours and get the culverins rigged. Quick, men! Look alive, for there's not a minute to waste."

The master gunner bawled at the frigate's men, who gave a cheer and then fell to work with a will.

"Master, what'll we do with 'un?" said one of the two holding Boteler.

O'Brien glanced at the latter, and there was a gray, chill look in his face. He waved the men away, took Boteler by the arm and gently urged him across the deck to the farther rail.

"Hark you, Philip Boteler! God forgive you, I know well that you're the Ormond Butler who betrayed Lord Burke's regiment to the enemy, after Boyne Water, and got you a title and a place at court by your damned treachery. Aye, turn white, you black-guard!"

There came toward them a tall, gaunt man, gray of hair but with O'Brien's bright blue and eager eyes. O'Brien beckoned him.

"Phelim, you're fresh from long years of slavery, so you've not heard of this man. Sir Philip, this is my brother Phelim. Look you, Phelim, at one of the Butlers who betrayed a regiment of horse and got him a title by it! Get below, you damned rogue—out of sight!"

Sir Philip scuttled away, in no little fear.

"Come, Phelim—" and O'Brien led the way to where the master gunner was at work with the hastily rigged shears. "Take charge of this ship. Master Gunner, here's your captain; fight your own king's ship! I'll give you a dozen men. Work those of the guns you can fight—"

"We've no powder," said the gunner.

"Get some from aboard us, we've lashings of it. Are those wounded men I hear calling from below? Get 'em up. We've wounded men too, and by the saints, they're fighting still! Look alive, man!" He turned. "Phelim, pick your men and quick about it. Are ye suited?"

"Aye," said Phelim, squinting at the approaching ships. "And what if they lay us aboard? They'll have ten men to our one, Jack."

O'Brien nodded.

"Double-shot every gun you can bring to bear, Phelim; empty 'em into the half-galley yonder as she comes up. Not a shot into the big one, mind! I want her for my own. You know their tongue, so shout at them in Arabic that they'll have quarter if they surrender—"

"Devil take you, Jack! You talk as if they were striking to you now!"

O'Brien laughed.

"What? D'ye think I'd talk as though anything else would happen? If they get aboard here, defend the quarterdeck with the swivel guns and cold steel. And every shot into the smaller one, but hold your fire until I begin. Understand?"

Phelim nodded and went to pick his dozen men.

Both ships were in a fever of activity. As the culverins were swung aboard the galley, St. Rocher got the carriages lashed into place; powder was broken out, shot was laid ready. The two approaching rovers were now not a mile away. The smaller was like O'Brien's captured craft; the larger was a splendid craft, a hundred and sixty feet in length, her thirty-five banks of oars flashing with precision; but the smaller ship was in the lead. They were angling out slightly, to come on either side of the two craft lying together, helpless before them.

Here, as O'Brien well knew, was the making or breaking of his entire future. He had jerked his few remaining men out of Moorish hands, but shot had played sad havoc with his captured galley; and any king's ship that came upon him would gobble him up and hang him for the buccaneer he had been. By this time, he knew, word of him had spread far abroad. Beat off these two rovers he might, with small trouble; but he must do more than beat them off. They came from Sallee, were in search of him, so he could not hope to trick them.

Standing there watching, he swiftly made up his mind what they would do, and what he must do.

"St. Rocher! Ready for a gamble, old friend?"

The Frenchman laughed.

"Ready enough, Jack."

O'Brien swiftly told what was in his mind, and St. Rocher whistled thoughtfully.

"*Diantre!* I thought you meant to lay out and fight with the heavy guns. We'd be throwing away all our advantage—"

"Aye, to beat them off. What use in casting dice unless you can throw a double main?"

"Right!" The other chuckled. "You have luck at that, I grant. Agreed, then. We stake everything on the work of a minute."

"Faith, it's not for the first time," said O'Brien, his eyes dancing. "To work, then!"

As though to emphasize his words, a bow chaser blazed out from the smaller craft in the lead, and before the report reached them the ball whistled overhead.

St. Rocher, a skilled artillerist in the old days, sent his voice blaring down the deck. The *Bristol* lay with her stern to the oncoming rovers, O'Brien's galley on her larboard side. Now the lines were cast off and the galley worked ahead of her a little, and turned so that her starboard broadside came full to bear, as though she were about to cross the bows of the frigate; but she lay there motionless.

Swiftly the culverins were shifted, rolled across on their carriages. Ten had come aboard, and all of these were double-shotted, laid along her starboard rail. St. Rocher picked his gunners, sent two to each gun, one man with match alight.

"Every other man to the oars," commanded O'Brien. "Double

bank them. Starboard sweeps only; larboard sweeps trailing until I give the word to let go."

So they waited, and presently O'Brien's pulses leaped, perceiving he had guessed aright. The large galley was reaching out to come alongside the frigate and board from her starboard quarter. The half-galley was coming straight in, to lie alongside that of O'Brien.

A smile touched his lips as he stood watching. The men were at the oars, at the guns, every eye fastened upon him, St. Rocher awaiting the word to fire. Now the half-galley was almost under the frigate's quarter, yelling men clustered thick about her rail, oars driving her ahead rapidly.

O'Brien lifted his hand.

The galley rocked and reeled; a white cloud vomited from her rail. O'Brien's voice pierced through the smoke, and the oars dipped, surged, swung her head around. Then came a crash of guns from the frigate, gun after gun in a ragged broadside, shot hurtling down into the corsair.

The galley swung. The double banks were abandoned, her larboard sweeps bit at the water. Screams and yells arose through the smoke. O'Brien spoke to the helmsman beside him. Swiftly spinning about, the galley gathered way, burst through the smoke-cloud dead ahead of her, the half-galley was drifting in under the high side of the frigate.

"Ready, men! Ready and 'ware shock!" shouted O'Brien.

Fusils banged out feebly from the corsair, one of her guns vomited vain smoke and flame. A frightful chorus of yells arose from her crowded decks when O'Brien's prow came driving straight for her, and then lifted in a surge as the oars hurled her forward. A roaring crash, one terrific shock that flung half the men sprawling—another shock as the corsair was smashed against the high side of the frigate. Caught thus, she was instantly crushed like an eggshell.

"Back, starboard oars!" rang O'Brien's voice, and St. Rocher repeated the order from the bow. Then he shouted shrilly: "We're done, Jack! Bows all stove in—"

"Give way!" ordered O'Brien, regardless.

Her men torn by that double storm of shot, her sides crushed and stove in, the corsair drifted on a little way past the frigate; O'Brien looked back to see her going down fast, men in the water or clutching at the side of the *Bristol.* Then he faced around, as his own craft, rapidly going down by the head, came in past the frigate's stern.

The large galley was just swinging in, flinging grappling irons, oars trailing, the excited crew crowded along her larboard rail to leap aboard the frigate as she closed.

"Way enough!" shouted O'Brien. "Board her, lads—we must take her or swim!"

The broken hull was settling under them as they surged in alongside, with a crash of snapping oar blades. Everything had been staked on the work of a moment, indeed. O'Brien saw his men pouring up over the side of the corsair, and he followed them, two of the men helping him. And, when he came over the rail and got out his rapier in his one good hand, St. Rocher's headlong rush had split the crowded Moslems asunder.

The rest was work; hard, driving butcher's work under the tropic sun. It was not ended until Phelim, from the frigate's rail above, emptied two swivel guns into the massed Moors and then led his dozen men down to smite them in rear.

After this, however, it was quickly finished.

UNDER A blazing noonday sun, with a light breeze springing up from the north, O'Brien sat beneath an awning of canvas and took stock of his winnings.

He was undisputed master of the *Bristol,* on whose quarterdeck he sat, comfortably smoking one of Boteler's pipes; it was his first taste of tobacco in many weeks. He had a frigate, but she was in such deplorable condition that he could make no use of her. St. Rocher was now busy breaking out the gold dust and ivory and stowing it aboard the galley.

In the bow of the frigate were crowded some three score Arabs and renegades—all that remained of above three hundred men on the two corsairs. In the waist, delighted with their freedom, moved as many liberated slaves, with over a score of seamen captured by the rover and destined to the Barbary slave barracks. O'Brien looked at the splendid galley alongside, and his pulse quickened at the size and lines of her. Phelim, who had been making an inspection and interrogating the prisoners and freed slaves, strode up and dropped on the deck in the shade beside his brother.

"It's a wild divil ye are, Shamus, and with the divil's own luck!" he observed admiringly. "Stuffed with plunder, she is; took an Indiaman off Biscay, and most of those poor souls yonder are from aboard her. There's a rich lading, but she's out of water and has poor provisions."

"Which can be remedied from this frigate," said O'Brien. "Eighteen guns, eh?"

"All fine brass culverins out of Spanish ships," and Phelim nodded. "I remember having heard of her among the Moors; their newest and proudest craft. What's your intent with her?"

O'Brien chuckled.

"Take her to the Main and go adventuring. The Spanish have galleys on the coast; why should not a buccaneer have oars? Faith, it's an idea."

"Hm!" grunted Phelim. "Shamus, I'll be frank with you. I'm for Ireland and the old place again beyond Kinsale. Does it mislike you?"

"It's not for me, Phelim. If Ireland calls you, well and good. You're safe there; and you can go with jewels out of Morocco and gold dust out of Guinea to load you down. God love you! After years of slavery, go back and be a fine old Irish gentleman! Me, I'll live and die adventuring."

"Agreed, then," said Phelim, obviously relieved. "Now, as to crew: out of your men, twenty-six remain; from this frigate's crew, thirty including wounded. Ten of the captives will sign with us, and all the freed slaves—"

"Don't want 'em," intervened O'Brien. "No Greeks or Levantines, thanks."

"There are thirty good stock, French and English, then. That gives us full ninety men, enough to go adventuring."

"To hell and back," said O'Brien, with a glance at the horizon. "And sooner than any one here thinks, most like. Will ye do me a favor, Phelim? Get all our men aboard the galley, arrange stations, pick squads to load aboard water, powder and stores from the frigate. And do it on the jump."

"Eh?" Phelim stared at him. "Art in earnest?"

"Deadly earnest," said O'Brien, and his tone brooked no protest. Phelim cursed, then rose and stalked away. "St. Rocher! Drop everything and come here."

The saturnine St. Rocher swaggered up. O'Brien indicated the galley.

"My friend, d'ye see she's heavy laden, probably foul from long cruising? And the other craft ran away from her getting here, if you remember."

"True," said St. Rocher, perplexed.

"Well, think it over," said O'Brien with a grim smile. "You'll see the reason soon enough. Phelim's getting the men aboard her. Those prisoners are tied?"

"Aye, their arms at least."

"Leave 'em so. Where's that damned traitor Boteler?"

"Sulking in the main cabin."

"I'm off to see him. Get aboard our galley, pick out your gun crews, get ready for action."

"Eh? Man, are you mad?" exclaimed St. Rocher.

"Aye. Send twenty of those king's men back aboard here. And send me that master gunner."

St. Rocher turned to obey. He swept a puzzled glance about the ship, about the horizon—and then he was gone in a flash.

O'Brien smiled, and was still smiling when the master gunner stood before him and saluted.

"You want me, your Worship?"

"Yes," said O'Brien. "You're a true man. I'm giving you this ship, which ye can work into the Canaries. You'll have some of the freed slaves, some of the rescued prisoners, and all the Moors yonder."

A flash of joy lighted the dour features of the seaman.

"God bless you, Master O'Brien!" he exclaimed. O'Brien cut him short and pointed to the western sea rim.

"The breeze is freshening. Look what's coming up with the wind."

The other looked, then sprang to the bulwark and took a longer look. Only O'Brien, of all those aboard the two craft, had noticed the three white specks.

"Lord, sir!" said the other, rejoining him with wondering eyes. "Ye know?"

"Aye. King's ships. Do they look like it to you?"

"Sure enough, your Worship. We had orders to join the squadron at the Canaries—we went to the Gambia River fort, and were to join up at the Canaries—"

"Your captain is new to the fleet?"

The master gunner spat disgustedly.

"He never seen a ship afore, sir. Appointed out of the court, he was, and came aboard the day we sailed. Junior captain, he was, but old Cap'n Delancey died two days out, and it's his fault we're in this shape. What them Admiralty lords can be about—"

O'Brien's face cleared.

"D'ye know what those ships are?"

"Aye, sir. The *St. Michael*, 96, the *Victory*, 84, and the old *Unicorne*. She be going out o' commission. Laid down in '33, she was."

"Right." O'Brien stood up suddenly. "Master Gunner, you

know the navy usage. Stand by me, give me the right advice; and afterward, tell that I forced you into it. Give me your word?"

"Not to fight British ships, your Worship!"

"Upon my honor, no. Merely to save myself and my galley and men—and leave you to take this frigate in. Agreed?"

"Agreed, sir."

"Then, from this moment I'm your captain—remember that!"

"Aye, sir. Shall I prepare a salute, navy style?"

"Yes. A score of your old men are coming aboard from my ship. Take charge."

O'Brien strode aft, well assured that he could trust this man's simple honor. Also, he was well assured that his one slim chance of escape lay in sheerest audacity. Nothing else could avail him now. Colonel James O'Brien was under ban and arrière ban of British law, until King James came into his own again and, if caught, his head was forfeit.

And Colonel James O'Brien was well content to accept the gamble.

He came into the main cabin where the stoutish Sir Philip sat over biscuit and a decanter of port, deserted even by his manservant. O'Brien wasted no words on the man, who was half drunk already. Jerking Sir Philip to his feet, he drove in his fist to the heavy jaw, and let the other crash down. In three minutes Sir Philip was trussed hand and foot, a napkin stuffed into his mouth, and rolled under a bunk.

Some fifteen minutes later O'Brien came out on the quarterdeck. The three ships were within half a mile, bringing a smart breeze with them; already sail was being taken in. The blue flag was going up on the stump of the *Bristol's* main.

"St. Rocher! Attend me!"

It was a new O'Brien who met the astonished gaze of all. He had found garments that fitted passably, wore Sir Philip's dress hat, and the great jewel of the Garter blazed on his breast. Guns were speaking from the huge *St. Michael,* and the master gunner came quickly to him.

"Odd or even, your Worship?"

"Eh? What mean you?" said O'Brien.

"Reply to the signal, sir. Navy custom. Even number if disaster has happened—"

"Does this look like disaster?" O'Brien laughed. "Odd number!"

Three guns boomed out from the waist. Five replied from the ship of the line, and again three from the *Bristol*. O'Brien turned to St. Rocher, spoke swiftly.

"We've a bare chance. Be ready to go aboard her with me. Unless we can hold 'em off until night and then slip away with the galley, we're lost. Understand? Warn Phelim—he seems busy as the devil aboard the galley. We've sunk two Moors and captured one. Master Gunner!"

"Aye, sir!"

"Those spars from the sunken galleys are pounding under the counter. Get 'em fished up and start to work putting jury rig on this ship. St. Rocher will send more men to help you from the galley."

St. Rocher strode away. As the wounded lieutenant, the sole other surviving officer of the *Bristol*, was below decks with the worst of the wounded, O'Brien found his coast clear enough. Now the *St. Michael* came under the stern, luffed smartly, and three cheers went up from her crowded decks and rigging. A hail came from her quarterdeck.

"What ship is that?"

"The *Bristol*, Captain Sir Philip Boteler," returned O'Brien.

"Compliments of Sir Clowdisley Shovell, and will ye send a boat aboard?"

"Compliments of Captain Boteler, and why the devil can't ye see I haven't a boat left?"

There was a burst of laughter from the great ship.

"Sending a boat for Captain Boteler. Do ye need help?"

"I may look it but I don't need it," shouted O'Brien. More

laughter from the other ship, and as she drew off, her barge was smartly lowered and manned.

"You don't talk like a navy captain," said St. Rocher. O'Brien chuckled.

"Faith, didn't I get 'em laughing? And that's half the battle. Stick close, now. And mind, you were a prisoner aboard the galley and I rescued you. Lord, Lord! I hate to be lying about it all—but it's neck or nothing. Mind, St. Rocher, your three Moors came upon us as we lay disabled. Ye know nothing about what happened to us yesterday."

"You're devilish confused, but I get the drift," and the Frenchman smiled. O'Brien went to the rail, nearest and above the long galley.

"Phelim! Shoot any man that tries to communicate with the ships, ye understand? We must have until night. Get your hands aboard with sunset, if I'm not back."

Phelim waved his arm in comprehension.

The barge came under the counter and, as the *Bristol* had no gangway left, O'Brien went down to her in a sling, the lieutenant in command catching him and wringing his unhurt hand.

"Well fought, sir, well fought! You've overcome her, eh?"

"Overcome what?" said O'Brien in disdain. "That galley yonder? Faith, we took her, and sunk two more of the rascals, after two Frenchmen had pounded us to a hulk. Coming, St. Rocher? That's right. Who's your squadron commander—Sir Clowdisley Shovell? The same who broke the French fleet at Barfleur last year?"

"Aye, sir, and proud he'll be of this day's work!" said the garrulous lieutenant. "We've been on station the past six months, and not a shot fired. What news from home?"

"None," said O'Brien, and was silent for the rest of the journey to the *St. Michael*.

So he came into the very maw of the lion.

SIR CLOWDISLEY SHOVELL, then rear admiral

of the blue and hero of the British navy, was a quiet, sharp eyed man of forty-three. He sat in his cabin with his captains and, while the decanters passed around the table and long clay pipes filled the place with smoke, heard O'Brien's tale with obvious delight. St. Rocher, welcomed by all as a rescued captive, was made thoroughly at his ease; and when O'Brien's one fear that some of these men might know Sir Philip Boteler by sight had passed, he relaxed and began to enjoy himself.

The company, for their part, enjoyed O'Brien immensely. He noted that, when the health of their Majesties was drunk, more than one of those present unostentatiously passed the wine glass "over the water", and that these same men eyed him with a curious restraint. One of them plumped out the question at him, presently.

"Sir Philip, did ye not have some share in the Irish war? I seem to recall the name."

O'Brien's eyes twinkled.

"Faith," he exclaimed, "you couldn't travel a league in Ireland without hearing the name of Butler damned a dozen ways and spelled in as many! It's like the name of O'Brien in that respect."

"You must pardon our interest, Sir Philip," said the admiral. "You see, we had letters stating merely that you had been appointed to the Navy List and were to join us at the Canaries. Unluckily, we haven't had the honor of meeting you before this."

"That's your loss and my own, then," said O'Brien gaily.

He made light of the *Bristol's* huge losses, since he did not desire Shovell to send a complement of men aboard her, and glossed over the matter excellently.

"It's odd you should mention the name of O'Brien," said the admiral, after arranging that the *Bristol* should be worked into the Canaries with her prize, where the squadron would meet her. "We've had orders regarding one of that name—a most pestilent rogue who's turned buccaneer."

"Aye, sir?" said O'Brien with interest. "In these parts?"

"We're warned to look out for him. A fellow of ability, they say, who probably fancies himself another Prince Rupert, being a Jacobite. All rank scoundrels, these Jacobites," and the eyes of Shovell twinkled at his officers. "Well, this O'Brien is to be hanged, gentleman or not, when he's caught; that's settled on already. He's played the Dons a dirty trick or two, and we spoke to a Spaniard the other day bound for Santa Cruz, where they think O'Brien may show up. This Don is going to cruise off Teneriffe a whole month, seeking filibusters in general and O'Brien in particular."

O'Brien's blue eyes sparkled.

"Yes?" he prompted. "A Spanish admiral?"

"Hardly, yet prouder than any," and the admiral laughed. "He's the Duke of Torres or some such name; damme if I recall it. By the way, shall I give ye a letter to the governor at Santa Cruz? He's a touchy rogue, and as ye may be there ahead of us, 'twould serve ye well."

O'Brien accepted the offer with hearty thanks, which were entirely unfeigned. The letter was being written, and St. Rocher was telling a most diverting story of certain adventures by no means military, during his service in Flanders, when an officer of marines presented himself at the door and saluted the captain of the *St. Michael*, who was seated next O'Brien.

"Your pardon, sir," he said. "The Irisher who's at the capstan for not smoking his pipe over a tub of water, as the regulations order, asks to speak with Sir Philip Boteler. At least, that's what we think he means, for it's hard to understand his speech—"

There was a burst of laughter. The captain, however, reddened angrily.

"Why, damn his insolence!" he exclaimed. "We've had enough trouble with that rogue. Give him thirty lashes—"

"Your pardon, sir," intervened O'Brien suavely. "It may be some poor devil who knew me in Ireland, eh? I'd be honored, sir, if you'd give me permission to speak with the man."

"Eh? Of course, of course, my dear fellow! I thought ye might be affronted by his cursed insolence. Have the rascal in."

Five minutes later a man was shoved into the cabin. He was still constricted and muscle bound by the intolerable torture of the punishment; but when his eyes fell upon O'Brien, they lighted suddenly and he broke into a torrent of Irish—which, fortunately, was entirely unknown to the officers present.

"So it's you, Shamus my heart! And will yourself look at me now, the man who fought with your regiment of the brigade and who saved your life the day we charged—"

"For the love of the saints, close your mouth before you ruin me!" said O'Brien sharply, in the same tongue. "Aye, Denis O'Neill, I remember you."

"Then save me from this place of torture and hell," cried the other. "There be half a dozen of us here, all true men; and if yourself will take us off, there'll be blessings on every day of your life if you live to be a hundred!"

"I'll do that," said O'Brien promptly. "But don't mention my name or we're all lost."

Affecting an amused laugh, he turned to the captain.

"My dear sir, will you do me a favor that will place me eternally in your debt? This man was once my servant, and because I am from Ireland, he begs that I'll take him and a few others into my ship. I know how to get along with the rogues, and if you'd send them over to join me, I'll be happy to return other men in their place at the Canaries."

"Why, with all my heart!" exclaimed the captain. "That is, if Sir Clowdisley does not object—"

"Any man who sinks two rovers and captures another," said the admiral, "can have anything I possess, from men to boots. So you speak that outlandish tongue, Boteler? Damme if I ever heard anything like it! Positively inhuman, upon my word. Here's your letter, and be so good as to convey my compliments to the governor and his lady. We'll see you again in a week or ten days, God willing."

O'Brien and St. Rocher took their leave formally, and found the afternoon nearly spent. The *St. Michael* stood up toward the

Bristol and lowered away her barge. O'Neill and five other Irishmen were sent down with their few possessions, and the barge set them aboard the wounded frigate right speedily, then returned.

Guns from the three ships saluted the *Bristol,* trumpeters played her a rousing call, and to the roar of her answering salute, O'Brien saw the squadron fill and stand away to the southward. Phelim came striding up to him, with a grin, and surveyed the six recruits.

"So not content with bearding the admiral himself, ye carried off some of his men? Faith, Shamus, it's a wonder ye did not borrow his shirt and boots!"

"I thought of it," said O'Brien, "but they seemed a trifle small. Get aboard with you and all our men, Phelim. Ho, Master Gunner! A word with you. St. Rocher, will you take these six men and carry Sir Philip aboard us? I've a mind to keep him."

"Best hang him," said Phelim darkly. "You'll have no good of keeping him."

"Nay, I'm no hangman," said O'Brien, and turned to the master gunner. "You kept your word; I'll keep mine. Take your ship into Santa Cruz; I'll give you the proper course and you can't miss it, we're so near there now. I'll have a letter waiting with the governor for the admiral when he returns, taking all blame for what's happened. Tell the truth and you'll come out all right."

An hour later the galley was standing into the sunset, her Moorish canvas bellying out, while the happy master gunner sent a five-gun salute roaring after her. And O'Brien, with close to a hundred men and a ship that fetched a song into his heart, fingered the admiral's letter and faced ahead to an adventure that was after his own heart. The *Bristol* would not reach the islands for some days, with her sorry jury rig, whereas he would raise the peak of Teneriffe on the following day, with luck.

"What I don't like about it," said O'Brien that night, as he sat with Phelim and St. Rocher over their meal, "is making this scoundrel Boteler a hero. I'll have to fix that with a letter. I was sorry to be lying to those gentry, also; I'll fix that as well."

"And what about Boteler?" said St. Rocher. "He's locked in a small cabin yonder."

"Turn him for'ard with the men. About a third of the crew is Irish. See that they know who he is, but with orders to use no weapon on him; they'll make his life a hell, and he deserves it; I'll set him ashore at the Tortugas or put him on an English ship, and be rid of him. He's not worth the rope to hang him."

And so it was done, the next morning. It was a sorry day for Sir Philip Boteler when he became a comrade of the men he had commanded, and of the Irish who knew him for a traitor; but it was like to prove a sorrier day still for James O'Brien, had he but known it.

The matter of discipline was quickly settled, as it is when men are willing; and the crew were promised a day of carousing ashore at Santa Cruz. The galley had been crammed with loot from the Indies by the corsairs, and added to this was the dust and ivory taken from the *Bristol;* while O'Brien had jewels he had fetched out of Morocco. These, with certain specie found aboard, he laid aside and prepared privately for Phelim, in case there were any ship now at Santa Cruz. The men consented readily enough, for O'Brien did nothing without consulting them, at least in appearance.

On the following morning they picked up a frightened fisherman and learned that a Spanish ship was in harbor, loading for Cadiz, and none other but the *Santa Trinidad,* the frigate of which the admiral had told O'Brien. So, pushing boldly in, beneath the high peak, they came into Santa Cruz harbor an hour before sunset, with the blue flag of England at the main to quell the apprehension caused by their appearance.

The port captain came aboard and insisted upon embracing O'Brien; and hearing that he bore a letter to the governor, hastened ashore with the document. Another boat put out presently, inviting O'Brien and his officers to a ball at the governor's house that evening, and providing him with a barge and smaller boats, since the galley carried none.

"So the town is at our disposal," chuckled O'Brien, as he sat at meat with Phelim and St. Rocher. "Faith, if they but knew we were buccaneers, eh?"

"And to what end?" queried Phelim, frowning. "You're risking your head every day you're here, Shamus. What use?"

"Plenty," said O'Brien. "First, we'll get you off by the ship leaving tomorrow. You can have my share of the wealth aboard, and if I ever win back to Ireland, I'll claim it, mayhap. Second, we clean out our cargo of plunder to the merchants here; that's your business, St. Rocher, so make a sharp job of it. Third—my dear Vicomte, have ye looked at the Spanish frigate yonder?"

"Of course," said St. Rocher, with a sniff. "Messy. No gun ports, slovenly rigging, all the gilded carving off her stern— what's it mean?"

O'Brien grinned.

"I was talking wi' the port captain. She's fast as the devil's own, he says. This Duke de Torres is on the hunt for filibusters, d'ye comprehend? Not a bad idea, either. They see a merchant-man separated from her convoy, and bear down to gather in the prey. Presto! In a flash she becomes a forty-gun frigate wi' three hundred men aboard."

"So!" said Phelim, while St. Rocher frowned thoughtfully. "And what has this to do with you?"

"Much, my honest brother, much! Look at St. Rocher, here; note the sallow cheek, the sunken eye, the gloomy frown! And why, think you? Because he, a noble of France, must serve as second in command to a wild divil of an Irishman. And what's the cure? Faith, are ye both so dumb and blind?" O'Brien broke into a sudden laugh, and clapped St. Rocher on the shoulder. "There's your ship yonder, comrade! We'll take her, and sail her to the Caribbees together wi' the galley, egad! Why shouldn't Jack O'Brien have a fleet at his back, will ye tell me that?"

"*Diantre!*" swore St. Rocher, his dark eyes suddenly afire.

"You're in earnest? But I see you are; splendid! Another bumper of that wine, and we'll sack Santa Cruz itself!"

O'Brien shrugged.

"It could be done; but I'll have no sacking of towns in my day's work, unless forced to it. I've seen enough of hell without causing more of it."

"Thank God ye have some limits!" said Phelim. O'Brien gave him a laughing glance.

"Thank God ye'll be off for Ireland in the morning! I'll have the governor supply ye with papers; and stay aboard tonight, Phelim. Your pose is that of an honest merchant rescued from the Moors, mind. St. Rocher, we'll take this arm of mine out of the sling—the wound is far from healed, but it'll mend quick enough. And this way it's devilish unhandy."

THE GALLEY, which O'Brien had christened the *Black Rose* in a sentimental moment, induced by certain talk of Ireland, lay within the Mole, no great distance from the spot where one Nelson was to lose an arm in later years.

The crowds that had thronged to see the captured Moorish galley were long departed. Moonlight bathed the great peak far above, and poured down across the cactus blackened plain, lightening the volcanic rocks and touching the dark town with magic fingers. Lanterns studded the great Mole with its battery of heavy guns, twinkled aboard the frigate, where the work of transformation went forward incessantly, and glimmered along the shore and the main square of the town. In front of the governor's residence burned huge smoky torches, and a crowd was gathered, talking excitedly about the two handsomely dressed men who had come from the captured galley. Two score men had come ashore also, dispersing among the wine shops and mingling in comradely fashion with the Spanish soldiers who thronged everywhere.

Within the mansion of the governor, healths were drunk to their Majesties of England and to Charles of Spain; there was much stately ceremony, and O'Brien got through it with a

courtly grace that well became him. Then he handed the governor's lady through a minuet, turned her over to St. Rocher,
and presently strolled in the patio with the Duke of Torres,
talking earnestly.

Torres was an impatient and haughty young man of twenty-
odd, who had vowed to hang five hundred buccaneers within
the space of a year, and was hot to be about the business. O'Brien
would have clapped him heartily on the back, had this vow been
made for a lady or to the saints; but Torres seemed arrogantly
proud that it was made in order to win a wager of five thousand
doubloons with the Duke of Alba, and this smacked too much
of hangman's pay to suit an Irish stomach. Not that O'Brien
showed it in the least. On the contrary, his hauteur equaled that
of the Spaniard, so that presently Torres felt like a brother to
him, and talked eagerly and at length, waxing eloquent upon
the subject of one O'Brien.

"A very son of the Evil One, *Señor Capitan!*" he exclaimed.
"We have had word of him from the Americas. He has sacked
towns, raped women, conducted himself with all the excesses
of his devilish nature. He shot ten priests with his own hand,
gave an entire convent of nuns to his men, was guilty of the
basest treachery to men who trusted in his word!"

"Here's news, devil fly away with me if it isn't!" thought
O'Brien, and banished his last lingering scruple. He took the
other confidentially by the arm.

"Listen—perhaps I can help you," he said. "Early this
morning, as we were standing in for the Peak, we picked up a
sloop containing five men. They said they came from a small
trader which had sprung a leak near one of the islands, but they
lied. It mattered not to me. I pressed them into service with
my crew, since they were English. Now, it strikes me that they
may have come from some filibuster or buccaneer, to spy out
the harbor—eh? You know how those rascals work. What say
you?"

"By the saints, señor, it is probable enough!" exclaimed the other. "If I had those men, I'd put them to the question soon enough and learn the truth!"

"Excellent idea! I'll do it tomorrow," said O'Brien eagerly. "Will you come aboard me and hear what they have to say? After the siesta?"

Torres was overjoyed, and so eager he could scarce contain himself.

That evening, O'Brien accomplished much; chiefly in arranging with the governor for Phelim's departure aboard the Spanish ship in the morning, but he also got permission to sell the lading of his prize. Nothing was too good for the brave Sir Philip Boteler, in fact, and if the eyes of the ladies followed his slender, handsome figure, the eyes of the men warmed to his quick smile and straight, whimsical gaze. In all this St. Rocher backed him mightily, being a very courtly gentleman when the mood took him and he could shake off his somber cynicism.

Later, however, aboard the *Black Rose*, O'Brien sat in the cabin and questioned man after man of those who had been ashore, while St. Rocher pricked down upon paper, the items of their responses—chiefly in regard to guns and men, and gossip they had picked up. So closed that day, and none heeded a haggard, unshaven wretch forward, who slept on a pile of rags to ease his bruised body and shattered self-respect.

Shortly before noon next day, with goods pouring ashore from the galley into the booths of merchants, O'Brien took his brother aboard the Spanish ship, whose captain had received explicit letters from the governor concerning him. The two men looked into each other's eyes, and their hands gripped.

"God be with ye, Shamus," said Phelim hoarsely. "And when ye come home, ye'll find all waiting for you, praise be!"

"Home's where honor is, Phelim," responded O'Brien. "And that's in my own heart. God bless you! Goodby."

So he turned and was gone to the galley again, where St. Rocher awaited him; and if the heart was sore in him, none could find hint of it in his thin chiseled features or his quick blue eyes.

That afternoon the Duke of Torres came aboard, with half a dozen of his officers, all stately Spanish men, and when they had drunk wine in the cabin, five blood spattered wretches were dragged in, groaning, and cast down before O'Brien, who gave them a wink and a stern word.

They straightway confessed all, to the amazed delight of the Spaniards. They were in truth buccaneers, and their captain was one O'Brien. They had been sent to spy out what ships were in the harbor, and their own ship was to meet them in two more days at a certain point off the coast of Grand Canary.

They were dragged away; more wine was fetched in, and the cabin echoed to loud voices. The vision of two hundred buccaneers falling into his hands at one blow, and the infamous O'Brien their commander, quite carried Torres away with its splendor. Then O'Brien made himself heard, and they listened eagerly to his words.

He pointed out that the rascal O'Brien evidently had all the craft of the Evil One, and would not shirk a fight; it were pity to spill more Spanish blood than might be necessary in taking him. Also, Torres was much set on taking him alive and hanging him. If he might venture to offer the help of himself and his men, said O'Brien, not to speak of the really good guns mounted by this galley—

Torres was delighted, for the proffer was most delicately phrased and flattered his vanity. So O'Brien outlined his plan.

Let the two ships go forth on the second morning, said he, to meet the infamous O'Brien. Aboard there was great store of Arab garments, and more could be found ashore. The crew of the frigate could be hid below decks, and she could be manned by some of the English crew in Moorish garb. Those aboard the galley, also, would be costumed in the same wise. To all appearance, here would be a Sallee rover with a prize—and mighty few men would be in sight. With a little ingenuity, evidences of a hard fight might be made to show. The buccaneer would think both craft an easy prey, and would certainly swoop down upon them; with most surprising results, to him.

Torres sprang to his feet, eyes blazing with delight, applause pouring from him in a torrent; and when he departed with his officers, he was walking on air. But St. Rocher surveyed his friend with a grim and saturnine smile.

"Well, Jack? One would think they were children, to fall for such a lure! Your intent?"

"Simplicity itself," said O'Brien quietly. "We go out with the Dons below deck—and we keep 'em battened down until we set 'em ashore on one of the islands. If these gilded popinjays show fight, which I much doubt, well and good. There'll be a dozen or so shut in their main cabin, and we'll turn a gun against the door if they insist. That's all. There'll not be a shot fired, I'll wager you."

The other nodded.

"I believe you. And not a bit of shame, friend?"

"Aye," confessed O'Brien. "I could not do it, had not the rogue prated of his vow. Vow, forsooth! Hangman's wages, that's what it is; hanging men for money, no less. Yet I'd not harm him or his gentlemen if I can help it, for they're men of honor—all save that fool. How seems the plan to you?"

"Perfect," said St. Rocher, and looked at the *Santa Trinidad.* "A magnificent ship there, my friend. With her, and with this galley—what could we not do?"

"Not could, but will," and O'Brien smiled. "How goes the bargaining?"

"All the stuff will be cleaned out of her, and ballast of water and stores put in by noon tomorrow," said St. Rocher. "And I'm afraid to think of the wealth we've won; I'm taking bills of credit on Havana where I can't get cash, but I'll be able to discount most of them with the Jews here. There are two, both wealthy rogues, who've pretended to be converted. What'll ye do if the squadron shows up unexpectedly, Jack?"

O'Brien glanced at the horizon, then at St. Rocher.

"Faith, I'd do what any wise man would do—run as though the devil himself had me by the tail! Let's fall to work, for we dine aboard the frigate tonight, ye mind."

BY THE following noon, most of the *Black Rose's* cargo was gone, and she was loaded and trimmed with provision, water, powder and stores in general; further, she had taken aboard a huge amount of specie, and St. Rocher had bills on Havana for other amounts, and the gold dust of the *Bristol* was still aboard. The men, who had caroused to their hearts' content, were well satisfied to await further spendings until they reached the Antilles.

O'Brien settled all details that afternoon with the Duke de Torres. He and his officers were living aboard the frigate, almost alone; most of his crew were quartered ashore, for the work being done on her was performed by shore carpenters and workmen. By dark, according to Torres, she would be in readiness. He planned to bring his men aboard at daybreak, with two hundred soldiers from the garrison, and to sail with O'Brien at sunrise. By noon, he figured, they would come up with the buccaneer. Returning to the galley toward sunset, O'Brien recounted all this to St. Rocher.

"And no squadron returning, either," he concluded jubilantly. "All going well. The old *Bristol* should appear tomorrow, but we'll be gone. I've left a letter ashore for the admiral; I'd like to see his face when he reads it! The governor's secretary has it."

"Signed by your name?" queried St. Rocher.

O'Brien nodded.

"Aye, but it's sealed; they'll not read it, before delivery." He looked at the Mole and shore batteries, and nodded with relief. "I'll admit I've been a bit worried, but now all's past. A bad position, if aught went wrong."

True enough. The *Santa Trinidad* lay against the great Mole, moored stem and stern. At the outer end of the Mole was one heavy battery, at the shore end another, and batteries on the shore and higher ground beyond commanded the harbor. With these guns, and those of the frigate, the galley would be in a tight place had anything gone amiss.

"Any shore leave tonight, your honor?" queried one of the men who had been appointed boatswain. O'Brien nodded.

"A score of men from the larboard watch. I promised 'em yesterday. Until ten o'clock."

The galley lay some fifty feet from the *Santa Trinidad,* and inshore from her. The men went ashore; the night was fine and clear, without a breath of air stirring, the stars all in a white blaze overhead and the full moon promising to be up in an hour's time.

O'Brien and St. Rocher were bidden that night to a banquet with the governor, given in honor of the departing heroes, and Torres had promised to call for them with his boat. When the barge came from the frigate, O'Brien was still settling details of the morning's work with his men. Torres and two of his officers came aboard, and St. Rocher took them down to the cabin while O'Brien departed hastily to shave and dress.

He was nearly finished, and on the point of joining his guests, when the boatswain appeared hurriedly.

"Master, summat is up ashore. There have been light signals from the station on the Peak, where they watch for ships; and the port captain's barge just went out o' the harbor with her oars dipping fast."

"Well, that's nothing to us," said O'Brien good humoredly. "If we find—"

Another man came leaping down the companion.

"He's gone, Bosun!" he exclaimed, and ducked his head at O'Brien. "There's a line over the side for'ard. He must ha' slipped over and swum for it—"

"Eh?" said O'Brien sharply. "Who?"

"That English captain, Sir Philip—"

"We'd missed him, Cap'n," explained the boatswain, "and now it seems like—"

O'Brien brushed them aside and was leaping for the deck on the instant. He stood there in the starlight, glancing around, listening. If Boteler had indeed got ashore, it meant the devil to pay. Lights were still winking from the signal station on the Peak, but he could not read their message. Boats were being rowed across the water—one was just at the frigate's side, hailing for Torres. Ashore, from the town, rose confused sounds, sharp outcries, that might mean anything or nothing.

"Bosun! All hands—silently about it!" exclaimed O'Brien. "Serve out arms. Send me three men here with pistols. Quick!"

"Aye, sir."

The galley's deck became a scramble of padding figures. The boat from the frigate was now coming across the water, and a voice came from her in a hail.

"Ahoy the galley! We have an urgent message for his Grace the Duke of Torres. Is he aboard?"

"*Si, señor,*" responded O'Brien. "Come with your message."

The boat drew in beside Torres' barge, and a man mounted to the deck in breathless haste. O'Brien met him, turned to the three men who had just come up, armed.

"Take care of this fellow—hit him on the head! Then down to the cabin."

He darted for the companionway, and a moment later broke into the cabin where St. Rocher and the three Spaniards sat about the table. At sight of him, St. Rocher came to his feet.

"Señores!" cracked O'Brien's voice. "Remain where you are. On deck, St. Rocher!" The three men came crowding in at the door, and O'Brien turned to them. "Stay here. If these men give any alarm or show fight, pistol them. Señores, you are my prisoners."

Then he was gone, with St. Rocher beside him, explaining as he went.

"The devil to pay now. Boteler's gone ashore, given the alarm. The governor's read my letter and verified his story. Not an instant to lose—"

"*Diantre!* And our two score men ashore?" cried St. Rocher. O'Brien was on deck now, among the crowding men.

"Take those boats alongside!" he snapped. "Quick! Down into them!"

A chorus of shouts from the water, drowned by the oaths and cries alongside, as into the barge and boat dropped men from the galley, striking down the amazed Spaniards, clearing the two small craft. Lights were flashing in the batteries ashore, whistles were shrilling, a drum began its quick, ardent beat.

"Barge a-coming, sir!" rose a voice. "Looks like our shore party!"

A barge was indeed racing out, crowded with men, who shouted as they rowed. O'Brien caught St. Rocher's arm, and his voice leaped.

"I'm going aboard the frigate. Slip the cables, get out the sweeps. Have a hawser ready to put into that barge. You'll have to tow her out; give the battery a broadside quick as you come opposite. Go!"

"You're mad!" cried St. Rocher. O'Brien laughed, excitedly.

"Aye. The moon's trembling under the horizon—we can just make it."

He darted to the rail, hailed the approaching barge. A voice made answer.

"They jumped us, Cap'n! Sojers all over the place—stabbed our men right and left! We broke away—murdered us, Cap'n! Bloody murder, it was! And sojers are loading into boats and barges—"

"Lay alongside and pick me up," ordered O'Brien. He counted swiftly; over a score of men in the barge coming under the rail. The others were lost. "Hawser coming down; lay hold of it!"

The barge drew in, with the long sweeps of the galley already reaching out into the water. O'Brien was down quickly, among the men in the barge.

"To the frigate, men! Aboard her, make fast that hawser, cut her shore lines. Put your backs into it, now!"

The barge darted from the galley's side, the heavy hawser dipping into the water behind, slowing her down. The silver notes of a trumpet rang out musically from ashore. Lights were springing in the great battery on the Mole; torches and flambeaux were breaking out ruddily ashore.

At O'Brien's heart tore the thought of those signal lights from the Peak, and the port captain's barge that had gone leaping from the harbor.

IN UNDER the towering frigate's side now, with a sleepy hail from above to greet them. The men went up like cats, and O'Brien followed, for the gangway was out. The hawser was hauled up. Shouts, oaths, cries rang up as his men scattered over the decks and struck down the few workmen and guards in sight. Out along the Mole showed a dark mass of men—soldiers marching out to board the frigate.

The galley was on the move now, her sweeps dipping.

O'Brien darted to one of the shore lines, severed it with his knife, sawing through the tough manila. An officer from the dark mass of soldiers shouted, gave an order; musketry blazed, and bullets tore around. The other lines were severed. Excited voices leaped from the battery up beyond. The frigate moved, slewed out from the Mole.

"Hawser fast, men?" shouted O'Brien. "Find shot and powder if ye can—lay a gun or two on the Mole battery!"

For the moment, both ships lay between the battery on the Mole and those ashore, so the latter could not fire. The *Black Rose* was gathering way rapidly, but this fell off as the hawser drew up and the weight of the frigate had to be overcome. And meantime, the boats and barges from ashore were crawling out over the water. O'Brien heard St. Rocher's voice.

"Starboard watch, stand by for boarders!"

Now was the crucial moment. The galley alone might have won clear without a struggle, but the dead weight of the *Santa Trinidad* was a terrific handicap. Yet it was being overcome foot by foot, while the barges swept up toward the two ships. One of them had cut over and was heading for the frigate.

"Two guns laid, sir!" rose a voice exultantly from the waist.

"Plump 'em into the battery then," ordered O'Brien.

Luckily, Torres had made everything ready against the morrow, even to powder and shot laid ready. A man came running from the lantern where he had been lighting slow matches. The red pin points glimmered. Then, almost together, two guns in the waist crashed out; yells and shrieks arose from the battery on the Mole.

St. Rocher was engaged now; two of the barges were under his counter, sending up men. A yell warned O'Brien. Musketry blazed from the barge creeping up, and bullets whistled all around. One of his men coughed and sank down. The others swarmed at the rail as the barge came in alongside.

"Over with 'em!" said a voice, and man after man lifted, strained,. got the heavy shot over the side. Crashes from the barge, wild yells, as the roundshot tore through her bottom. She fell behind in drifting wreckage.

"Good men!" cried O'Brien. "Another gun if ye can!"

They could and did, working like mad. Now both ships were picking up speed, with the sweeps bending desperately and forcing them ahead. St. Rocher had beaten off his assailants, but his guns were still silent—he could spare few men from the oars and bulwarks. They were nearly opposite the great battery on the Mole now, and with luck, those heavy guns could blow them out of the water. Tense, strained, O'Brien waited.

A crash, and the frigate reeled. The first gun of the battery had spoken. The two guns in the waist made answer. Then, without warning, the galley's starboard battery vomited flame with a great roar, and no mean eye had laid those guns. Bags of bullets screamed about the Mole battery, struck down men right and left, silenced the guns ere they had spoken. A cheer went up from O'Brien's score of men, swabbing desperately at their two guns. These were run out once more, and once more stormed shot into the hapless battery, not a hundred feet distant.

Then the shore batteries began to speak.

The moon was just coming up. Already the towering Peak was silvered with her light, and the long hills behind the town, running up to Point Anaga, bathed in splendor. The guns spat red flame along the shore. Another gun and another from the Mole roared out terribly. An entire shore battery erupted into thunder.

The two ships drew out.

Shot ploughed the water around them, smashed into them, rocked them; for the second time, the galley's guns volleyed, and this time with roundshot that wrought death and ruin in the Mole battery, where lay the greatest menace. Steadily, oars dipping like mad, the galley drew out, fetching along the great ship behind her. The barges, and boats had given up the vain chase now. Guns roared from the fort on the hill, but did no damage.

"Ahoy, Cap'n!" It was St. Rocher's voice, shrill and eager. "We're clear! All right aboard?"

"Right enough," answered O'Brien. "Well done, friend! Better come alongside, once we're well out. No wind ahead."

There was none, indeed. The sea lay glimmering like molten lead in the level light of the rising moon; not a catspaw ruffled the face of the water. The oars dipped and dipped, and phosphorescent swirls of fire trailed behind. The guns were silent now, their prey escaped from them as by a miracle.

The oars ceased to dip. The frigate forged ahead still, came in alongside; lines were flung, fenders put out, the ships touched. O'Brien leaped to his own deck, and a wild yell of exultant delight went up from the men.

"We've paid for our murdered comrades, lads," he exclaimed. "Any killed aboard?"

"Five," said St. Rocher. "And a dozen wounded."

"Three down on the frigate. A cheap enough price for such an escape! If we—"

The words died on his lips. St. Rocher, reading his face in the moonlight, swung around. The men turned to stare. A dead silence fell upon them all in this moment, so that the gentle grind and squeak of the fenders was the only sound. A man cursed, and fell silent again.

For there, coming out around Point Anaga to the north, was the squadron of Sir Clowdisley Shovell, the towering *St. Michael* in the lead, clearcut in the moonlight.

"They made out the squadron from the Peak," muttered O'Brien. "And the port captain's boat bore 'em word—"

Then his voice lifted like a trumpet blare.

"All hands! Gather around!"

THE SQUADRON was two miles away and heading down for them, half a dozen boats out ahead of each frigate, towing them rapidly along, navy style. O'Brien saw at a glance, however, that the topsails of the frigates hung listless. There was ho breath of wind.

"Lads," he said quietly, "we can get away in the galley, but damned if I'll give up such a prize as we have yonder! We have one chance. Get out the boats of the *Santa Trinidad*. Those of you who are navy men, take charge, man the boats, lay out lines. Work with a will, kill yourselves at the oars—and we can manage it! St. Rocher, take your ship. Head southward."

A wild yell made response.

"And you, Jack?" said St. Rocher.

"You'll see. Go at once!"

St. Rocher and another score men went aboard the frigate, and her boats were cast loose. O'Brien called the boatswain.

"Load the guns—bags of bullets, lads. No shot. Wait! Every other gun, double-shot with grape."

The frigate began to move, as her boats drew out with their

lines. The boatswain's whistle told O'Brien that the guns were loaded.

"Out oars. I'll take the helm. Gunners, stand by with your matches. Every other man to the oars."

The galley darted through the water. She swept around, then headed straight for the approaching squadron.

O'Brien looked over his ship. Here and there a shot had done damage enough, but the spars were untouched. With the "Haw-haw! Haw-haw!" of the timer, the oars dipped regularly, evenly, sending her spurting ahead through the water. The *Santa Trinidad* was standing now for the south, gathering way fast.

The three ships of the squadron were close together, the boats spread out fanwise ahead of each ship. The barge of the port captain was alongside the admiral. Straight for them went the galley, closer and closer; within half a mile now, and heading forward unfalteringly. A puff of smoke came from the *St. Michael*—her bow-chaser, the only gun she could bring to bear. A shot plumped into the sea.

The galley made no response.

"Steady as she is, Bosun," said O'Brien, turning over the helm.

He strode rapidly along the deck, giving the gunners their instructions. Another heavy boom from the *St. Michael*. This time the shot whirred and screamed overhead. He came back to the poop and took the helm.

"Trail larboard oars!" leaped out his voice. "Two strokes more, starboard benches!"

The galley headed around in a swerving sweep across the pathway of the three ships and their boats. She lost way. The gunners sighted, laid their guns. She reeled and rocked as the pieces thundered out, and through the smoke appeared jets of spurting water all around the boats.

"Give way, larboard oars!"

The galley spun as she rocked, came about. Now her larboard broadside roared forth in a ragged volley. The stricken boats clumped together, those unhurt picking up survivors from the smashed craft. Trumpets sounded aboard the frigates. Their bow-chasers boomed out. One shot plumped into the galley's bow, crumpling her forward bulwarks and sending splinters flying.

"All hands to the oars! Give way!"

She shot down athwart the silvery moon lane, and leaped into speed. From the poop, O'Brien shook his fist at the three ships, whose bow-chasers roared with futile voice, and laughed as he sped away from them. The pursuit was checked, smashed, ended.

And the *Black Rose* headed down to pick up her consort.

Sunrise saw the two ships off Roxa Point, the Peak towering up into the sky behind, and a breeze coming down from the north. Three miles to larboard, coming past Grand Canary, was a large ship under jury rig. The frigate ran down and came close.

"Ahoy, Cap'n!" hailed St. Rocher. "Yonder's the *Bristol.* D'ye want her?"

"Nay, she's promised already!" and O'Brien laughed. "Give her three guns."

He brought the galley into the wind. In response to his order, St. Rocher sent over a boat which came aboard, and with his gangway still out, O'Brien ordered up Torres and his two officers. They came on deck, with all the fight taken out of them, for they had long since learned the truth of their position. Nor had Torres a word to say when he was shoved down into the boat with his officers, and O'Brien pointed to the *Bristol.*

"There's a craft will take you aboard," he called down. "Row for her! All right, men. Up wi' the canvas!"

The men toiled on the lines. The lateen sails bellied out to the breeze, and O'Brien looked back to see no sign of the squadron in pursuit. The thought of Sir Philip Boteler came to him, and he chuckled whimsically.

"After all, why worry about the rascal!" he reflected. "He'll have worse punishment ahead than if I'd hung him. But faith,

I'd give a fortune to be present when Shovell and the others learn the truth about him and me! Bosun, three guns for salute!"

The three guns crashed, and from the *Santa Trinidad* came three more. The two craft came side by side, and headed to the westward.

Behind, the master gunner of the *Bristol* answered their salute with a hail and farewell of five guns—navy style—and brought in his jury rig to pick up the small boat.

"Where bound, Master?" asked the boatswain curiously. O'Brien looked at him and laughed.

"For glory and the Spanish Main, Bosun!"

And as the word was passed on a cheer rippled along the deck.

VI

SIR BUCCANEER

A Novelette of the Sea Rovers.

UPON THE restless Caribbean was fallen a flat calm. The sea heaved slowly, monotonously, sullenly, like bluish molten glass under the white-hot sun of noon. Away in the north, like a purple cloud breaking the horizon, showed the mountaintops of Hispaniola. Not a breath of wind stirred. Not a catspaw ruffled the smooth, fiery blue water.

Yet, across that molten surface, a ship was moving, and moving rapidly. A strange sight, in this Year of Grace 1693, and in these waters. For she was, all too obviously, a galley of the Barbary rovers, and a double bank of oars drove her with a bone in her teeth. Drove her toward the helpless thing awaiting her, drove her relentlessly upon her prey. Nine guns to a side she showed, long Spanish culverins of glittering brass. And presently they began to speak, vomiting forth powder smoke that clung heavily to the water.

A stout ship was the Dutchman, stout and massive, with a score and more of heavy guns—but helpless for lack of wind. Smack under her stern lay the galley, and drove the heavy shot into her until her barred flag fluttered down.

Now, as it so happened, there were two other sail lying idle upon those waters. One, to the south, was the forty-gun frigate *Jacobus*, taken from the Spaniards by O'Brien, and in command of his very good friend Vicomte de St. Rocher; who, with his buccaneers, fired a gun of congratulation as they saw the Dutchman strike to O'Brien. And off to the northwest, where she had been following the Dutchman like a sullen hound until becalmed, lay a small brig—so small as to get scant notice from any, buccaneer or Dutch.

O'Brien boarded his prize. He was a slim, straight man, his bleached yellowish hair framing a thinly aquiline face, his blue eyes very level and unafraid and merry. Lace fell at wrists and throat, his blue suit of Genoa velvet was spotless, and the sun glinted from his diamond buckles as he bowed gravely to the men and women assembled on the quarterdeck.

"You are no Moor, sir!" said the Dutch captain, staring at him.

"The saints forbid!" exclaimed O'Brien, and laughed a little. "Tell your men to throw down their arms. No harm or insult comes to any of ye here, unless I desire prisoners. Your ship's lading is mine. Your private goods are your own. Your ship is mine as well, if I want her."

"And who may you be, sirrah?" said an angry man, stepping out and speaking in English.

O'Brien eyed him.

"I am Colonel James O'Brien, my good fellow. And you?"

"Sir Archibald Murray, newly appointed vice-governor of Jamaica, with express orders to hang all pestilent buccaneers, and chiefest among them one Colonel O'Brien. And how does that suit you?"

O'Brien looked at the hard eyed, thin lipped Murray and, seeing that the man feared him not, laughed in frank delight. He strode up to the other and clapped him on the shoulder.

"Aye, here's a dour Scot for ye! Come you and the master down below for a talk over a glass of wine." He turned, with an order to his men, who were by now swarming aboard. "Ho, lads! No private goods looted, no man to be harmed. Denis O'Neill, come aft with me and see to the lading and manifests. Ten men take charge of the quarterdeck and harm no one."

So they went down to the cabin, where O'Brien looked at the manifests and saw that his prize held little he desired, except for the minted dollars in the lazaret and certain shipments of arms below. Ordering O'Neill to break these out and leave the rest, he reached for his wine cup and lifted it.

"King James!" he exclaimed, and drank. "What, Murray? Ye'll not toast a Stuart?"

"Aye, the Stuart who sits in Whitehall," said Murray grimly. "Well, I've told ye what you'd ha' found out for yourself, so what about it?"

"I suppose you think I'll hang you, since your chief commission is to hang me?" O'Brien smiled whimsically. "Why so intent upon it, sir?"

The Dutch captain leaned forward and spoke earnestly, in broken French.

"It is his family, *M'sieu le Capitaine*. They are aboard, the lady and daughters, and he is a brave man."

O'Brien nodded and held out his hand to Murray with the warm friendliness that so lifted him into men's hearts.

"For this time there's truce between us, eh?" he said. "You'll go your ways and hang me if you can. I'll go mine and hang you next time we catch you. Agreed?"

"You mean it? Then with all my heart," said the Scot promptly. "What sort of buccaneer are you, O'Brien? You're not what we've heard, that's plain enough."

O'Brien shrugged.

"You'll find out, if our paths cross again. Today I'm bartering your lives and personal property for news from Europe. I've been on the Barbary coast and the Main for a long while. There's still war?"

"There always will be, aye," said Murray, gloom in his dour, sharp visage. "The Empire, England, Spain, Holland, all leagued against France—and damme if I can see aught in it for any one!"

When he had questioned them further, O'Brien lighted a pipe that the skipper furnished and nodded to the Scot.

"You have letters? Hand them over. I'll read and return them—aye, no matter how they speak of the pestilent buccaneer! Upon my honor, Murray."

It was a singular scene. Murray and the Dutch captain, finding their people unhurt or unmolested by the buccaneers, who were chiefly French and Jacobites, both English and Irish, watched O'Brien in no little amazement as he read their letters and handed them back. Time passed. Presently O'Neill appeared with a word to O'Brien.

"Everything's out of her we want, Cap'n. But that brig is coming up, fetching a wind."

O'Brien hastened on deck. He had learned, among other things, that the Dutchman had been part of a convoy bound for the West Indies, had been blown south and separated from the fleet, and his first thought was that the brig had come from the convoy also. She was approaching slowly, bringing a very light air with her.

"A filibustering rascal," said the Dutch captain. O'Brien shrugged.

"No danger from her."

"No danger?" repeated the other. "Wait till you see her vomit men and you'll change your mind! I'd sooner meet five hundred Spaniards than fifty buccaneers. Ye'll not hand us over to them, m'sieu?"

"Not I," said O'Brien, with a glance at the women clustered aft. "I'll detain her till you catch the breeze. After that, fight your own battle—you're well able. Make the Windward Passage and bear up for Jamaica. *Adios!*"

So he departed, and as he waved to them from the deck of the galley the women gave him a fluttering cheer and the Dutchmen swelled it to a roar of farewell.

O'Brien cast a glance to the southward where St. Rocher lingered helplessly, and headed his galley for the approaching brig.

M E N W E R E wetting down the topsails of the brig to catch the light air when O'Brien ran alongside after an exchange of hails. She carried close to three hundred men, as the Dutch master had predicted, but had only four small guns, being "found" for the Guadeloupe filibusters by M. de Choiseul of Basse Terre. They had yet to make an initial capture.

Their two leaders came aboard the galley, and O'Brien stood off for a little. The actual captain of the brig was one Chevalier de Beauchene—a huge, swarthy, violent man of Canadian origin, with a very thin veneer of gentility. Associated with him was one Morpain, an older man of considerable repute, small and restrained in speech, with a shrewd eye.

The two were filled with curiosity regarding the galley, and followed O'Brien down to the main cabin where a noonday meal was being set forth. They were amazed and a little awed by the profusion of white linen and silver dishes, by the deference of the servitors, and by the comfort and cleanliness of everything in sight. O'Brien, who had observed the wild savagery of the crowd aboard the brig, redoubled his politeness.

"*Ma foi, m'sieu,*" exclaimed the chevalier, "you live more like a king here than a democratic buccaneer!"

"No," said O'Brien. "I am a gentleman and live like one. Devil take all democrats!"

"Ah!" said Morpain. "I have it now. You are the O'Brien who killed Vernier and took his ship. I remember some of his men telling about it. Beauchene is just back from the south seas and Peru, with great tales of that coast."

Beauchene had tales, sure enough. He had been raiding New Spain with Watkins and the English buccaneers, and mouthed a story of massacre, obscenity and plunder. In the midst of his narrative he started up and went to the stern window.

"Hold! We must be after that Dutchman," he exclaimed. "The breeze is coming up. You are with us, m'sieu?"

"Not at all," said O'Brien coolly. "The Dutchman, as you observed, was boarded by me, and is now going his way under my safe-conduct. He's not worth your while."

"His ship is," said Morpain. "Come, M. O'Brien! You're not in earnest?"

O'Brien looked at the pair of them, with his thin smile.

"I gave you no safe-conduct aboard here, gentlemen," he said significantly.

There was a moment of silence, then Morpain spoke in his low voice.

"Oh, I catch your drift, O'Brien! You prefer to have us join you against that Spaniard to the south, eh? What do you say, Chevalier?"

Beauchene shrugged.

"Fair enough, by all means. Between us, we can handle her."

"Will you send a hail aboard your brig, then?" said O'Brien, chuckling.

The chevalier stamped to the deck, roared an order at his men, and the two craft headed toward the frigate, the galley slowly rowing along with the brig. O'Brien glanced out the stern window, saw the Dutchman catching the breeze and bearing away, and smiled to himself.

"You have a fine craft here," said Beauchene, "and well able to cope with the Spanish galleys along the coast; useful, too, in a calm. But what the devil! You'd never get free buccaneers to turn themselves into galley slaves."

"Proving the advantage of my discipline over your democracy," said O'Brien. "Well? Why are you two exchanging looks?"

Morpain laughed and nodded to the other, who spoke.

"Look you, m'sieu! We've caught drift of something worthwhile, but too hard for our teeth. A fisherman told us this morning that inside Saona Isle, up yonder at the tip of Hispaniola, there are two craft moored. They left San Domingo three days ago, but ran foul of one another in the night and put in under shelter of the isle to repair. They'll be there for a day or two. One is an English fifty-four, probably the *Yarmouth;* we heard she was newly come out to the Jamaica station, and has been cruising off Hispaniola. The other is our meat. She's a Panama galleon, blown away from the Plate Fleet during that storm of two weeks since, and put into San Domingo. No doubt the *Yarmouth* is convoying her on her way, or until they meet with some other ship to give her company to Cadiz. With this galley and our brig—are you game for the venture?"

O'Brien reflected. His own two craft were richly enough laden, for off Caracas he had picked up a Portuguese carrack fresh from the Indies. None the less, thought of a Panama galleon was arresting in its possibilities.

"You're mad," he answered slowly, puffing at his long pipe. "The *Yarmouth* would blow us both out of the water!"

"What about the Spaniard yonder?" said Beauchene eagerly. "We'll take her, and then bear up for Saona Isle. All we want is to lay alongside that galleon."

"Say you so?" responded O'Brien.

"Aye! And we must be closing with the Spaniard by this time. What say you?"

"Let's on deck, gentlemen."

The three came out on the quarterdeck of the galley, whose oars had been put up by this time, and her two lateen sails dropped to catch the freshening breeze. She had drawn well ahead of the brig and was holding straight for the frigate, now not a mile distant. Morpain caught the arm of O'Brien.

"Hold! Wait for our brig—tackle her together! She can't get away from us."

O'Brien turned to him, laughing a little.

"You mean your brig can't get away from her! Ho, there, O'Neill! Signal M. de St. Rocher to heave to and lower away a boat and come aboard."

The two buccaneers stood thunderstruck as they perceived the exchange of signals, and realized that this frigate was no prize for the taking, but in company with O'Brien. A new and splendid ship of forty guns, taken almost without a shot and little damaged, she made with the *Black Rose,* as the galley was named, a pair of fighting craft that might well go raiding down the mainland coast and singeing the beard of Spain, as O'Brien dreamed to do.

"If you mean to nip our brig," said Beauchene sullenly, "you'll get naught but hard knocks, I warn you."

O'Brien clapped him on his hulking shoulders.

"Here comes St. Rocher, and if he says the word we'll nip the galleon—but on my own terms, mind you. So chew on that awhile, my fighting cocks! My terms."

St. Rocher, tall and dark and saturnine, was coming in a boat that danced across the freshening seas. The brig luffed uncertainly, but Beauchene waved her on and then fell into talk with the old filibuster by the rail.

When St. Rocher came over the rail O'Brien welcomed him eagerly.

"Swing in your boat and come along, Vicomte. Tell you later about the Dutchman. Here's something else again. Chevalier!"

St. Rocher was presented, and the four of them returned to

the cabin, where O'Brien set the tale of the galleon before his companion.

"There's the lay of it," he concluded, "and I'll leave the answer to you, for the *Jacobus* is your own ship, my friend. If you'd not risk her, small blame to you."

"What's worth having is worth risking," and St. Rocher showed his white teeth in his reckless smile. "I say yes!"

O'Brien turned to the two filibusters.

"Agreed, gentlemen. Now listen to my terms. I'm to be in command; you're to lead your men under my orders, whether ye like 'em or not. And when it comes to looting the galleon, I'm to have first say as to my share o' the spoil, whether it be half the proceeds or what-not; I'll ask no more than half, mayhap not that much. Last, there's to be no killing except in fight, no ransoming of prisoners without my consent; and as there may be women aboard the galleon, I'll say now that they're not to be touched."

Beauchene leaped to his feet angrily.

"Death of my life!" he roared, passion swelling in his eyes. "Impossible! It's filibuster law that everything be sold at the mainmast. As for the ship, she must be taken into Basse Terre and sold, for the Admiralty gets a tenth part. I'll have none of your terms!"

O'Brien gestured ironic assent.

"Very well. Then go your ways—and we'll take the galleon without you."

The shrewder Morpain intervened and argued his companion into compliance. There was, in fact, nothing to do but accept the terms laid down, or else be left out of it; so that presently they were going aboard the brig to put the matter to the vote of their men. At the rail, awaiting the agreed signal from them, O'Brien told St. Rocher about the loot of the Dutchman and what happened aboard her.

"If you agree," he went on, "it's in my mind to leave the galley standing off and on, and walk in on the galleon with the frigate and brig. We'll be proud Spaniards and can fool these British well enough. We need not visit the galleon until we're ready to take her. There's a good breeze coming up and we should reach the isle before dark."

"Agreed," said St. Rocher simply. "There's the signal."

The galley swung in close to the brig, into whose chains leaped Beauchene.

"Are ye meaning to go straight in and board them?" he demanded.

"Not unless I have to," rejoined O'Brien, while the savage, unkempt men aboard the other craft eyed him in wonder. They were little better than wild beasts of the sea, those men, and looked the part. "I'll take the frigate in. You follow, with only a dozen men showing on deck. I'll say you're a prize. They'll take us for Spaniards. During the night we'll walk off with the galleon. Understand?"

The buccaneers yelled wild approval, for this sort of strategy was new to them. They had no equals at seamanship, and once aboard an enemy their wild ferocity bore down all opposition; but all their tactics consisted in a straight and savage combat.

So it was settled, and all three craft trimmed sail for Saona Isle, to the northeast. When they raised the land, most of O'Brien's hundred men were shifted aboard the frigate, leaving only enough to work the galley, and the *Jacobus*, to all appearance a stately Spanish ship, hoisted the white banner with the arms of Spain, and held in for the isle and the cape behind. But little did O'Brien dream of what destiny there lay in wait to snare him.

JUST INSIDE the long Saona Isle, whose trees cut off any view of the sea, the *Yarmouth* lay anchored, her men spending most of their time ranging the sandy shore or hunting wild cattle along the edge of the savanna. The *Santa Maria*, a glorious but unwieldy creature all scarlet and gold and blue, towered above her.

Bluff Captain Killigrew, a nephew of the admiral of that

name, was on courteous but not too intimate terms with the Spaniards, whom he distrusted as allies and disdained as seamen. Here he was right enough. The sailing master of the *Santa Maria* had died en route from Panama, and her titular captain, the Conde de San Lucar, was a very gallant soldier but a very poor ship's master. However, with help from the *Yarmouth* he managed to get his smashed rudder post repaired and his riven bowsprit spliced.

"Sink me," said Killigrew to his officers, "if I can see how the Dons could smash up both ends of a ship at once! And never hurt us by so much as a scratch."

O'Brien did not walk in upon his prey by any means, for Killigrew had men on watch and came out stripped for action to meet him; but with the Spanish frigate had come the allied signals, so the courteous guns of salute rolled, and Killigrew put back into the shelter of the island with the *Jacobus* following and the little brig trailing her. There was no lack of Spanish garments aboard the frigate, and presently O'Brien lowered the barge and was rowed over to the *Yarmouth* to dine with Killigrew, his men hailing the galleon in right good Spanish as they passed.

Twenty-four men in the world had the right to wear the collar of the Toison d'Or, and O'Brien was not one of them; but he wore the Fleece none the less, the golden drop on its pink ribbon standing out against his slashed black velvet. This, too, had come to him with the frigate from the Duke de Torres. Daylight was still lingering when he passed aboard the *Yarmouth,* sending back his boat lest unwittingly the men betray the imposture.

He bowed low to Killigrew and the gathered officers, and spoke in English.

"Gentlemen, it gives me great pleasure to meet with you. I learned at San Domingo that you were here, for fishermen had brought in word, and I came in order to relieve you of the galleon yonder," and he smiled cheerfully as he said this.

"Sink me!" exclaimed Killigrew. "You speak English well, Señor Don!"

"Was I not a captive in your charming country for two years?" said O'Brien. "But I forget. I am the Duke de Torres, and yonder is a rascally filibustering brig which I took on the way hither today."

Killigrew introduced himself and his officers, and O'Brien was escorted below to where the punchbowl was brewing and dinner presently to be served. Within the space of a drink or two O'Brien was a prime favorite with all present—accounted for, he said, by his Irish blood. Not a few nobles of Spain but could boast it.

"Aye, he's right," spoke up the jolly chaplain. "D'ye mind, Captain Killigrew, the great lady aboard the galleon, who speaks English? Ye should have invited her and the count over, sink me if ye shouldn't!"

"Not to mention the two señoritas!" said another. Killigrew grew red in the face.

"Damme, gentlemen! I'll thank you to know that I'm aware of whom I want here, and no rascally Spaniard—oh, devil take it! Your pardon, Señor Don—"

O'Brien broke into hearty laughter and slapped Killigrew on the back.

"Faith, here's to the king, gentlemen! Whether he be your king or my king, it's all one among friends. Who's the lady ye mention aboard the galleon?"

"Sink me to hell if I can think of her name," said the blunt captain. "Her husband was some big noble in New Spain—a viceroy, didn't they say? Anyhow, he's dead, and she's a rare one. None of your affected court beauties, and not a day over thirty-five. She's from some great Irish family—what's the name of it, Dillon? You know all those barbaric names."

"O'Donnell," said the laughing lieutenant. "She's from the O'Donnells. And, gentlemen, that's the same in Ireland as the Plantagenets in England, no less!"

"True for you!" exclaimed O'Brien. "Only better, praise be. Your health, gentlemen! I've been at wars too long to have much courtly polish left, so I don't mind saying it's lucky I'm aboard here, rather than the galleon yonder."

"Luckier than you know," said Killigrew with a wry face. "This Count of San Lucar is a great gentleman and all that, but a cursed poor sailor, and devilish bad company. He's not a friend of yours, maybe? No offense intended."

"Never heard of him before," said O'Brien truthfully. "I'm fresh from the Canaries and have never seen New Spain. Have you had any news of the pirate O'Brien?"

"He's not been heard of for months," returned Killigrew, "but when he turns up he'll be hanged. Every ship on the station is watching out for him; the coastguard galleys as well. A special vice-governor is coming out, I've heard, to hunt down O'Brien and get rid of him."

O'Brien lifted his glass.

"All luck to him, then!"

"To whom—O'Brien or the vice-governor?" spoke up Dillon with a laugh. The blue eyes of O'Brien twinkled merrily at him.

"Ye'll know before morning, I hope. What's this—dinner? An honest roastbeef dinner; so you've been killing wild cattle ashore, eh? Bucan some of it over a woodfire, then you'll be a buccaneer and on even terms with O'Brien if you meet him—"

So they drank and jested, and one and all vowed that this Spanish nobleman was the most gallant gentleman they had ever known. After dinner came a boat from St. Rocher with a great hamper of Spanish wines out of the frigate, and all must needs sample them, and after that was the usual Saturday night punch of navy custom, for the morrow was Sunday. What with one thing and another, most of the gentlemen were under the table when O'Brien took his leave toward midnight.

He seemed sober enough, however, and they remembered afterward that he paused at the gangway and asked when came the turn of the tide here.

"The next ebb, your Worship," answered the sailing master, "will come at two in the morning. And your ship has swung in upon us, master."

"She'll be far from you with morning," said O'Brien, and went down to his boat.

It was not by chance, however, that the *Jacobus* had swung in upon her hawser, so that she lay squarely athwart the bow of the frigate, nor that a kedge had been put out astern to hold her there.

Across and in toward the mainland shore was moored the galleon, and close to her the brig had dropped anchor. St. Rocher had his orders, so O'Brien went directly aboard the brig, sending the boat after the dozen men from his own crew who were to join him. He found the hatches off and the decks aswarm with men sleeping under the stars. Chevalier de Beauchene met him as he came over the side.

"All well, m'sieu?"

"Perfect," said O'Brien cheerfully. "Two in the morning. We'll sleep until then. Have you picked out the men and assigned them to their places?"

"Everything arranged, mon ami."

"Then I'll stretch out on the deck for an hour. When my men come, let them join me."

As he lay there, looking up at the silent stars, with the snores of sleeping men from the decks and hold, there stole the tinkle of a lute from the high stern windows of the galleon close by. A voice came to him, a slow, faint voice singing Irish words of an old song his nurse had sung to him many a time in the far days of childhood; and it drifted again to him now so that he came to one elbow, incredulous, listening:

"The rose that you gave
Is withered and dead;
Yet even in death
It brings me a breath
Of the sweetness I crave—

Though its beauty be fled."

And suddenly, as the lute tinkled on, impulse seized O'Brien. He lifted his voice softly and carried the Irish words of the little song, as though there were no peril or watchers around, nor cursing buccaneers nor wondering Spaniards, but only some one yonder in the towering gilded poop of the galleon to hear his words:

> "The love that you gave
> Abides with me yet.
> You have perished, men say;
> What knowledge have they?
> I know that the grave
> Can not make you forget."

The lute ceased its tinkle. Somewhere a man laughed, another cursed. Beauchene came aft to where O'Brien lay and stopped beside him.

"Are you mad?" he demanded fiercely. "Your men are here."

"Mad? Of course," and O'Brien laughed. "All Irishmen are mad, my friend. Did my men bring my sword with them? Good. Send them along, and do you see that your sea wolves carry no pistols. Cold steel and naught else."

And presently, with his dozen men around him, he was sleeping, dreaming still of the voice that drifted across the water in ancient Irish words.

WERE THIS a tale of the galleon's taking only, much might be made of it; but there was destiny here, hidden behind Saona Isle, for a deal more was to come of the whole affair than was spelled in the tale of blood and loot.

From the moment he cast anchor, O'Brien's plan had been clear cut in every detail and of the utmost simplicity. It was carried out with a beautiful precision—thanks largely to the fact that St. Rocher had carefully laid every gun of the frigate's broadside.

At two in the morning, with the tide just on the ebb, the brig moved silently. A swimmer, unseen, had bent on a line to the hawser of the galleon, and she was almost alongside before a startled Spaniard realized the fact and hailed. Grappling irons were flung; a moment later men were swarming over the galleon's high side, spreading to their stations, cutting down all whom they encountered. Almost before the first alarm yells had died, the deck was theirs. The hatches were clapped on, the cables were slipped or hacked asunder, and scores of men were aloft, loosing the sails to catch the offshore breeze. Galleon and brig, grappled together, moved out on the ebb tide.

Behind them trumpets and drums waked wild echoes from the shores about, battle lanterns sprang alight, the *Yarmouth* shrilled to a boatswain's whistle. St. Rocher, aboard the *Jacobus*, gave the word, and slow-matches glimmered. Gun after gun vomited flame; crash upon crash reechoed from the hapless king's ship. Down came the tophamper, bags of bullets cut the rigging to shreds, laying spars and canvas across the deck, cloaking guns and passage. She lay there crippled and helpless in the starlight, while the frigate went out in stately silence upon the tide, with none to follow.

And later, when he came into Kingston harbor, Captain Killigrew would compare notes with Sir Archibald Murray, and curse the very name of Colonel James O'Brien.

Dawn found Hispaniola a shadow to the northwest, the *Black Rose* galley two miles to starboard, St. Rocher in the van, and the galleon lumbering along with the brig grinding against her counter. O'Brien sent the men to the lines, and brought the great ship into the wind, and set about his work. He was on the poop with his own men, Beauchene and Morpain with him. The frantic hammerings on cabin doors and hatches had long since died away into silence.

Over three hundred Spaniards, soldiers and sailors, were battened below. When the way was cleared, they came up with pike and fusil and sword to meet swinging cutlasses; and when a dozen of them had tumbled below again no more poured up. Instead, came shouts, to which the buccaneers answered, and presently the Spaniards came up two by two, without arms, as ordered.

O'Brien went forward. When the first pair of Spaniards appeared a blood spattered Frenchman leaped, and one of the two fell with a split head. O'Brien's long rapier flickered in the gray light and drove through the buccaneer's throat. There was a growl and a yell, as the circle of savage men faced him.

"Disobedience is death," said O'Brien coolly. "Right or wrong, my lads?"

"Right!" yelled a voice, and the curses died away in wild disputing.

Thereafter his orders met with no protest, and the Spaniards came up unharmed and were sent into the brig. Long ere it was finished, the buccaneers were at their looting.

O'Brien came back to the lower poop, and the door leading into the main cabin was unbarred. The sun was just rising over the eastern sea rim. Into the open doorway, blinking at them, came a Spaniard in half-armor, rapier in hand, a man whose jet beard and arrogant features, no less than his splendid attire, proclaimed his rank.

"What means this, dogs?" he exclaimed in French.

"It means what you will, señor," returned O'Brien in stately Castilian. "I am Colonel O'Brien, and your ship is mine. Hand over your sword, you and those men behind you. I offer you your lives and freedom within the hour."

"San Lucar does not surrender," said the other in proud scorn. Though he must have seen the numbers of the buccaneers now flooding hastily aft, and that his ship was utterly lost, it all mattered no whit to him. "Filibusters, eh? By the saints! Come, señores, cut down these dogs—"

"One moment!" snapped O'Brien. "Stop and think, fool! The ship's mine. If you have women to defend, they shall not be harmed, upon my honor—"

The only answer of San Lucar was to step forward and let

drive with his rapier—a deadly soldier's blade which O'Brien barely caught with his own.

"All right, fool," said he, lunging in. "If you'll have it, then take it!"

Yell upon yell went up; not so easily was San Lucar brought down, for he had survived many a stricken field in New Spain, and knew his business. Twice his corselet saved him from O'Brien's point. The big galleon rolled and dipped suddenly, and San Lucar lost his balance. O'Brien drew back a pace.

"Your last chance, señor! I would not kill a brave man—"

With a snarling oath, the Spaniard's blade drove in. At the same instant, some one in the passage behind him fired a pistol, whose ball sang past the face of O'Brien. That was the last San Lucar saw of the bright sunlight, for he caught at his throat, and the blood gushed over his hands as he fell.

With that the giant Beauchene was rushing headlong into the passage, cutlass a-swing.

Men fell there and asked no quarter—Spanish officers of the ship and of the soldiers aboard. In the passage was hot work, savage work. Presently O'Brien came into the main cabin, and his dozen men choked the passage behind, as he had ordered them, so that the buccaneers could not follow.

Here, in the huge cabin with carved and gilded walls, Beauchene and Morpain, with a pair of their men, were joined by O'Brien. Facing them were two wounded officers, swords in hand, and behind them three stern eyed friars, unarmed. Crowded behind these, again, were half a dozen women.

Beauchene hurled himself at the two officers. One he cut down. The other wounded him, but fell to the back sweep of the crimsoned cutlass. A wild shriek burst from the women as Beauchene swung his weapon to strike down the foremost friar—and then one of those women had leaped out before the three friars, facing the savage buccaneer, a poniard in her hand.

"Stop!" she ordered, a ring of authority in her voice. "Are you a mad dog, not knowing whom you bite?"

Beauchene checked his blow and laughed wildly as he gazed upon her. O'Brien gazed too, but he did not laugh. Instead, a flame came into his heart, and his blue eyes leaped, and something sang in his pulses. He knew this was the woman who had sung in the night.

She was neither tall nor short, but held her head very high, and when one looked into her eyes it became clear that she had not been one of those who screamed, for there shone in them as it were the flash of a sword. About her head was bound red gold hair, though her brows were dark. Her face held an eagerness beyond words, that gave even the wild Beauchene pause. Then, with another laugh, he feinted—and struck the poniard from her hand and caught her by the wrist.

Just then the point of O'Brien's rapier touched his throat, so that he looked sidelong and met the blue eyes—and loosed his grasp.

"I am master here, not you," said O'Brien. "Step back."

Those blue eyes chilled the man's passion. He saw Morpain and his pair of rascals at one side, and he saw two of O'Brien's men with pistols ready, and he lowered his blade.

"God save all here!" said O'Brien in Irish, stepping past Beauchene, and then spoke in Spanish. "There is nothing to fear. Your lives are safe; you, padres, will escort these women into the boat alongside, where your men are waiting for you. All, that is, save this one woman."

He met the proud eyes of the woman before him, and then Beauchene uttered a wild oath.

"Aye, and what's this now? You said no woman molested—and if there's any to be glutted here, it's me and not you!"

For an instant longer O'Brien looked into the woman's eyes, then he turned and looked at Beauchene and stood laughing a little.

"Have you forgot our bargain, Chevalier?" he said mockingly. "I call Morpain yonder to witness it. First share of the spoil to me, not to exceed a full half. Aye, Morpain?"

"That is so, Cap'n," said Morpain, but his hand was at the knife in his belt.

"Then," said O'Brien, speaking now in Spanish that all might understand, "I claim this woman and all her possessions aboard this galleon, as my share; and with it, a full third of whatever treasure may be aboard, for my men. The rest is yours, Chevalier."

"Oh!" said Beauchene, with a grunt of surprise. He looked suspiciously at O'Brien. "No trick to this, is there?"

O'Brien bowed to him gravely.

"Upon my honor, none. This woman stays here, or rather, she comes aboard my ship, with all her belongings. The others go in safety aboard the brig, to sail whither they will; you'll put water and stores aboard her to last the crowd. You will sail this ship to Basse Terre with your men, and Captain Morpain yonder will be my agent to see that I am not cheated in the division of the spoil. You will so honor me, m'sieu?"

"With all my heart, monsieur," said the astonished Morpain, amazed and flattered that O'Brien should so trust him.

"Then let's be about it, and no more time wasted," said O'Brien, and sheathed his rapier. He turned to the passage and called in Irish, "Ho, there! To me, all O'Brien's men!"

They came crowding in, and he swept off his hat to the lady with the red hair.

"Give these men your orders," he said, and saw in her face that she understood the Irish words. "Let them make ready all your goods to go aboard my ship, for here you are among wild beasts. Do you understand me, daughter of the O'Donnells?"

"Surely you are the Red Earl come to life again!" she replied. "You have the face and the eyes of his portrait that was in my father's hall—good. I agree. Come with me, you men."

They went, for they were all Irish picked for their loyalty by O'Brien, and she led them into one of the cabins. Chevalier de Beauchene looked after her darkly.

"By my faith," he said, "I am not sure but that woman is worth more than a third of this ship's plunder!"

O'Brien laughed at this, and escorted the friars and women to the deck, with two or three officers who had been only wounded. The women cried out at him, and one of the stern friars demanded what would become of the marquesa.

"Suffice it to know she will not be harmed," said O'Brien, and had them put aboard the brig.

Marquesa, eh? Of the O'Donnell blood, too. He had heard often of the Flight of the Earls, seventy years ago—how O'Neill and O'Donnell had fled away out of Ireland to Spain, dying there or in Rome, and their houses perishing with them. And he was like Red Hugh's portrait, was he? Men had said that same thing ere this, how like he was to the Red Earl, the greatest Tyrone of them all. Some trend of O'Neill blood in him, perhaps. What matter now?

So, with a shrug, O'Brien had a signal made, and St. Rocher came in person with the boat for him, mounting on the galleon's deck and looking about. The brig had cast off and was heading northward again toward Hispaniola.

"I have sad news for you, old friend," said O'Brien, his eyes dancing. "I've claimed a third of the treasure aboard here, if there is any, for you and the men. For myself, I've claimed a woman."

"Yes, a likely tale," said St. Rocher with a careless laugh, and glanced aft. "You've been through the cabins? There'll be pearls from Panama and Caracas, beyond doubt—"

"Nay, I'm in earnest," broke in O'Brien. "We've plunder enough aboard our own craft to serve me. Morpain will act as our agent here, and I think honestly. But here she comes, and our men with her. We lost not a man in taking the craft, by the way, though I slew one of these savages. Madame, may I present my friend and comrade, Vicomte de St. Rocher? He'll take us aboard my own ship, where we may break our fast with more pleasure than here."

As he was speaking, the woman with the red-gold hair came from the after cabins toward them, followed by O'Brien's men carrying packages and trunks. A cloak was wrapped about her, but St. Rocher could only stare until he recollected himself, and bowed over the hand she extended to him. Then her violet eyes turned to O'Brien.

"They are pillaging in there," she said. "Should you not join them?"

"I have plundered all the world in finding you," said O'Brien. "May I hand you into the boat, or shall I carry you down the ladder? It is a long way down."

"Hell is farther," said she, with a silvery laugh. "I am able enough."

And refusing aid, she passed down the ladder herself, though it was no easy matter. St. Rocher looked at O'Brien and swallowed hard, then shrugged and followed in silence.

NO WORD was exchanged until they sat in the cabin of the *Black Rose,* though a smile touched the lips of the woman as she heard the galley's name. Wine and bread were set before them, and O'Brien saw that she looked very sharply at the man who bore it—an old man who had served in the Irish Brigade and in Flanders in times past.

"Wait," she said, as he was withdrawing, and she spoke in Irish. "Is your name Turlough, by any chance, once called Turlough of the Black Eyes?"

The man looked at her; his jaw fell and his hands shook a little.

"By the Rock of Doon!" said he, staring. "None has called me by that name in thirty years and more, since I was servant to the O'Donnell in Madrid!"

"Twenty years," said she, and laughed. "Twenty years ago you were my father's servant, Turlough of the Black Eyes—"

The old man fell on his knees to her, and tears leaped to his cheeks, and O'Brien had to put him out of the cabin by force.

But she looked at him and at St. Rocher and smiled as she broke bread with them.

"Well?" she said. "I know you not, nor you me—"

"I heard a voice in the night across the water," said O'Brien quietly, "and had need to know no more. But I know you are a daughter of the O'Donnells, and that is enough."

"I have a Spanish name, and it is not badly regarded in Spain," she said, "but we will not mention it here. Once I was called Roisin, Little Rose; that's name enough. And when I saw you in that cabin, and you like the picture of the Red Earl, Hugh Ruadh, it was enough."

St. Rocher understood, for they spoke English. He reached out for a pipe from the rack and stuffed tobacco into it.

"I think both of you are stark mad," he said gravely.

"What right has this man to think?" said Roisin, regarding him.

"The right of my friend for many years, and my comrade," said O'Brien. At this, Roisin put out her hand to that of St. Rocher and smiled in her eager, lively manner.

"You should have said that in the first place, O'Brien—but I remember now, you did. The fault is my own."

St. Rocher blinked a little.

"But—what the devil?" he exclaimed, with a helpless gesture. "Why is she here, Jack? Let's be blunt about it; I must get back to the frigate. Are you taking her to Basse Terre?"

"That depends on her," said O'Brien. "Faith, I don't know."

"I think you do know," she said suddenly, and rose. "And if you don't, I do. I'll go out and speak with old Turlough and leave you to talk it over."

When the door shut behind her St. Rocher swore fervently.

"I don't know what to make of it," he said. "Look here! I know well enough you're no man for wenches; you never look twice at a woman. You seem to have gone mad; what's worse, she seems mad also. Are you bewitched!"

O'Brien held a coal to his pipe.

"St. Rocher, it's past explanation. I'd bid any other man to the devil; but I'll tell you the truth. That woman and I will go to the end of the world together. Don't get me amiss, my friend. It's no business of man and woman, of two sexes merely. Well ye know I had a wife once, and loved her, and lost her. This is something else again. Something bigger and deeper. There's an understanding between us, and no word spoken."

"Aye," said St. Rocher. "But I take it she's a great woman in Spain. She'll not be able to forget it and to be comrades with a buccaneer, if that's what ye mean. Devil fly away with me! She's too fine a woman to be dragged down. Ye must not let her be carried away—"

He frowned savagely at O'Brien, but the latter broke into a peal of laughter.

"Oh, man, man! Can ye not see that it's a joy to be in her hand. She's a comrade, aye. All her past life is broken and laid away like a cloth folded on a shelf."

"What?" said the other, glowering. "Will she wear boots and small clothes?"

O'Brien laughed till the tears came to his eyes, then sobered, suddenly.

"She'll wear the heart's devotion of every man aboard here," he said gravely. "And she'll carry me to hell or heaven, and I her, and that's the whole of it."

St. Rocher nodded thoughtfully, laid down his pipe and rose.

"It's one of two things," he said. "Either you're raving mad, or else fate has come into your life. I'll think it over between here and Basse Terre. *Adios!*"

He saluted Roisin as he went to the ladder, and so was gone aboard his own ship, and the three vessels headed together toward Guadeloupe.

On sober reflection, O'Brien thought that he might be a little mad indeed, but as the days drew on he found otherwise, and became convinced that he was remarkably sane. Long before the peaks of Basse Terre broke the horizon, he had found his first impulses confirmed and strengthened into solidity. Between himself and this woman was friendship and something deeper, beyond words, which he could not explain or analyze. It was as though the same eager spirit lived in them both, and had united them.

As for the past, that was cleared away between them and then left for the dead to bury their dead. The Marquesa de Guimares had left a son in Spain, and a husband in New Spain, but it was the son whose memory chiefly lingered; here, as she said, was life to be begun anew, and happiness for the first time in twenty years, and freedom. And if there was any more than this in the hearts of either of them, it did not come to the surface or reveal itself.

O'Brien, in truth, had found something to live for, and the old gods were dead. If he had wanted gold, there was plenty of that aboard his two ships, and he cared nothing about the galleon's freight. While Roisin had gold and jewels to spare in her trunks, and great wealth in Spain if she wanted it. What was more to the point, he found her at one with him in his search, his questing beyond the horizon. She talked with him of Caracas and raids on the Brazilian coast beyond, and the keen thrill of adventuring drew them both—not what might be had from the venture. So, for the first time, Colonel James O'Brien found himself all aflame with what lay in the future.

So they came into Basse Terre, and let Beauchene lead the way in the galleon, with great saluting of guns and blazing of trumpets. Because of a certain relationship between the O'Donnells and the O'Briens, it was not amiss that the marquesa should be presented to the governor as O'Brien's cousin. She made it plain to all that, while she might accept a house ashore and the women slaves that were offered her, when O'Brien sailed again she would sail with him; and the officers and planters who looked into her eyes thought nothing strange in this, for Guadeloupe lived a merry, happy life wherein criticism of others played no part. Indeed, it was Madame de

Choiseul herself, a relative of Pontchartrain, who took the marquesa under her wing.

NEXT DAY St. Rocher came aboard the galley and wakened O'Brien, who was sleeping after dancing and gambling at the governor's house till late in the night.

"Wake up and to business, Jack," he said. "I've been at work this morning. Owing to his connection with Pontchartrain, this M. de Choiseul is the real power in these parts. He's offered to get us letters of marque from the governor, which puts us safely inside the piracy pale. Yes or no?"

"Yes, of course," said O'Brien. "Turlough! Where the devil is my morning draft?"

"Here's the cup, so put it down," said St. Rocher. "Now, clear your head and listen. The island's full of filibusters, French and English, and all of them begging to come aboard us. Say the word, and we can take on a couple of hundred men, which will put the *Jacobus* on a fighting basis."

"Leave that to me," said O'Brien. "Faith, you have the energy of the devil this morning! Yes, I'll ship men, if they suit me. Why not? We need them. By the way, do you still think I'm a madman?"

St. Rocher shrugged in his saturnine fashion.

"My brain says you are. My heart says you're the luckiest man in this world, and here's my hand on it."

"Well said." And O'Brien gripped his hand.

Turlough knocked and came in.

"Your Honors, there's a man come aboard to speak with Captain St. Rocher."

"Send him in."

A little man clad in black entered and bowed low, and asked whether he were speaking with M. Philippe Jean Paul Asseline, Vicomte de St. Rocher.

"You are," said St. Rocher, laughing. "Though how you ferreted out my full name is more than I can see."

"Then, m'sieu, I beg to present the compliments of my master, M. Cassat, avocat, who lives at the third house up the street from the wine shop of the Laughing Nymphs. He requests that you call upon him at the first occasion befitting your convenience, upon a matter of most urgent importance."

"Eh?" St. Rocher stared at him. "What have I to do with an avocat? What's the business?"

The lawyer's clerk spread his hands in air.

"But, m'sieu, how should I know? I have a boat waiting, and if you would honor me with your company—"

"Very well," said St. Rocher, and at this O'Brien leaped out of bed.

"Wait a moment, and I'll go ashore with you. Better be getting some of those men signed up, or at least spread the word. What's all the noise on deck?"

St. Rocher chuckled.

"The hatches are off and our lading is going ashore, with merchants fighting to get it. You'd better keep your eye on that galleon, also, for those rascals are sending barges of loot ashore, I hear."

"To the devil with the galleon," said O'Brien, hurrying into his clothes.

He found the whole island in turmoil, indeed. What with the rich lading of three ships coming ashore, all sorts of fantastic tales about the galleon and her cargo of gold, and the sale of the galleon herself, according to filibustering rules, the harbor and town was filled with hurrying men and rushing boats and staring folk.

Applying himself to business, O'Brien did not see St. Rocher again until late in the afternoon, when he came back to the galley. He found that he could get a full crew for both craft without the least trouble, and spent a pleasant hour with Roisin and Madame de Choiseul. No sooner had he regained the *Black Rose* than St. Rocher hurriedly joined him from the frigate and waved aside all his questions.

"Come below, Jack. I have news for you."

Wondering at the unaccustomed gravity of his friend, O'Brien assented. Once in the cabin, St. Rocher closed the door.

"Jack, may I take this galley for a trip to Martinique?"

"Aye," said O'Brien. "It's yours as much as mine. What's up?"

St. Rocher exploded with laughter, caught him by the arms, hugged him with sudden exuberance.

"My faith, Jack! Over at Martinique everything's waiting for me—the governor there has documents, everything! You remember I've told you of that rascally old uncle of mine? He's gone, and look at me! The Marquis de Manneville, no less, lord of high and middle justice, of waters and forests, and the fairest lands in all Touraine! Fortune comes all at once, showers us with favor to repletion—"

O'Brien shouted his delight, called for wine, then bore St. Rocher ashore to celebrate in more fitting fashion. Yet, within himself he knew that St. Rocher was gone forever from his company.

With morning, St. Rocher took the emptied galley and departed, mustering a crew from ashore. O'Brien moved into the *Jacobus* with his own men, most of whom were engaged in wild carousal ashore; and, between shipping a full complement and getting the plunder ashore, was a busy man.

He remained busy during the following days, also. As his own business came to a close, he recollected the galleon, and set out to find Beauchene. In this he had small trouble, and found the chevalier and Morpain together, shortly after they had concluded the sale of the galleon. They greeted him none too warmly, but Morpain had been honest enough in the matter, and turned over bills of exchange to a staggering sum. Beauchene, who with his men had been made rich enough to buy half the island, put down the flagon of wine and looked hard at O'Brien.

"I am leaving tonight in a brig outfitting up the coast," he said. "I am taking her out on a trial cruise. Do you wish to go as my lieutenant?"

"Thank you, I have other business," said O'Brien, reading hostility in the man but not comprehending it.

"So I have heard," said Beauchene, and laughed. "How about taking your fine frigate and cruising in company with me?"

Seeing that the man was leading up to something, O'Brien drove in ahead of him.

"I don't care for your company, Chevalier," he said coolly. "To tell the truth, it rather pollutes the air—"

With a roar of rage, Beauchene was on his feet, knife lashing out. O'Brien hit him across the face with a pewter mug and dropped him with the blood spurting. A crowd intervened hastily, and Morpain drew O'Brien aside.

"You'll have to meet him for this, m'sieu. To be frank, it is a question of a lady—"

"I will not," said O'Brien, with a shrug. "I meet whom I choose. If he bothers me again, I'll kill him. So let it lie at that."

He went his ways, but the affair had turned him a little sick, and when he met the healing warmth of Roisin's eyes, he felt impelled to get away from this place, out of it all.

"What say you, Roisin?" he exclaimed on impulse. "When St. Rocher will be back, is hard to tell. Shall we slap a crew aboard the *Jacobus* and take her for a cruise? We might go to meet St. Rocher, for that matter—anything to be away from here, out to sea!"

"When?" was all she said.

"Tomorrow noon."

"Agreed, Shamus."

O'Brien hastened back to the frigate, picked Denis O'Neill for lieutenant, and sent him to fetch men aboard.

All that night they poured in, and some of them O'Brien took, but more he did not. English there were plenty, and he took these rather than French or Spanish, for the filibusters were drawn from all races. Ere midnight he had a full two hundred men aboard, had appointed his officers, and had only stores and fresh water to get aboard with morning. His letters of marque had already been sent down from the governor's house.

Of Beauchene he heard nothing more, except that the man had left to take out his new brig.

So it happened that with the next day O'Brien found himself sailing out of Basse Terre again. Roisin stood beside him on the poop, and not in boots and small clothes either, but wrapped in a gorgeous cloak of crimson and gold that became her handsomely. When the salutes had ceased reechoing and the *Jacobus* was standing out, O'Brien turned to her and smiled.

"Off, Little Rose! We'll meet St. Rocher and the galley, and make our plans for Caracas and the Brazil coasts, eh?"

"Perchance," she said. "And perchance things will turn out otherwise, Shamus. It is in my mind that destiny is hard upon you and upon us all, but I do not know why I think so."

O'Brien laughed a little at this saying, but he remembered it two mornings afterward.

UPON THE third morning out from Basse Terre, a crepitation of gunfire came rolling down the sea.

Whence it came was hard to say. A light air filled the topsails of the *Jacobus*, but close to the water clung the mist of morning, rolling heavily along the waves. The guns came again; this time in a full throated broadside that came with shattering effect through the mist. O'Brien went hastily up the rigging at a call from the man on lookout in the top.

There, above the worst of the cloaking vapors, he sighted the topsails of a ship dead ahead, and not half a mile distant. Then they were gone in a swirl of white. He focused his glass on the point, and after a moment was rewarded as the mist opened out for a moment and gave him full sight of what was passing there.

An exclamation burst from him. There were two vessels—a small brig, turning in frantic flight, no doubt a filibuster; and behind her, with foremast down and a wild tangle of spars and canvas over her foredeck, a frigate which O'Brien recognized at a glance. She was the *Yarmouth*, now repaired and refitted, her canvas glittering new and white.

"Killigrew, as I live!" exclaimed O'Brien, as the mist closed down upon the scene once more. "And if only Sir Archibald Murray is aboard her—ha!"

He descended to the deck. Easy enough to guess what had happened. Some French buccaneer had run foul of the *Yarmouth*, or had mistaken her in the mist for a merchantman, and in swift panic had slapped a ragged fire into her, then taking a full crashing broadside as she went veering away. But she had left the frigate crippled, unable to pursue.

"And now, egad, I have her!" he exclaimed eagerly, as he told Roisin and O'Neill what he had seen. "Killigrew's helpless, he can't maneuver, and the mist is going off to the eastward. The wind's freshening fast. I'd give a good deal to see his face when we come bowling out of the fog on top of him!"

"Yet he's helpless, Shamus," said she, looking him in the eyes. O'Brien nodded.

"Oh, I'll not kick a poor devil when he's down, Roisin. But I'll have a bit o' fun with him. And I hope he has the Scot aboard. I like Murray—"

"There is a nice boy aboard that ship, Shamus," she broke in quietly. "A gentle spoken Irish lad, a young officer. I talked with him once or twice, and I'd be sorry to have any hurt come to him from our guns."

O'Brien nodded cheerfully.

"I remember him; one Dillon, a lieutenant. We'll have him aboard. O'Neill! Get your signals ready. When we come up on the ship yonder, let him know we want to speak him. No flag, however. All hands! Clear for action."

Irish and English alike fell to work with a will, whistles shrilled, the ports were triced up, the decks cleared. With all hands at quarters but no colors displayed, the *Jacobus* forged on. The mist was gradually thinning behind arid about her as the fresher wind struck, and the sun smote the water with warmth.

So they came suddenly on the *Yarmouth,* not two cables away, and with shouts and drums and trumpets ringing out from her, O'Brien luffed and came up into the wind, across her stern. He leaped to the rail; she was so close that he could have tossed a biscuit aboard her, and saw Killigrew there at the stern rail, and Sir Archibald Murray and other officers.

"Ahoy, Killigrew!" he called, and waved a hand. "Good morning to you, Sir Archibald! Will ye lower a boat and come aboard us for a return visit? And Lieutenant Dillon is bid likewise, for there's a lady would speak with him."

They stared down at him in silence, all aghast for a moment. O'Brien laughed gaily.

"Come, Killigrew, call truce for an hour! I'd like a word with you and Murray."

"It's you, O'Brien?" roared Killigrew. "More of your tricks?"

"Devil a trick," said O'Brien. "If ye owe me ill will for shooting the spars oust of you at Saona Isle, be thankful I didn't put shot into your decks. Come along and break a bottle and leave the guns rest until the both of us are on an even footing."

"Sink me if he isn't a gentleman!" he heard Killigrew exclaim. "Aye, of course we'll come aboard. Truce if ye like, O'Brien."

So a boat was swung out from the *Yarmouth,* and presently Killigrew and Murray came up the gangway of the *Jacobus,* with young Dillon following them. They greeted O'Brien stiffly, but Murray, flushing a little, put out a hand to him.

"I'll be sorry to hang you when the day comes, O'Brien."

O'Brien smiled.

"Faith, the sorrow will be mine! But come below a moment, for there's a lady waiting."

He led them to the cabin, where Roisin met their amazed eyes, and they bowed over her hand clumsily.

"The marquesa!" exclaimed Dillon. "Madame, I have been sore at heart, thinking of you in the hands of buccaneers—"

"Faith, it's the buccaneers are in her hands!" said O'Brien blithely. "Sit you down, gentlemen, and—"

He paused, at sound of an uproar of voices from the deck. As they looked one at another, O'Neill came hastily breaking in upon them, his face a blaze of excitement.

"Cap'n! On deck!" he burst out. "The fog's opened up—there's a fleet in sight and bearing down on us from the south'ard!"

It was scarce two minutes since they had left the deck. In this short time the mist had suddenly been rolled away by the wind and sun, opening out across a vast stretch of sea, shredding off into scattered banks of vapor.

And there, a mile or a little more to the south, and bearing up for them under towering masses of canvas, were five great ships, and a smaller one trailing with them—the same brig which had poured her shot into the *Yarmouth*. When all of them had come out to the rail, a bitter oath burst from Killigrew.

"Frenchmen, by the Lord Harry!" he said, and put up his hands, shouting lustily at his own craft. "Cut away, there, cut away! Clear for action!"

O'Brien turned to him.

"Man, you can't fight five of them—all forty-gun ships or larger. And you're unable to run—"

Killigrew faced him and squared his burly shoulders. His jaw snapped like that of a bulldog.

"Damme if I'll run!" he said slowly. "True, I can't run—but I can fight. And fight 'em I will. There'll be no striking aboard the *Yarmouth* this day. Murray, are you with me?"

"Aye," said the dour Scot, a flash in his eye. "To the end, gentlemen. Let's aboard."

THEY STARTED for the waist, calling their boat's crew and Dillon after them. Then Roisin came up to O'Brien and touched his arm.

"Don't let the boy go, Shamus. It's death for him."

"What's he to you?" said O'Brien, meeting her level gaze.

"Like my own dead son, Shamus."

He groaned a little.

"Faith, ye know not what you ask, woman—"

"Nonetheless, I ask it."

He strode along the deck swiftly and caught Dillon by the arm as the latter was following the others over the rail. He jerked Dillon aside.

"Wait here," he said. "I have need of you." Then he looked over at the boat. "Killigrew, I'm keeping Dillon here."

"Be damned to you!" roared up the Englishman angrily, and shook his fist. "Push off."

A dismayed oath burst from Dillon, and he would have gone headlong over the rail, but O'Brien seized him. Hot eyed with anger, Dillon turned on him; but just then Roisin came up, caught his arm and spoke quietly. Dillon saw the boat spurting away for the *Yarmouth,* and a groan came from his very heart for the dishonor that was upon him, and he let Roisin take has arm and lead him aft in silence.

The crew of the *Yarmouth* had swarmed aloft, working like madmen. Even before Killigrew regained her, the wreckage had been cleared away. Her foremast was gone a dozen feet above the deck, but lines had been hastily bent on, the big spritsail bellied out from its yard, and the great mainsail fell. The banner of England broke out from poop and maintruck, and she was underway—unable to run, indeed, unable to handle swiftly, but nonetheless able to fight.

And Killigrew would fight until the deck sank under him. O'Brien had seen it in the man's whole bearing. Striding aft, he was joined by O'Neill, the boatswain, and the other officers he had appointed, and they watched the French ships bearing down in a double line, the white flag running up aboard them, the brig making the third of one line. O'Neill touched O'Brien's arm.

"Yonder brig, Master," said he, "is Beauchene's ship."

O'Brien nodded and said no word, though his blue eyes

hardened a little. Presently Dillon came up to him, with face all drawn and strained.

"By God, O'Brien, can you see those men fight and not give help?" he cried. O'Brien looked at him curiously.

"My own flag is French," he answered with a shrug. "My king's in France. Every damned Englishman alive can be sunk before I'd turn a hand to help him. Do you know those ships? If so, name 'em over to me."

"I know all but one, for we've studied their types," said Dillon. "Damn you! Aye, I know 'em. That's the *Licorne*, fifty-six, with her ensign at the mizzen to show there's a vice-admiral in command. Two forty-eights, the *Couronne* and the *Guise*. The forty-two, leading the brig, is the *Biscaye*. The other's a thirty-six, but I don't know her. And any one of them more than a match for us! Why don't the damned dogs draw off and come one at a time?"

"They're not fools," said O'Brien coolly. "And Killigrew is, or he'd strike."

"Aye," said Denis O'Neill in Irish, giving him a sidelong look, "the same sort of fool as yourself, Shamus O'Brien, were your Honor in his place."

O'Brien said nothing to that. A gun spoke out from the *Licorne*, and Killigrew answered it; his frigate handled badly. The Frenchmen had the weather-gage of him now, but they disdained to take advantage of it. Opening out, they bore down to pass on either side of him. His yards swung about.

"By the lord, he's taking their challenge!" cried O'Brien eagerly. "The madman—his one chance was to avoid their broadsides!"

Roisin came and leaned over the rail beside him, her face was close to his.

"So very sane yourself, Shamus?" she said softly. "'Were your Honor in his place,' said that man of yours. And what would your Honor do, if you were in his place? Tell me."

"I'd not lie to and let 'em send me fighting to the bottom," said O'Brien, then he turned to her, for something in her voice drew him. "Eh? What mean you, Little Rose? You don't mean you have any sympathy for those cursed Englishmen?"

"No?" said she. "Have you?"

"Devil a bit."

"You lie, and you know it," she answered softly. "You find it hard to remember they're Englishmen, eh? Well, well, it's none of my affair."

Guns thundered suddenly, for white plumes of smoke had billowed out from the sides of the *Yarmouth* as the double line of ships came sweeping down, one on either hand. Now white came spouting from them also; they reeled to the shock of the recoil, the thunderous crashing lifting sullenly. None of them heeded the *Jacobus,* for beyond doubt Beauchene had told them already what she was.

It seemed that when this pall of smoke lifted there would be no *Yarmouth* left, after that murderous series of broadsides. Yet through the smoke pierced the red flashes of her guns, steadily, repeatedly; and when things cleared off she was there, her yards squared away, running almost yard to yard with the French thirty-six, pouring shot into her. Then she fell away, staggered, and her tophamper came down in a tangle.

"That ends her," said O'Brien, watching the men swarming out to cut away the wreckage, as the French line luffed and bore back. "Now they'll surround her and hammer her."

He became aware of Roisin's face turned toward him.

"I have heard many strange tales told of the great families of Ireland," said she, in her low, rich voice, "but I have not heard it said that any chieftain would stand by and see brave men die when he might aid them."

Color rushed into the face of O'Brien.

"Woman, would you make a fool of me?" he said harshly.

"God forbid! I'd have you be what you are, Shamus, whether fool or wise man."

"*Duar na Criosd!* It'd be throwing away all of life and hope and future—"

"What were they worth, if you could not look the past in the eye?" said she.

O'Brien looked out at the ships sweeping down on the *Yarmouth,* and bit his lip. White smoke puffed out, as Killigrew poured a broadside into the *Biscaye;* then, unexpectedly, he wore about so that his other broadside was emptied into the same ship pointblank. When the smoke cleared, the water all about the *Yarmouth* was spouting as shot from the other frigates thundered at her, but the *Biscaye* was staggering away down the wind, a reeling, stricken, thing out of control, leaning far over, and the filibuster brig standing by to her help.

"By the Lord, he tore the bottom out of her!" cried O'Brien. From his men clustered along the rail he heard a sudden wild, exultant cheer, and felt like echoing it himself.

Next moment silence fell again. The French ships had driven on, and were forming up once more, but behind them lay the *Yarmouth,* dismasted now, a sodden hulk. As they looked, a spot of color appeared forward. It was her ensign, being hammered to the stump of the foremast.

"All hands!" O'Brien's voice went blaring down the deck. "Clear for action. Two men to the helm with me. Shake out the topsails—look alive, all hands!"

A S H E stood by the helm, Roisin came up to him. He gave her a swift look.

"There'll be splinters flying here, Little Rose—"

"Here I stay," she said, and laughed. "So you're a fool, Shamus? God love ye for it! You'll put up the flag of England?"

"Damned if I will," he said. "I'm not fighting for England. Dillon, will you take command of the starboard tier below?"

"I will that, praise be!" yelled Dillon eagerly.

"Double shot every gun," said O'Brien, and shouted the order at his men in the waist. When he turned to the woman again, there was a blaze in his eyes and a laughing exultation in his face that transfigured him.

"Here's an end to us all, Roisin," he cried, "but be sure of one thing, my lass! It's you that were made for me, aye, from the start of the world; and if we were young again with the blackbirds whistling down the road, it's myself would prove it to you. But there's naught to hear us now but the guns, Roisin, and each other, and what I have in my soul to say to you, will be said elsewhere. Good comrade!"

"Good comrade, Shamus," she said, her eyes shining. "Faith, there's no need of words between us."

Nor was there, indeed; and no further chance for them either.

The four towering Frenchmen had come down upon the *Yarmouth* and, as Killigrew's guns thundered out at them, their broadsides began to crash. They came about her, all four of them, their starboard broadsides double manned, and in the rising cloud of smoke they did not see the *Jacobus* heading toward them across the wind. A mile away the *Biscaye* had gone down, and the brig was picking up her men.

O'Brien swung the helm, and at his voice the whistle shrilled and men tailed on the lines and the frigate swung sharply about. They were in the smoke now, and O'Brien thought once of St. Rocher, and wished that stout heart were with him—then the great shape of the *Licorne* loomed up ahead and, as they drove past her, he gave the word to fire.

Crash! Yells made response, and the *Jacobus* reeled to the shock of recoil. The wind came down in a puff that cleared away the smoke for a moment. The *Guise* lay to starboard, and so close came O'Brien that he could see the powder grimed men looking through the open ports and over her rail at him. Again Dillon's guns crashed and thundered, then the helm spun and she came about, and the larboard broadside spoke in a shattering detonation. But with this, the French had taken warning, and the *Couronne* let fly a broadside that smashed slap into the frigate, and the unknown thirty-six drew up and let fly another.

She took a reply from Dillon's guns that swept her decks in red ruin.

Then, for a little space, O'Brien was clear of them all, and wore about to find them drawing away from the battered *Yarmouth*. He looked about for Roisin, saw her lying on the deck and leaped to her. A splinter had shattered the man beside her and knocked her senseless. O'Neill came running up at his call.

"Carry her below to the cabin—the little one amidships, where it's safest," he ordered, and breathed more freely at seeing her off the deck.

Then to the helm again, and the *Jacobus* drove square down at the Frenchmen as though to meet them yardarm to yardarm. Well enough did O'Brien know that in choosing his part this day he had broken irrevocably with all the past, and had naught to expect from the future either. If he drew out of this affair at all, he could hope for nothing more than the status of a rank pirate—but he had cast reason overboard, and bore on, a smile curving his lips and his blue eyes blazing.

And now, when the four great ships were dead ahead of him, he suddenly began to fight; not with his guns, but with his head and wheel and ship, for he had gained the weathergage of them and meant to take full advantage of it.

Vainly the four of them tried to corner him. He luffed and wore, took every chance of wind and sea, while the guns thundered and the shot crashed into him. He caught the thirty-six unawares and sent two smashing broadsides slap into her stern, sent her drifting away down the wind with her rudder gone and her masts overside, then ran in alongside the huge *Licorne*, gave her gun for gun, and two for one, and was gone before she could reload. And still the *Yarmouth* fought on amid them all, as the *Guise* tried to lay her aboard and was hammered off.

Now the *Couronne* came driving in amid the smoke, and ran along within twenty feet of the *Jacobus*, broadside roaring away, balls plowing the deck, musketry striking down men with hails of bullets from poop and top. O'Brien groaned as he looked along his decks, which had become a red shambles.

Naked men, black with powder, brought up kegs, swabbed the hot guns, ran with water to sluice them down, tailed on the lines. The *Couronne* drew ahead, and O'Brien suddenly luffed under her stern and poured a full broadside across her decks. With a roar and a crash, her splintered masts and canvas came down; a dismantled, reeling wreck, she went careening away, to fetch up almost alongside the *Yarmouth.* Killigrew promptly engaged her in a death grapple.

The *Jacobus* shivered suddenly, heeled over, erupted in shrieks and splinters. A full broadside from the *Licorne* had caught her to larboard, dismounting and silencing her entire upper tier of guns there, blowing her forecastle into a splintered chaos, killing a score of men. Dillon appeared suddenly in the smoke beside O'Brien, blood pumping from a wound across his breast.

"Give me—a chance!" he yelled frenziedly. "We've got red hot shot ready to load! Run us close in—"

"Load," shouted O'Brien, putting his strength at the helm. "Your chance is coming now."

It was coming indeed. The smoke blew down to leeward, to show the big *Licorne* lying caught in stays, taken aback, momentarily helpless. O'Brien held for her, and Denis O'Neill came staggering up to him, wild eyed.

"We've not sixty men left—"

"Man every starboard gun, and quick about it!" blared O'Brien. "Quick!"

The other dashed off. Sunk was the *Biscaye,* the thirty-six was drifting downwind, Killigrew had grappled the *Couronne.* The *Guise* was wearing, coming about to engage O'Brien, but she was too late to save her consort. O'Brien luffed under the stern of the huge *Licorne,* her musketeers and stern-chasers blazing away in futile wrath, and so closely that his yards almost scraped her high poop.

The blast of his full starboard broadside, alow and aloft, ripped into her, tore all her stern and poop to shreds, raked her lower tier. A great scream of wounded men came out of her, and she went heaving away like a hideous hurt creature as the *Guise* came driving down.

"Larboard guns all useless," panted a man, stumbling up. "Hardly a full gun crew left to man 'em—"

"All hands to the starboard batteries," said O'Brien, coolly. The other cried out:

"Cap'n! You're wounded—there's blood—"

"Shut your mouth, ye fool!" snapped O'Brien. "All hands to starboard!"

The man darted away hastily. A seaman came up to help with the helm, but as he gripped it he lurched. A hail of bullets tore all around. A crash of guns, a wild medley of yells—and O'Brien swung around to see the forgotten brig crossing under his stern, raking him with her small arms and her brass culverins, Beauchene standing in her chains to throw a grappling iron.

Desperately O'Brien swung on the wheel. He had overlooked Beauchene, but now he had him. He sent a yell forward, the men passing it on as they swabbed. The *Jacobus* came about and an instant later reeled to a crunching shock as she collided with the brig, which lay under her forefoot. And Dillon's lower tier blazed into the brig, guns depressed, bags of bullets sweeping the crowded decks. She sheered off and away. Beauchene was wounded, and after that bitter pill his men had no heart for more.

In her place loomed up the *Guise*. No escaping her now; she caught O'Brien on his wounded counter, sent a storm of shot hurtling into the *Jacobus*. Down came yards and tophamper; the whole larboard side was a stricken wreck; some one passed up word that Dillon was dead and O'Neill dying.

O'Brien worked with the few men at hand, slashing away, reeving lines; they got the wreckage cleared and the fore-yard up again, just as the smoke lifted momentarily. A feeble cheer came from larboard, and O'Brien saw that Killigrew had taken his prey, for the English flag was up above the *Couronne* now.

"Starboard batteries—all hands!" blared O'Brien's voice, and he was alone as they went stumbling away to obey him. He was looking out at where the *Licorne* lay, with men slung over repairing her rudder post, and the *Guise* standing by her before returning to the fight. The wheel jerked at him, and his hands felt weak on the spokes, until suddenly they spun freely, and he looked to see Roisin there at his side, lending her strength.

"Aye, this is the place for you, after all," said O'Brien hoarsely, and laughed. "Down! We must take their broadside—down, I say!"

"*O'Donnell Abu!*" rang out her voice. "Never down, O'Brien of my heart, never down, but up and take it! I'll hold her now—"

She staggered and her voice died. White clouds erupted from the *Licorne* and the *Guise*, and there was a whistle and screaming in the air all about. The rigging was rent and ripped, the sails torn into ribbons; but the *Jacobus* held on, answered her helm. A red mist was before O'Brien's eyes. With an effort he straightened up, swung on the spokes—and as she came around, the starboard guns thundered one by one, pouring death into the two Frenchmen. A ripping, rending crash, and over the rail went the foremast, taking the sprit along.

A last gun or two from the *Guise*. O'Brien staggered. The helm was smashed and splintered out of his hands. He groped out blindly, and felt soft strong hands clutch him and heard the voice of Roisin ringing in sudden wild exultation.

"English ships to starboard! Two of them standing for us—the smoke's going—"

O'Brien tried to see, but blood had filled his eyes and his head drooped.

"Aye, the smoke's going," he muttered. "And life's going, and all else; and well spent, Roisin, well spent! And if not, then Murray will get his wish and hang me—"

He laughed wildly and then slumped down to the deck, above the pieces of his splintered wheel. And beneath him the *Jacobus* heaved sullenly to the long swells, and wounded men yelled frantically that she was going down under them.

She was, indeed, but O'Brien was past knowing or caring.

"AYE, MISTRESS, it's my duty to hang him, and hang him I will," said dour Sir Archibald Murray, as he talked with the Marquesa de Guimares. "But it's not said when he's to be hanged, and I'll not hang him until the next ship comes from England. He'll not be ready for hanging until then, either."

"And when will that be?" said she.

"Mayhap next week, or next month, or next year," said Murray, and took his leave with a very low bow.

Many weeks had passed, and all this while O'Brien lay in the pleasant house of the vice-governor, above Kingston harbor, and those that lived of his men lay in the great jail on the plain outside Kingston. The marquesa, cured of her own slight wounds, had become O'Brien's nurse; for his wounds had been slow in healing, since Jamaica was very hot, and had passed into a fever that all but took his life. He knew not a soul around him, nor anything that passed, and was become a shadow of a man.

So the marquesa, helpless, knew that Murray was awaiting word from London, and would surely hang O'Brien when the word came.

Another fortnight passed, and a Dutch ship put into Kingston and dropped a single passenger, and went her ways again. The passenger displayed his papers and paid his respects to Government House; he was a noble Spaniard, a relative of the Marquesa de Guimares, who had come from Havana upon learning that she was here. A tall, saturnine man, he was escorted to Murray's house, and the marquesa received him, alone.

"You!" she exclaimed as she came into the room. "M. de St. Rocher—"

"No," he said, bowing over her hand. "The Marquis de Manneville, if it please you; but here, a Spaniard and your relative. Where is he?"

She made a helpless gesture.

"Sleeping quietly, for the first time. The governor's surgeon says he will waken either to life or death, and knows not which."

"The devil!" said St. Rocher, strode up and down the room, and halted. "Look you, madame, I am ready to carry him off. A ship is waiting, his own Barbary galley. At a signal from me, boats will land up the coast—"

"He can not be moved," she said quietly. "And Murray will hang him," she added, and went on to tell of Murray's words. St. Rocher frowned.

"Bad news," he said. "We passed two English frigates yesterday, coming from England. I can see him?"

"Better not, until he wakes," she said. "I will summon you. Remember, the black servants carry tales."

St. Rocher assented grudgingly. He was assigned quarters in Murray's house, however, for the marquesa said that he was her cousin.

With the next sunrise, signal guns told that the London frigates were sighted standing in for the harbor, and O'Brien wakened.

He looked up at St. Rocher, and a thin smile touched his pallid lips. He met the eyes of the marquesa, clasped her hand, and life came into his face. She bent over him.

"No talk, no talk, *mo mhuirnin!*" she murmured in Irish. "Drink, sleep, and talk when you wake again."

He assented, and took the drink that the surgeon held to his lips, and closed his eyes. The surgeon bent over him for a space, then rose.

"Life," he said laconically. "I must advise Sir Archibald—he was most insistent that I bring him word at once."

He departed; and from the terrace before the house St. Rocher and the marquesa watched the two frigates come to anchor and send in their boats. They breakfasted there, and were talking together an hour later, when Sir Archibald Murray came striding up, with his wig all askew, his coat half buttoned and a packet of papers in his hand. He joined them and, panting a little, took a paper from the packet and opened it in trembling hands.

"Here it is," he said harshly, and did not observe that St. Rocher fingered something inside his coat, as it might be a poniard there. A black man came running.

"Master!" he cried. "He's wakened again and asking—"

"Be silent," said Murray, and turned to the marquesa. He thrust the paper it her. "There, madame," he said. "Take it. Let him have it from your own hand. The attainder's wiped out, a full pardon granted him—and he's Sir James O'Brien, with the thanks of Parliament and of their Majesties for his gallantry."

With a quick, sharp little cry, Roisin seized the document and was gone. Murray dropped into a chair.

"Thank God!" he said. "I'd have hanged the damned rascal if it was my last act—and it would have broken my heart." He drew a deep breath, and glanced up at St. Rocher. "Eh, eh? You heard, señor?" he asked in Spanish.

"I do not understand English, señor," said St. Rocher, and went to the edge of the terrace, turning his back for a moment. He tossed something into the flowering bushes—a little jeweled poniard, a splendid toy to be thus flung away by a careless Spanish Don.

He stood looking out at the sea, then swung around suddenly. Murray straightened up. Their eyes went to Roisin, who had appeared in the doorway. She said no word, but her hand went out toward Murray, and from it fluttered the document, torn across and across.

Murray started to his feet, and then a grimace twisted his thin lips.

"Oh, aye?" he exclaimed. "If King James had half the spirit of those who serve him, he'd be in Whitehall today. Well, madame, whether the paper be torn or not doesn't affect the matter a whit. I can't hang him for refusing a knighthood from my king, thank God!"

And he stooped to pick up the scraps of paper, looking very cheerful about it, too.

H. BEDFORD-JONES

BEDFORD-JONES IS a Canadian by birth, but not by profession, having removed to the United States at the age of one year. For over twenty years he has been more or less profitably engaged in writing and traveling. As he has seldom resided in one place longer than a year or so and is a person of retiring habits, he is somewhat a man of mystery; more than once he has suffered from unscrupulous gentlemen who impersonated him—one of whom murdered a wife and was subsequently shot by the police, luckily after losing his alias.

The real Bedford-Jones is an elderly man, whose gray hair and precise attire give him rather the appearance of a retired foreign diplomat. His hobby is stamp collecting, and his collection of Japan is said to be one of the finest in existence. At present writing he is en route to Morocco, and when this appears in print he will probably be somewhere on the Mojave Desert in company with Erle Stanley Gardner.

Questioned as to the main facts in his life, he declared there was only one main fact, but it was not for publication; that his life had been uneventful except for numerous financial losses, and that his only adventures lay in evading adventurers. In his younger years he was something of an athlete, but the encroachments of age preclude any active pursuits except that of motoring. He is usually to be found poring over his stamps, working at his typewriter, or laboring in his California rose garden, which is one of the sights of Cathedral Cañon, near Palm Springs.

Bedford-Jones has written stories laid in many corners of the earth, but among his most popular tales were the John Solomon stories which started many years ago in the *Argosy.*

www.ingramcontent.com/pod-product-compliance
Lightning Source LLC
Chambersburg PA
CBHW061518020726
47502CB00006B/2121